TRINKETS, TREASURES,
and other
BLOODY MAGIC

TRINKETS, TREASURES & OTHER BLOODY MAGIC
Copyright © 2013 Meghan Ciana Doidge
Published by Old Man in the CrossWalk
Productions 2013
Vancouver, BC, Canada
www.oldmaninthecrosswalk.com

All rights reserved under International and Pan-American Copyright Conventions. No part of this book may be produced in any form or by any electronic or mechanical means, including information storage and retrieval systems, without permission in writing from the author, except by reviewer, who may quote brief passages in a review.

This is a work of fiction. All names, characters, places, objects, and incidents herein are the products of the author's imagination or are used fictitiously. Any resemblance to actual things, events, locales, or persons living or dead is entirely coincidental.

Library and Archives Canada
Doidge, Meghan Ciana, 1973 —
Trinkets, Treasures, & Other Bloody Magic/Meghan Ciana Doidge — Paperback

Cover image & design by Elizabeth Mackey

ISBN 978-1-927850-05-3

Dowser Series · Book 2

TRINKETS, TREASURES, and other BLOODY MAGIC

Meghan Ciana Doidge

Published by Old Man in the CrossWalk Productions
Vancouver, BC, Canada

www.oldmaninthecrosswalk.com

For Michael
with you every kiss is a good kiss

Three months ago, I lost my foster sister, Sienna, to the darkness. As in blood magic and chaos and general mayhem. No one saw it until it was too late, but I should have. Now, I have a wounded heart and soul that I can't even reveal to anyone around me, because I'm supposed to hate Sienna with the fiery passion of the justified. And I do. I just wish I didn't feel so lost without her, so unsure of the path I thought I had carved for myself, and so outclassed by the powerful Adepts constantly by my side these days. I'm not even sure if they're with me for my own protection or because my shiny new powers are rare and valuable. Assuming I ever figure out who or what I am, and how my magic actually works.

Even chocolate can't save the day every time ... just most of the time. At least I've got that going for me.

Chapter One

Fully aware that the vampire was watching me from somewhere deeper in the woods, I placed my second to last piece of single-origin Madagascar chocolate on my tongue and lovingly sucked on it. The smooth, creamy, dark-roasted cocoa teased my taste buds and I instantly relaxed.

I wasn't going to freak out about being stranded in the Squamish forest. I wasn't going to freak out about being damp from my blond curls to my perfectly painted pink toenails. And I really, really wasn't going to freak out about running out of chocolate in the middle of bloody nowhere while being harassed by a vampire and stalked by a werewolf.

Okay. I was exaggerating, but only a little. My toes, crammed into clunky, very practical — but ultimately ugly — hiking boots were bone dry.

Everything else was the utter truth, from my perspective at least. Except the werewolf would say 'training,' not stalking. And the vampire would — if he bothered to explain at all — call harassment 'education.'

The last of the chocolate melted in my mouth with no hint of bitter aftertaste, and I opened my indigo eyes, ready to move forward. I was good at moving forward — baby steps, at least — because if I really paused to think or take mental stock, I was afraid I wouldn't ever get going again.

I was sitting on a fallen, moss-covered tree — a cedar, maybe — surrounded by more trees. Though these ones were still upright and thick enough that I wouldn't be able to wrap my arms around them. You know, if I felt like hugging trees. I was currently somewhere in a valley that cut between multiple mountains and led eventually, I thought, to Whistler ski resort. I could see three snow-covered peaks without turning my head. Whistler, known for its world-class skiing and fantastic restaurants, would be a great location for a second Cake in a Cup bakery. That is, if I ever got out of this forest and felt like working for more than twelve hours a day, six days a week. I was close enough to a river — the Squamish River, I hoped — that I could hear but not see it. No trails cut through the underbrush. The sun, which had just made an appearance, glinted off water droplets caught on fern leaves. My phone declared the time to be 2:23 P.M., but I had no signal.

So, yeah. I was lost.

The vampire wasn't in a helpful mood, which was usually fine by me, because whenever he was helpful, it creeped me out. Helpful usually meant he was satiated. And what satiated vampires? Blood. Not mine, so far at least. Not that he wouldn't fang me in a split second, even if he was all detached with his cool peppermint magic and carved-ice features. A girl just knows — with guys or vampires, though other girls, not so much.

Anyway, lost.

I scanned the immediate area. I could feel the vampire nearby, but he had a super annoying ability to somehow contain or cloak his magic, so that I wasn't sure of direction or proximity. I couldn't pick up any trace of the green-haired werewolf. Kandy moved way faster than me through the forest, so she'd probably found the end range of my dowser senses. Plus, she had practically inhaled — even while driving — the dozen cupcakes I'd brought for the hike before we'd even parked the SUV at Alice Lake, so she had a lot of fuel to burn.

A shimmer of sunlight caught my eye ... no, not sunlight. What was that? I was done with the sulking and on my feet before I even made the decision. Wow, that was me in a nutshell.

The glimmer of magic beckoned from the side of a cedar tree, as if something supernatural had brushed against it at shoulder height. I usually didn't see such incidental traces, but I was learning to just go with the heightened-powers persona instead of freaking out about it all the time.

"Gotcha," I murmured, thinking Kandy had inadvertently left me a clue. Though I wasn't totally clear if I was actually playing hide-and-seek with the werewolf, or if she'd just gotten fed up being around the vampire and had taken off. Both scenarios were equally possible.

Except that as I got closer, the glimmer didn't look exactly like Kandy's magic ... its base color was green, but leafy, not grassy. It was too dim for me to pick up any taste —

"The foremost magical authority ..."

I actually jumped as the vampire's cool voice sounded right next to my ear. God, I hated it when he did that. I spun around but the immediate area was vampire free.

"The foremost magical authority," Kett prompted again. His voice floated in from the right, but I stopped myself from spinning in that direction. Everything was a test with him, but I couldn't complain because I'd asked for it. Yep, I had promised to treasure hunt for the vampire if he agreed to fill in some of the holes in my magical education.

There were a lot of holes. And Gran was still spitting mad about bargaining with a vampire. If she'd had her way, Kett would have been ash three months ago. Hell, she probably would have let the untethered magic of Sienna's pentagram just swallow him.

Ah, Sienna. What was that? A full five minutes without thinking of my foster sister and the black magic that destroyed her? I shoved the ache in my throat back down to its permanent place in my heart, then turned to scan for Kett's magic.

"We went over all that already, vampire," I said, hoping to get him to talk again. "Like thirty minutes ago."

"Perhaps I wasn't happy with your answer."

There he was — a rapidly fading wash of red in the shadows, three trees to my left.

"Perhaps you fell asleep and forgot, old man," I teased. Then I took three quick steps only to grab thin air.

He laughed. I could feel his breath on my neck. "Answer, dowser."

I spun. The taste of cool, clean peppermint with something spicy and dark underneath — not cinnamon or nutmeg; I hadn't quite figured it out yet — hung ever so briefly in the air, then dissipated.

"The witches Convocation, vampire Conclave, and shapeshifter Assembly are all overseen by the Grand Council," I said, "which is comprised of members from all the Adept communities, though not all the species." I hadn't caught Kett once in the three months we'd been playing this game. At least Kandy wasn't here to curl her lip at me.

I paused between fir trees to wrap my fingers around the hilt of the invisible knife I always wore across my right hip. Actually, the knife wasn't invisible. It was hand carved out of jade rock I'd found near Lillooet, and about the length of my forearm and the thickness of my thumb. The sheath — a birthday gift from Gran because such spells were beyond me — was invisible.

"Going to stab me, dowser?" the vampire asked.

"Nope," I said as I closed my eyes and unzipped my Gore-Tex jacket a few inches. I weaved my fingers through the wedding rings I wore soldered like charms onto a thick gold chain around my neck. The necklace was an accumulation of nearly two years of work. Today, I wore it looped three times around my neck, so that it lay across my collarbone over my T-shirt. The T-shirt proclaimed me a spin-the-bottle champion in faded white lettering.

"The knife is your best offense. Revealing its existence, even a second too soon, could be a fatal mistake."

"But you can see through such magic, vampire."

"I'm not teaching you to fight me —"

I pivoted and then lunged between two closely spaced trees to slap the vampire with the flat of my hand right in the middle of his chest. "Tag, you're it!"

He stared at me, surprised. It was subtle, but it was surprise. His white blond hair, unnaturally pale skin, and ice-blue eyes stood out starkly against the wet green and brown backdrop of the forest. Kett had been human once, hundreds of years ago — though he had yet to actually confirm his age — but he hadn't retained much natural expression. His eyes were slightly wider than normal, hence surprised. I'd beaten him.

"You used the magic in the knife and the necklace to amplify your dowser senses."

The wedding rings of the necklace and the jade stone of the knife contained natural or residual magic that I had — unknowingly at the time — reshaped with my own magic to create a new magical object. This exceedingly unique talent was the reason I now had a self-appointed vampire mentor and a werewolf bodyguard. 'Alchemy,' as the vampire called it, was so rare that I hadn't even heard that such a talent existed among the Adept. It was most likely an inherited ability — my father's biological contribution to my magical genetics — but seeing as not even my mother knew who dear old dad was I didn't know for sure.

"Is that praise I hear?"

"No. It is a lesson you should have learned within our first week of training."

Ouch. "Nasty," I said.

Kett shrugged. A human gesture he seemed to be trying on lately. I think it was difficult for him to be around so many people all the time.

"You're just pissed that —"

"Now, where is the werewolf?"

"Slave driver," I muttered. "Fine. It's not like I want to keep tromping around here in the moss and mud. You promised me treasure, vampire. You lied, again."

"I'm not the dowser."

I huffed and turned away from him, so as not to be continually distracted by the magic I could see dancing on his skin. I reached out with my dowser senses again — once more anchoring myself within the stores of magic in the necklace and the knife — to seek the flavor of Kandy's magic. I came up with nothing except a hint of that same unknown glimmer a few tree trunks away.

"You really cannot sense the werewolf, dowser?" Kett sounded genuinely perplexed.

"Maybe she's gone too far." I moved toward the new glimmer to look at it more closely.

"The wolf should not have been able to test the limits of your range within the short time she has been gone."

Kett wrapped his fingers around my elbow to stop me from continuing to clomp around. I didn't exactly move lightly through the underbrush. Then he paused as if listening.

"Should you be able to hear her?" I asked.

Kett's eyebrows lowered a sixteenth-of-an-inch, which I took as an admonishment to be quiet. The vampire scanned slowly left, then right. He then repeated the gesture. "No wolves," he said.

The forest was suddenly much quieter around us. As if the prey within had all sensed the presence of a predator. It was frightening how Kett could hide that so effectively if he wished.

"You can't track her?"

"And how would I track her, dowser?"

"You're a vampire. You hunt."

"Not by scent. If that is what you are suggesting." He was really affronted. But how the hell was I supposed to know? He wasn't exactly forthcoming about his abilities. None of the Adept were, but vampires were practically xenophobic.

"By what then?" I asked, laying on the snark. "Heartbeat?"

"Yes," he answered. His voice dipped into that occupied quality it got right before his fangs made an appearance.

I'd been joking about the heartbeat thing. Yeah, it wasn't funny if it was true. I took a step away and touched the hilt of my knife for reassurance. The vampire — though sometimes freaky — wasn't going to attack me ... not right now, at least. Usually there was a bit more warning. I hated that I occasionally forgot who and what he was. It didn't help that he was nice to look at and his magic was unique and distracting, to me at least.

"What's that?" Kett murmured. His head canted to one side.

I reached out with my dowser senses in the vague direction he seemed to be listening. I picked up more glimmers of the unknown but slightly familiar magic.

"You mean the glimmers? I thought it was just trace left by Kandy, but it's something else."

"Something else you should have mentioned?"

"Would you have allowed the interruption when there were such important questions to answer and games to play?"

Kett sighed. Such a thing always seemed heavier when he did it. Probably because he didn't actually need to breathe. "I don't see any glimmers, dowser," he said. "But to the east there is ... something."

Well, that was informative. "I'm not a compass."

Kett pointed in the direction he'd been looking, then turned his gaze on me. "Use the necklace," he coaxed. He had a real thing for my necklace. But then, so did I.

For years, I had sought out wedding rings that contained residual magic in antique stores or pawnshops. I preferred to collect the rings in pairs, but I occasionally added singles if it felt like the right thing to do. I ran the pad of my thumb across a new solder join where I'd recently repaired the necklace and tried, once again, to quash my immediate thoughts of my dead sister, Sienna. A glimmer of her magic was embedded within this ring. But it would take more than a divorced man's wedding ring and a hank of hair to find her now. I tried to not believe in absolutes such as heaven and hell, but I was fairly certain she was as deep into the darkness as a soul could go.

Focus, focus …

Once again anchored in the magic of the knife and the necklace, I stretched my senses through the dense forest. I couldn't pick up anything nonmagical, such as animals, as I assumed Kett could. But I also guessed he hadn't asked me to dowse for owls when he pointed east.

There … just on the very edge of my reach I could sense a … grouping?

"How far is that?" I asked. My eyes were narrowed at the tree a few feet from me, but I wasn't seeing the grooves in the bark or the dried needles that created a crunchy carpet underneath. I was trying to resolve the feeling of the grouping into a taste I could identify.

"Miles," Kett answered. His voice was soft and yet focused, deadly focused.

"You think I can dowse for miles?"

"Pay attention, half-witch. What is that? Or who?" The vampire downgraded my title from 'dowser' to 'half-witch' only when he was chastising me. Though you couldn't hear any chastisement in his tone, or I couldn't, anyway. Maybe to other vampires, he'd be dripping with condemnation.

"Well," I said. "They'd have to be magical for me to pick them up."

The vampire didn't sigh or pierce me with an icy glare, but I sensed it was a near thing. The sarcasm was a coping mechanism, as was the chocolate, and the baking, and the trinket making. Just because I recognized the behavior didn't mean I could stop. I had a lot of coping to do.

"Magical, as in the same magic as these glimmers you failed to mention?"

"Maybe. I'd have to get closer."

Kett grinned. I could see this smile in my peripheral vision, and even though it wasn't directed at me, it made me freeze like an over-lit deer. It wasn't a nice smile. It was a predator baring its teeth. Nice, straight, very white teeth that I was pleased weren't currently anticipating biting me.

"Let's get closer," he whispered. And then he was gone.

Okay, the vampire didn't just disappear, but he did blur off eastward into the forest.

And great. Now with the running. The running always led places I really didn't want to go. Like into blood and mayhem. Well, I guess I had just walked into the last batch of that ...

I tightened the strap of my sling pack and moved farther into the woods after the vampire. I quickened my pace with each stride until I was running as fast as I dared through the undergrowth. The needles and moss were slippery underfoot. The forest wasn't my natural environment and running wasn't my favorite activity. I was more at home in my bakery or on a yoga mat. But my body didn't mind running. I could, in fact, run farther and faster than I'd ever tried before. Kett and Kandy had been forcing physical training on me. Though I still hadn't managed to slice the vampire with my knife in our sparring sessions.

I leaped up and over a fallen tree, then cleared the huckleberry bushes on the other side without really trying. I made a mental note to collect some of the red berries before we returned home. Though it took numerous handfuls to make anything substantial, I was thinking of a limited edition cupcake for the bakery ...

Though I was still chasing his magic, I couldn't see or hear the vampire ahead of me among the cedar and fir trees. Of course, I couldn't really hear anything over the sound of my own labored crashing around. I had probably already scared away any animals that hadn't fled from the vampire.

I focused on the gathering ahead. I wasn't sure I could run all the supposed miles between here and there, even though ever since Sienna had forced me — inadvertently or not — to open the portal in my basement, I'd been stronger and faster than I ever had before. Contact with the portal magic had ... well, not strengthened my magic, because I think I'd always been this way without knowing. But it had connected me with more of my magical abilities. So I was stronger and faster than I thought, and I healed quickly, though I hadn't tested that voluntarily.

Maybe I could run miles if I needed to. I just knew that a vampire on the hunt shouldn't go unchecked. Not that I could check Kett — not if he ever really lost it. But maybe he would hesitate to slaughter too much, too wantonly in front of me, seeing as how he was my self-appointed mentor and all.

The grouping was nearer now, but I still couldn't distinguish their magic. I hadn't tasted it before. It was earthy like shifter or witch magic — but then, most of the Adept drew their power from the earth. The spirit of the earth, as Gran called it, was dying, and the powers and numbers of the Adept along with it. Whether this was a natural evolution or something to do with climate change and the poisoning of the earth, I didn't know. Beyond its earthy base, the magic of the gathering up ahead was tart like the huckleberries that grew in wild abundance in these mountains. And spicy like some sort of red pepper. No, maybe like a sweet-edged onion?

I couldn't manage to catch up to the vampire without going all out, and I was afraid I'd run out of steam if I did.

The gathering resolved into individual magical signatures as I neared. I picked up my pace as I sensed Kett do the same ahead of me. The low branches of some junior evergreens whipped across my face, but the scrapes healed within seconds. That was still weird. I mean, I was certainly happy to not be walking around with a scratched up face, but feeling yourself heal was definitely freaky. I had been putting off asking Kandy about it. Werewolves healed quickly as well, though Kandy had taken a good week to heal after her run-in with Sienna. 'Run in,' was completely understating the actual situation, but I was still having a difficult time dealing with the aftermath of it all in my head.

I could make out five individuals up ahead. But I was also flagging, my breathing quickening and my stride shortening. I pushed through, knowing my mind would give out before my body actually did, because the vampire was pulling too far ahead of me now. He would reach the group easily five, maybe ten minutes before me. It was difficult to judge. I'd never been in a foot race with a vampire before.

Certainly he wouldn't go barreling into a group of unknown magic users? He was too careful, too meticulous for that. Except that once on a hunt, what if he had a difficult time reining himself in ... ? Damn. How did I get myself into these situations? Right, I wandered around alone in the forest with a vampire. I was practically begging for it.

Chapter Two

I caught a taste of Kandy's magic. It was faint, as if shielded. That brought me up short, because it wasn't in the same direction as the gathering. Kett — though I could still only sense his magic rather than see him — didn't even pause. Maybe he hadn't noticed, or maybe he didn't care. The vampire was just as much of a collector as I was, but while I obsessively gathered glimmers of magic — including the jade stones in my pocket that I'd fished out of the river an hour ago — he collected information on unusual Adepts such as myself.

So, did I leave the gathering ahead to the vampire and the possible slaughter that lay at the end of his run? Or did I ignore Kandy, though her magic felt oddly sluggish and remote?

The vampire didn't typically go around slaughtering people. Though honestly, I had no idea how — or on who — he fed. Though I gathered it could be a mutual pleasure, nonlethal sort of arrangement. And Kandy was the nearest thing I had to a friend since Sienna had disintegrated before my eyes. I'd felt my sister's magic dissipate within the golden power of the portal. I'd let go. I'd let her die —

I veered off toward Kandy and left the unknown Adepts to the vampire and fate. I was barely able to take care of myself. The strangers would have to wait while I checked on the werewolf.

I could hear another river in this direction, and I found myself seriously hoping I hadn't somehow circled back. I was fairly certain we'd been following the Squamish River before, but now that was in some doubt. Logically, I'd been running through a valley surrounded by mountains, so chances were good that there'd be another river around here somewhere.

I almost ran over Kandy. Her magic was that dim. I managed to not step on the green-haired werewolf, but just barely.

"Kandy!" I cried, throwing myself down on my knees by her side. Yeah, I found it difficult not being completely typical all the time. Especially when faced with a friend curled in a fetal position on the damp ground in the middle of the freaking nowhere forest. Okay, I was aware that we were somewhere between Squamish and Whistler, but that was a long distance, like fifty or so miles. On foot.

Kandy moaned so quietly that I wasn't actually sure she'd made any noise, but the werewolf didn't open her eyes.

I hunched down to look her over. My first instinct was to touch her, but I was really trying to not just heed my every whim these days. Touching her could be bad for us both. If she'd been spelled, that magic could grab me or react badly to my interference. She didn't appear to be hurt, not that I could tell for sure given that she healed so quickly. Her jeans were ripped across her thighs, but I couldn't remember if they'd been like that before. Her snug-fitting, belly-baring T-shirt bore some obscene print as per usual.

I needed to figure out if she'd been spelled. Slowly, I ran my fingers down her taut, muscled arm, but picked up nothing beyond the abnormally sluggish pulse of werewolf magic.

I carefully rolled Kandy over onto her back. I could see a vein pulsing in her neck. It looked too rapid and intense — but then, I barely knew anything about human physiology, let alone werewolf. Where her short-cropped green hair grew out shaggily, it fell across her brow, but other than that, she didn't react. No roots, I noted, even though it wasn't vaguely relevant. Kandy must dye her hair every two weeks to maintain it so perfectly.

She was pale. She was usually so vibrant, so brash and ready with her predatory grin and easy swagger. My heart was attempting to climb up my throat, but I swallowed it back down. This wasn't the same situation. This wasn't the same as when Sienna had cut Kandy so badly —

Focus. Focus.

Kandy's hand lay across her belly, and I noticed her very human-looking fingers were tipped with wolf claws. Had she tried to change? Or had she just been practicing partially changing as she often did?

I touched her hand. Then I noticed the bright spots of magic underneath it, on her belly and across her chest. Five points that were partially diffused into Kandy's own magic. I could clearly identify the different colors of green.

I hovered my fingers over the brightest — the newest? — spot. The magic felt similar to the glimmers in the forest, and to the gathering in the east.

Though now that I widened my senses from being pinpoint-focused on Kandy, I noticed that the gathering had dispersed.

Then I got hit by a bear.

I didn't know it was a bear at the time it hit me, seeing as how I was curled into a ball in an attempt to protect my head and neck. It became clear after that, after I rolled away from Kandy to direct the bear away from the incapacitated werewolf. After I slammed against a two-hundred-year-old cedar and twisted my wrist in an attempt to break my badly handled fall. Kett would have lowered his eyebrows at least a quarter-of-an-inch over that tumble if this had been a sparring session. After I straightened, looked up, and kicked the bear in the gut then I saw it was a bear. A nine-hundred-pound, nine-foot-tall-on-its-hind-legs grizzly bear that I had just slammed into a neighboring tree.

I'd never seen a surprised grizzly hunch over and hold its bruised belly before. But then, I'd never seen a grizzly in the flesh at all.

I didn't stop to celebrate the fact that I'd just kicked a nine-hundred-pound bear ten feet or so, though the display of strength was impressive and unprecedented. Not knowing it was a big, freaking bear probably helped. I widened my stance and pulled my knife. The jade blade was more of a rapier than a sword, and held between the bear and me, it looked like I was threatening to poke it with a toothpick.

Kandy moaned and rolled back into her fetal position.

The bear swung its massive, broad head toward the werewolf. I remained calm, forcing myself to not just start shrieking for Kett. Could a vampire drop a grizzly bear? Could I even annoy it?

"Hey, big guy!" I shouted. "Look here. Look at me. See my shiny knife. No touchy the green-haired one, or I'll poke you." Geez. Poke you. Brilliant threat. Hopefully, my tone was doing the heavy lifting. Too bad I didn't have any bells. Bears didn't like bells, right?

The bear thumped down on all fours. Evidently, my kick wasn't a long-term sort of deterrent. Even flat on his feet, his head was higher than mine. Couldn't a grizzly take multiple rounds from a shotgun and still keep mauling its victim?

The bear was vacillating — yep, I pull out the big words when a weird situation gets weirder — as it swung its huge head between Kandy and me.

I waved my knife. The bear didn't even blink. Maybe he was nearsighted? I wasn't terribly interested in getting close enough to find out.

I stepped sideways. The bear watched me, though its head was turned toward Kandy. I took another step toward the unconscious werewolf —

Loud noises! Bears hated loud noises.

I clapped my hands together and stomped my feet. The clap was pathetic because I was still clutching my knife in one hand. The stomping was ineffective and muffled by the blanket of needles that covered the ground underneath all the trees.

The bear swung its head back at me. I took another step, attempting to place myself between it and Kandy.

The bear raised its head and opened its mouth. Its many teeth were wider and much more pointy than my fingers. It bellowed at me.

Its wet, hot breath buffeted me. But while I clenched my inner thighs and attempted to not pee my pants, I felt something underneath, something I'd been too pumped on adrenaline to notice right away. Namely, magic. Specifically, something magic on or around the bear. Was the animal spelled?

The bear lowered its head, rolled its massive shoulders forward, and lumbered toward me.

I tried to turn and execute another side kick. I didn't actually want to kill — if I even could — a confused, spelled bear. But the bear moved quicker than I anticipated. It batted me sideways, hooking me from hip to upper ribs with three-inch claws.

I brought the knife up and slashed it across the bear's shoulder as it flung me sideways again.

It bellowed with pain.

I tumbled then landed down on one knee, but half-turned as I caught myself to raise the knife between the bear and me.

Except it didn't attack further. It somehow — I saw it, but I still couldn't figure it out — rolled its head under Kandy and flipped the werewolf over its shoulder.

Kandy groaned as she hit the hard muscled meat of the bear's back, and for a brief moment, she opened her blazing green eyes to look at me.

"Shit!" I swore, scrambling to my feet.

The bear took off with the werewolf slung across its back.

Uh-huh. Yeah.

My feet kept moving, which was good because my brain was stuttering to a halt. A bear was kidnapping my friend. It was freaking insane.

The deep claw puncture wounds on my side closed, though my T-shirt and jeans were probably ripped and covered in blood.

With my knife still in hand, I chased after the bear.

Yeah, again. I chased. A bear.

The eyes of werewolves glowed green, as Kandy's had, only when they were accessing their shifter magic somehow. But Kandy wasn't changing forms, so her magic was doing something else. Perhaps burning off the foreign magic I'd seen on her belly and chest. I didn't know, and I certainly wasn't going to leave her at the mercy of an obviously deranged bear.

I caught up to the grizzly. It was fast, but I — as I was still learning — was faster.

I grabbed a fistful of its pelt on its right back haunch and yanked. The bear skidded right, but then attempted to twist away from me.

I was trying to wrestle a bear. Maybe I was the insane one.

I avoided another paw swipe. The bear seemed more interested in getting away than fighting, so it was easy to anticipate its half-hearted defensive strikes.

I reached for Kandy. She lifted her blazing green, unfocused eyes and raised her hand toward me. Her other hand was clenched tight in the bear's fur. The bear twisted away and I nearly lost my footing, and then my shoulder, as it veered by a large cedar tree. My fingers skidded down Kandy's forearm, keeping me from getting a grip on her. The bear was trying to scrape me off its back with the bark of the trees as if I was an annoying insect.

Asshole.

I'd show it.

I raised my knife, then plowed face first into a large block of dense ice.

I crashed to my knees and brought my hand up to my bloody, crushed nose. Pain ricocheted though my skull. Tears streamed from my eyes. Jesus. It felt like I'd bitten clear through my bottom lip.

I spat a mouthful of blood out all over a pair of Merrell hiking boots that were an exact match to the ones I currently wore, except for the size. What the hell?

I craned my neck and head upward. Expensive jeans, expensive leather belt, blue lightweight Gore-Tex jacket that was torn in a few places and spotted with dirt, bark, and leaves. Underneath the jacket was a gray T-shirt stretched over a trim, but clearly muscled upper chest. All of which led upward to a chiseled, angular, too-pale face.

Freaking Kett had just broken my nose.

"Kett!" I cried, because I have a difficult time not just stating the obvious when stressed. "I was wrestling that bear!" My voice was dreadfully nasal. I snapped my nose back into place. It instantly healed, though I saw spots floating before my eyes for a few blinks afterward. "It was a contest of wills, and Kandy was the prize."

I stumbled to my feet, using various bits of Kett's clothing as handholds. Well, one handhold. I kept the other hand, the one dripping with my blood, over my now healed nose. I wasn't sure that the sight of so much blood would sit well with the vampire.

I must have sheathed my knife at some point because I could feel its magic on my right hip. I didn't remember doing so.

Kett swayed on his feet.

Every bone in the front of my body felt bruised. "Kett," I said again. "Kandy is in —"

Red rolled over Kett's ice-blue eyes. The eyes that were currently fixed on mine. I'd never seen Kett's magic operate like that before. Usually his eyes filled with blood when he needed to feed, but this was different.

"Dowser," he murmured. "Found you." He reached up and brushed the curls away from my cheek. It was a lazy, intimate caress. The hackles on the back of my neck tingled a warning.

Predator alert. Predator alert.

Kett listed sideways and stumbled. His eyes, which flashed red again, never left my face.

He tugged my hand down from covering my nose, running his thumb thoughtfully across my blood-covered palm. Then he lifted his eyes back to mine. "All healed?" he asked. His tone was softer and deeper than usual.

"Yes," I answered, completely bewildered.

"You're going to have to run now, little dowser."

"Can we just skip the running and chasing part? You don't look hurt. You don't look like you need to feed. And Kandy —"

"Not me, dowser. You. You need to head southwest, back to the car —" He stumbled again, as if swooning. I grasped his upper arms, though I loathed to touch him while all covered in blood. His potent magic tingled all the way through his jacket into my hands.

"I don't know southwest. I don't know where the car is."

"Find a river. Follow it back."

"Kandy —"

"No. You're going to need your Gran. Get Pearl."

"Kett." He was really starting to freak me out. He was heavy — oddly heavy for his size relative to me — and getting difficult to hold steady.

"I'm right behind you." He stepped back so my hands fell away from him. "Go now, dowser." He swayed as if buffeted by a nonexistent wind.

"You don't seem okay."

"I can still keep up with you." He grinned. His teeth were too pointy for my liking. "You still move more like a human than you should."

"How would you know?" I snapped. Yes, the topic of my parentage was an instant trigger.

"It would be a shame for you to die. I would do anything in my power to save you. Don't make me save you, Jade."

A chill ran down my spine. His use of my name, and what I was pretty sure was a threat to my humanity — or whatever I was — completely unnerved me.

I turned and ran.

Kett followed, but he wasn't chasing me.

The bear had bulldozed a path through the underbrush, so I followed it. Least resistance and all that.

I all-out sprinted. Not really knowing where I was going, but still running as fast as I could.

I felt Kett falter behind me, and I slowed to hook my arm around his waist and pull him with me.

He snarled but didn't pull away.

I didn't look at him. I was afraid I'd see red eyes and full-on fangs. I was hyperaware that my neck was very exposed on my left side. I wrapped my right hand around my knife and pushed myself to run faster.

I wasn't too sure that following the bear's path and dragging Kett with me was the right thing to do, but I still hadn't given up hope of finding Kandy. Bears didn't eat humans, right? Right?

Kett stumbled, practically yanking my shoulder out of its socket. I clutched him tighter. Once again, though only a couple of inches taller than me, he was suddenly very heavy.

I heard the river just as Kett wrenched himself away from me and dashed ahead. I followed, my shoulder screaming in relief at losing his weight.

I sprinted out of the forest to find myself on the smooth-rocked edge of a large river. It was wide and full, but I had no idea if it was the Squamish or some other. A logging road, I guessed, ran parallel along the far side of the rushing, frothing water.

I couldn't see Kett anywhere, though I was fairly certain I'd just been right behind him. Nor could I see Kandy or evidence of the bear. I faltered, unsure whether to turn left, right, or attempt to swim across the river to the road. Because all roads led somewhere, right?

Something shrieked behind me. It didn't sound human, but I wasn't sure if animals screamed like that.

Involuntarily — or perhaps instinctively — I darted forward at the sound and stopped at the edge of the river with the water at my back. The water-worn stones were wet and well polished underneath my feet. It would be easy to lose my footing if I panicked, even in my thick-tread hiking boots. So I willed my heartbeat and breathing to slow as I glanced around.

Trees and more trees spread off from either side of the river and road. The river twisted, seemingly endlessly, in either direction. Multiple mountains loomed all around me.

I still had no idea where I was, but now I'd lost both my companions.

The river had to be crazy cold, seeing as how it was fed by the glaciers of those mountains, now more intimidating than beautiful. Their peaks were still snow capped even this late in July, though the summer had been warm and unusually dry in Vancouver so far. So, river, cold. Deadly cold, if one was stupid enough about it.

Focus. Focus.

I reached out with my dowser senses and looked for a glimmer of Kandy's or Kett's magic. I closed my eyes and slowly pivoted, though the movement was more psychologically than physically necessary.

There ... I felt Kandy not too far away, but on the other side of the river. I kept turning. Had Kett also crossed the water, thinking I'd follow? I couldn't feel him —

Oh, shit.

I opened my eyes.

A black bear, a coyote, and a red fox sat at the edge of the forest about fifteen feet away. The woods at their backs, the river at mine. Something shrieked at me from the trees. No, cawed — really, really loudly. A crow. A huge crow. A raven.

The raven shrieked a second time. It was perched on the lowest branch of a cedar tree just behind the other three animals.

What the fuck? Pardon my language, but please what the fuck?

"A bear, a coyote, and a fox walked into a bar ..."

The animals just watched me, but I was absolutely certain that watching might turn into rending in the blink of my eye. They all tasted of the same huckleberry and wild onion magic that had wafted off the grizzly bear. Had some sorcerer spelled all the freaking animals in the forest? Well, all the animals with teeth and claws? Of course, I hadn't seen any beavers yet. They usually stuck to rivers ... like the one at my back.

I settled my hand on my knife and took a step back. The river boiled up over the top of my boots, eagerly wetting my socks and calves. It had to have been a sorcerer, not a witch, of course. Witches were one with nature and would never endanger an animal. Well, most witches ...

The raven screamed again. I imagined it would go for my eyes. I liked my eyes. They were perfectly indigo blue, and very helpful for seeing and such.

"You guys seem to be missing your buddy. You know, nine feet tall, brown hair, a little on the heavy side?" The animals shifted but thankfully didn't talk back. The sarcasm was more for my benefit than theirs, anyway. Confidence building, you know. Seeing as I was about to do something crazy.

I took another step back, up to my knees in the river now and barely able to keep upright in its strong pull. I couldn't fight all of them if they attacked at the same time. Instant healing was probably only good if I wasn't torn to bits. Not that I wanted to test it.

The black bear — smaller than the grizzly by like 50 percent, but able to climb trees — reared up on its hind legs. Why I knew or thought of the tree-climbing thing, I didn't know. The raven could just fly over the river, of course. And maybe the bear could swim across?

It didn't matter.

The coyote and fox gathered themselves and leaped for my throat. Or so I imagined.

They missed as I jumped backward into the icy river and let it take me.

The water rolled over my head and sucked me down. I hit something with my leg, but my scream of pain was swallowed by the water. Then something else slammed into my shoulder … rocks, boulders in the river. I surfaced — though through no effort of my own — and managed to get a lungful of air after expelling a gallon of water.

I went under again, pulled effortlessly by the vicious current.

I lost all sense of up, down, sky, or water.

I slammed into more rocks, wrapping my arms around my head in a fleeting hope of protecting what little brains I had.

Then I prayed that drowning was a better death than being mauled and torn to pieces.

Chapter Three

After I didn't immediately drown — though once again, this wasn't due to any brilliant strategy on my part — I slowly figured out how to maneuver myself closer to the opposite side of the river.

I hauled my soaking-wet ass to shore. The sun had come out, but I was seriously freezing.

I was dignified enough to not simply flop face down on the rocky bank. Instead, I chose to perch on a boulder. Okay, I obscenely wrapped myself around it in an attempt to steal every iota of heat it had accumulated during the short amount of time the sun had been out today.

My clothing had survived the river fairly well. The left pocket of my Gore-Tex was ripped and the hood was missing. However, seeing as I still had two working feet, legs, and hands, as well as my head intact, I figured that potentially drowning had been a successful risk. Yes, I liked to justify my crazy decisions after the fact. Don't we all?

Unfortunately, now I really had no idea where Kandy and Kett were. I wasn't sure how far I'd been dragged downriver, but I couldn't sense either of them. I also couldn't sense any huckleberry-and-onion magic either, so I guessed that the spelled or ensnared animals weren't near. I wasn't fully certain an animal's behavior could be controlled with a spell or that their minds could be ensnared, but I also wasn't completely versed on all the powers of all the Adept.

Yeah, big surprise, huh?

Sorcerers, I knew, worked from books and with magical objects. The magic on Kandy and the animals didn't appear to come from an obvious object or weapon, but that didn't rule out a book of power. Sorcerer books weren't the same as the spellbooks Gran had collected from her ancestors or created herself. Witches were directly connected to the magic within the earth. Sorcerers needed a conduit. So, a sorcerer was stalking these woods? Even though everything I knew about sorcerers indicated they weren't much for hiking or roughing it in general? Plus, what would be the end game?

I also wasn't sure what river I'd just pulled myself out of. I'd gotten seriously turned around in the forest. Kett had said to head southeast, but that was entirely unhelpful without a compass. If I even knew how to work a compass. Which I didn't.

Oh! Maybe there was an app for that ... if my phone wasn't completely wet fried. Damn. I wasn't even six months into my three-year contract. And, of course, if I could have downloaded an app, I could probably just call someone instead. Sometimes my own stupidity seemed almost willfully ignorant. Like when Sienna had been — No. I wasn't dwelling there anymore.

I stood up — stiff in my wet, tight jeans — and stared at the river. I'd seen a logging road from my vantage point on the other bank. It might still be nearby if I headed back into the woods. But if this was the Squamish River — I was hoping the presence of the logging road verified that — then did it run toward or away from Squamish, Howe Sound, and therefore Vancouver?

Or did it run through this massive valley somewhere into ... I didn't know, Haida Gwaii?

I had no idea. I put off the course direction decision by heading straight back into the forest to find the logging road. Maybe I'd be lucky and find a marker or a sign telling me which way to turn.

I really, really just wanted to be warm and dry and making cupcakes. I'd been working on a cherry buttercream icing since getting my hands on fresh, fairly local — from the Okanagan — cherries this summer. There had been a late frost that had delayed the cherry season. I was waffling over possible cake bases, either my favorite dark chocolate cake or a fluffier white. Maybe I should do both and let the customers decide. I was also toying with the names *Kiss in a Cup* or *Harmony in a Cup*. Both concepts were wishful thinking on my part. However, to my dismay, so far I couldn't get the frosting thick enough to spread without the sweetness of the icing sugar overwhelming the cherry flavor. Kandy didn't mind eating the experiments, though.

I stumbled out of the woods onto a hard-packed dirt logging road. I'd missed the step down, hence the stumble. The road looked well used, and not badly overgrown. Two cars could pass easily if they were careful, but actual logging trucks would need to back up.

So ... right or left? I peered up at the mountains surrounding me, but they weren't helpful. I stretched out my dowser senses to feel for Kandy and Kett but couldn't find them, not even with my hands wrapped around my knife and necklace.

I dug into my unripped jacket pocket and pulled out the few jade rocks I'd collected from the river earlier. Could I somehow make a compass or some sort of tracking device to get me back to the car? I hadn't deliberately tried to make a magical object since the night I'd used the ring off my necklace and a hank of hair to track Sienna down. And most days — honestly — I regretted doing that more than just about anything I'd ever done.

That night, I found Rusty's half-eaten body, then had discovered that Sienna had done the eating. Most likely consuming the flesh of her boyfriend, a latent necromancer, to raise the corpse of my would-be boyfriend, Hudson. Hudson, a werewolf, had been in town with a few of his pack members to investigate the murder of another werewolf, who — it turned out — Sienna had also killed, somehow using the magic contained in my trinkets to anchor her own.

Yeah, it sounded just as insane in my head as it had been in front of my blind eyes.

I hadn't actually known before that night that I was capable of more than simply sensing magical objects or things — that I had the exceedingly rare ability to create them as well. It wasn't remotely an even trade, finding out that I'm possibly an alchemist, but losing my sister to her blood-magic addiction, and ... well, her need to be more. To be something special.

Ironically, she got her wish — along with a postmortem tribunal. She, along with her boyfriend Rusty, had been found guilty of three murders, four attempted murders, and the practicing of blood magic. None of the so-called attempts — namely Kandy, Kett, Desmond, or me — had wanted to be included in the charges. Wounded pride on the part of the other three made them underplay the severity of the evening. Perhaps they were embarrassed that a half-witch managed to lure, bind, and then practice blood magic on them. Or maybe it was the humiliation of being rescued by me, someone who was also way beneath them in the power department. And me ... well, I just couldn't believe that Sienna would actually try to kill me. Yes, I had justified to myself getting stabbed — twice — by my own sister.

The witches Convocation — headed, to my surprise, by Gran — had been unanimous. Scarlett, my mother — and this was even more surprising — had demanded to fill a vacant seat on the Convocation before the trial. A seat that had been available and offered to her every year for the previous ten years.

So, yeah. Sienna's actions had been extreme and damaging enough that my free spirit of a mother had tied herself to the Convocation for life, to make sure … what? That practitioners of blood magic were further ostracized? Sienna was already dead. There was no punishment beyond that, was there?

I shook off the dark thoughts and bounced the stones in my palm. I was starting to shiver again. I needed to keep moving. I couldn't create a magical compass or tracking device, because I didn't have anything to tie the stones to Kandy's or Kett's magic. I had nothing that would enable a stone to detect direction — specifically, southeast.

I turned and took a few steps left, against the flow of the river behind me. Then I stopped and turned in the other direction.

It was a freaking road. It led somewhere in either bloody direction.

So I walked, keeping all my senses on alert for magic … and bears, of course.

Turns out I was being wary of the wrong predator.

I wasn't sure how long I'd walked. It felt like hours, but the vampire would have called it minutes.

My clothes weren't dry yet, so I was still freezing every time the breeze picked up.

I still couldn't feel any trace of Kandy or Kett. No other magical glimmers, either. I was utterly useless. And utterly lost. Thank God my chocolate bar hadn't completely washed away. Yes, I checked. I'm aware that reflects badly on me.

Off to the right — so back toward the river, though the road had curved away from the bank at this point so I could only hear the water rather than see it — I felt a hint of the huckleberry and wild onion magic. I darted into the trees to the left, put a few feet and a few huge cedars between me and this new gathering of magic, and paused.

I waited to see if this grouping — I could feel four distinct magic users now — was tracking me, or if I'd just inadvertently happened upon them. They didn't seem to be moving closer ... maybe they were along the river's edge? I couldn't tell. This entire reaching out with my dowser senses and tracking magic was still way new to me.

I also couldn't tell if I was sensing the spelled animals from before — either the grizzly or the black bear, the coyote, the fox, or the raven — or if maybe I was sensing the spellcasters, or witches, or sorcerers themselves.

I wasn't a complete idiot. I mean, it was pretty obvious even to me that Kandy and then Kett had been hit and incapacitated by some spell. Even though werewolves and vampires were supposed to be quite resistant to magic. I remembered Kett and Desmond slowly breaking free of Sienna's blood-magic-fueled binding spell. And bindings had been her specialty, even without the blood magic power boost.

Okay, keeping with the I'm-not-a-complete-idiot train of thought ... I should keep off the road. If the magical signatures I could feel by the river — moving away from me now — were human and looking for me, they would eventually cut over to the road. If they were animals? Well, then I was probably screwed. But I couldn't completely leave the road or river because it was the only means I had to orientate myself at the moment.

I turned to scan the forest behind me. Perhaps there was another path?

Oh, yes. That looked like one. It was narrow, but obviously a commonly used path for forest animals and such.

Obviously, because there was currently a gigantic mountain lion stalking along it toward me.

The mountain lion — it was too large to simply be called a cougar — paused and lowered its head to glare at me.

Yes, glare. It was easily nine feet nose to tail and over two-hundred plus pounds. Its front paws were the size of side plates, claws retracted. Its broad shoulders, tawny fur, and green eyes would have been gorgeous if the cat hadn't been about to eat me.

Wait a second ... green eyes?

The mountain lion pulled its lips back in a low-pitched hiss that ended in a rumbling growl as it started stalking toward me again.

I would have, should have, been pissing my pants, except I knew this beast. It wasn't a friend, but it wasn't a foe ... at least, I didn't think so. It did seem really pissed. Not that I'd ever seen a pissed mountain lion before.

Indeed, as the beast stalked closer — taking its time and underlying its movement with a growl meant to freeze me in my tracks — I felt the shapeshifter magic gather and roll over me. This magic was spicy, dark hot chocolate with a thick creamy base. It gathered all sparkly green around the huge cat. Then in the moment I was forced to look away because it was too bright, the mountain lion transformed into Desmond Charles Llewelyn, Lord and Alpha of the West Coast North American Pack. I'd nicknamed him McGrowly — in my head — because he scared me and I needed to make him at least slightly ridiculous somehow.

Desmond was absolutely gorgeous and dangerous in cat form. But as a man, he was hard — almost overly muscled — and exceedingly difficult.

And completely naked.

Okay, Jesus. Of course he was naked.

And now I was staring.

He growled — his vocal cords still more cat than human — and padded the last few feet toward me. His broad toes curled in the dirt and leaves underfoot as if he still had claws. The hair on his head was darker than his tawny cat fur, but a similarly colored dusting of hair covered his chest, down his insane abs, and through to his ... Well. I seriously hoped he was a shower, not a grower, because ... err ... for his girlfriend's sake of course ... not me —

"What have you done with my wolf?" he asked with a snarl as he crossed the last couple of steps between us. "It felt like you were dying, dowser. And now I find you here, cowering in the woods. Half-soaked and without your protector, who I can't smell anywhere nearby."

I was forced by proximity to look him in the eye. It was a mistake. It had to be. Otherwise, I was somehow responsible for my next actions, rather than just being enchanted, or spelled, or mesmerized by the magic in those emerald-flecked golden brown eyes.

I opened my mouth to answer his questions. He curled his lip at me.

Then I reached out, stepped into him — close enough to touch chests but not — and wrapped my arms around his neck.

He had time to frown before I plastered my lips across his. It wasn't a soft kiss. It was a terrified, lost, I-just-almost-drowned-and-can't-find-my-friends kiss.

He didn't kiss me back.

I closed the inch of space between us, pressing my full length against his nakedness.

He grunted — surprised, I think — and I attempted to soften the desperation out of the kiss. Except I was scared and alone, and it had been months since I'd kissed anyone. I just needed to kiss someone.

He lifted his hands to unlatch me from his neck, I think, but got his fingers tangled in my wild, river-washed, sun-dried curls instead. His touch was light as he combed my hair through his fingers. His lips softened underneath mine and I opened my mouth ever so invitingly. He offered up his tongue and I slid mine across his.

His magic coated every inch of him. It was utterly delicious. The fear, the tension, I'd been holding at the ready for three months melted away into the kiss.

His hand cupped the back of my head and he deepened the lip lock.

I melted further, completely sinking my body against his with the tiniest of sighs. I ran my hands across his too-broad shoulders, feeling every edge of every muscle. His skin was hot. His magic tingled underneath my fingers and palms.

He was being too gentle, as if he was afraid of hurting me. I imagined that might often be a problem for him, but I wanted to be held, to be crushed, to be taken away from all the uncertainty and pain. If I was going to drown, I wanted to drown coated in his delicious magic.

I ground against him, biting lightly down on his bottom lip.

He reached down — sliding his hand along the side of my breast, waist, and hip — and tugged my leg up around his to settle his groin tighter against mine.

Oh, God. He was a grower. I could feel the hard length of him across my pubic bone and lower belly.

I darted my tongue in his mouth and lifted my other leg up around his hips, now completely wrapped around his nakedness with all my limbs.

He took two steps and pressed me against the tree I'd been hiding behind. I remembered the first tree he'd pressed me against that terrible day when my sense of the world cracked along with my heart. I remembered complaining. I didn't complain now. I pushed the thought away and clenched my hands into what little of his hair I could grab as I tried to devour his mouth and his magic.

He slipped his hands — his skin and magic were searingly hot — underneath my jacket and T-shirt as he ground against me. I could feel the girth of him even through my damp jeans, and I moaned quietly, welcoming the bloom of heat he generated between my legs. This pleasurable ache informed me that I was wearing way too much clothing.

I untangled my arms from his neck and wrestled with my jacket without removing my lips and tongue from his. He helped. Something tore. I paused the kissing to note that he'd ripped the arm of my Gore-Tex.

I chuckled and he grinned. The fabric, now freed from the shoulder seam, pooled down my arm and caught at my wrist.

I pulled my head back to focus on his face. He curled his lips into a toothless smile. His face was as relaxed and open as I'd ever seen it. He wasn't so inscrutable and overly chiseled now.

"Good kiss," he said.

I laughed. "Cool cat form."

"All the better to stalk you with."

I smiled and then leaned forward to continue the make-out session.

Desmond slapped his hand to his neck as if he'd just been bitten by a mosquito. I laughed again, but when he pulled his hand away, I felt something, some glimmer —

He slapped his hand to his neck a second time and took a step back. I loosened my legs from around his hips and dropped to the ground.

I felt another glimmer nearby, and without thinking, reached out and snatched it from the air.

Desmond and I stared at the wooden dart — more like a small arrow — I'd just caught. It dissolved into a pool of magic in my palm.

"What the hell?" I said. The dart had somehow been loaded with the magic I'd sensed earlier on Kandy. I tried to shake it from my fingers but didn't get it all off. I wiped the rest across the ass of my jeans.

More glimmers sparked from the forest around us. My knife was in my hand before I could even think to pull it out, and I cut three more down before they reached us.

Desmond slapped his chest once more and then growled. A low warning growl. "Where and what are they?" he asked. His beast was very present in his voice.

And by beast, I wasn't referring to his mountain lion form.

I knocked two more magic darts away before they could reach us. "I don't know. And four. Spread around us. Hidden beyond the trees there, there, and there. The fourth is moving … there." I pointed toward the huckleberry and wild onion magic that emanated from among the trees. I'd been too focused on Desmond, and the gathering by the river had found us.

"Be careful where you step," I said, just as Desmond trod on one of the downed darts. He stumbled and let out a fierce growl. Then his skin literally boiled with a blast of shifter magic, and his half-beast, half-man form poured forth.

This beast was no fuzzy kitty. No pretty, dangerous thing. This form was over seven feet tall — a trade-off between his human and cat forms, I guessed — and deadly ugly.

This beast was McGrowly in the terrible flesh. It was hard to look at him, all furred, clawed, and double fanged. I wasn't sure he could close his mouth fully in this state — all the better to chomp the heads off prey.

Magic glimmers hidden in more wooden darts winged toward us. I knocked down four and missed the fifth, which hit McGrowly in the chest.

"Five now," I shouted. "Two directly behind you."

McGrowly whirled toward the magical signatures I'd pointed out. It was more difficult to protect him as he stalked away from me. Two darts hit him. I grabbed one out of the thin air right before my left eye. "Freaking hell!" I yelled. "My freaking eye?"

McGrowly casually knocked over a tree in his way. It wasn't a two-hundred-year old, but was still a good forty or fifty years thick. He pushed it over like as normal person draws back blinds.

All the darts — five and then five more in quick release — winged toward McGrowly now. Four hit him. I wasn't fast enough, and he couldn't feel their magic as I could.

He stumbled. I tried to keep up with him, but walking backward was awkward. They weren't aiming for me anymore.

McGrowly snarled, reached up into the boughs of a cedar, and cracked a massive branch right off.

A man fell out at his feet. A perfectly normal-looking plaid shirt, hiking boots, and all — Native American male. He looked completely terrified — so would I if hell-on-claws was standing over me — but still managed to raise a blow pipe to his lips and hit McGrowly in the face with his last dart.

McGrowly, who had been leaning over the man at the time of the hit, didn't stop leaning.

I'd lost count, but I guessed even the alpha werecat of the West Coast North American pack couldn't withstand a dozen or more magical darts. Sleep-spelled darts.

McGrowly tumbled over onto the native guy, whose shout was abruptly cut off. Well, that was one bad guy down at least.

I closed the space to them in two bounding steps, ready to defend McGrowly, and got hit with four darts for my inattention. It was easier to keep count when the magic exploded against you.

It got harder and harder to avoid the darts, and I couldn't focus enough to burn off the foreign magic — though that was another hard-learned power I could now access. By the time I fell, I was surrounded by four more native people. First Nations actually, but I didn't feel like being particularly politically correct in this moment. Two women and two more men. Their ages ranged from sixteen to mid-forties at best guess. Their expressions were serious — unrelenting, and unforgiving of some transgression I didn't know of.

I didn't talk, didn't try to bargain. I simply tried to defend McGrowly. I suppose I should have run, but I was tired of being lost. I was tired of not fighting for what I thought was right. And I was really, really cupcake deprived. Not that I had any hope of waking to find myself in a kitchen with all the right ingredients, but still ... I had to be me to the bitter, tasteless end.

The huckleberry and onion magic flooded my senses, overwhelmed my body, and I fell.

Chapter Four

"Dowser," a cool voice murmured in my ear. "You're awake, dowser."

"I'm not awake," I answered, really pissed that I did seem to be coming out of some crazy deep sleep. Pissed, because I wasn't exactly sleeping well lately, the vampire shouldn't be in my bedroom, and my bed was made of sticks and rocks. Then I remembered.

I remembered that sleep was the least of my problems. That being sleep deprived was an issue from my old life. The nice, peaceful life where the cool voice of a vampire right next to my ear didn't wake me into fear and uncertainty.

"Don't open your eyes," Kett continued, ignoring as he always did my penchant for childish statements. "You're magically bound. You need to neutralize the magic, free yourself, and run."

It drove me crazy when the vampire issued impossibilities as if they were everyday instructions. Neutralize the binds? WTF? With what? Baking soda? But damn it, my feet and hands were tied and I was missing my knife. Not a surprise, but still, I didn't like to be without it.

"Dowser, now would be a good time. They appear to be arguing about our future. I've heard mention of fire. That wouldn't be pleasant."

Jesus, they were going to torch us? Who the hell would burn someone alive? Oh … the vampire was referring to himself. They'd obviously figured out what he was … but, I was fairly certain they were wrong about the fire thing in Kett's case. Vampires grew immune to sunlight and fire — to a certain extent — as they aged. So, the older the vampire, the more powerful the vampire. As far as I could figure, Kett was pretty damn old.

I attempted to push through my groggy senses — my natural human ones — to hear this so-called argument that was going on. I picked up the noises of the forest — wind through tree branches mostly. The crackle of the fire — so Kett was right about that. And breathing. By the low levels of magic I could feel as I became more aware, both Desmond and Kandy were close by. Kett was beside me.

I really, really wanted to open my eyes, and not just because the vampire told me not to. I was fairly certain I was lying on my left side with my back to the fire, facing the others. By 'others,' I meant the five — no, now six — Native Americans from the forest. Now that I recognized it, their magic was unmistakable. That tart berry and onion combo that some of them held in larger quantities than others. I guessed that the eldest was the most powerful, if magic worked for them the same way it often did for witches.

My hands, tied behind my back, were numb. My entire left arm, on which I was lying, was deadened as well. The air shifted, a slight breeze tickled my cheeks, and by the smell and coolness of it, I guessed it was after dark. Voices came on the breeze as well. The Native American's were indeed discussing us. I picked up concern and caution along with anger in their tone, but no actual words.

"Dowser," Kett said. "The shifter is waking. He won't react well to being bound. And they won't be able to sedate him a second time without violence."

Great, no pressure. Kett meant Desmond, though I didn't know how the vampire knew he was waking. Heartbeat or breathing, maybe? Shapeshifters were known to be resistant to magic — though obviously enough of it could take them down — but Kett seemed to be indicating that the sleep darts wouldn't work a second time. Damn. I was still hoping to get out of this alive.

I refocused on the magic binding my hands. I could feel rope of some kind on my skin, but it was magically imbued as well. Which made sense, because a vampire or werewolf could tear through normal rope like tissue paper. But obviously even Kett couldn't break these bindings, just as he'd had a difficult time breaking Sienna's binding spell in the bakery cellar. That magic had been fueled by blood and murder, but this magic was as earthbound as any true witch's.

I shoved thoughts of Sienna out of my mind, wishing I had a physical compartment I could close and lock thoughts of my sister in. Then I tried to figure out what Kett meant by neutralize.

Magic — or energy as some preferred to call it — couldn't be destroyed, but spells could be countered. Except I wasn't a spell sort of witch. I combined or channeled. I had channeled residual magic into my necklace before, but that had been my own magic. I didn't want to accidentally alter the protective power of the necklace by channeling the huckleberry magic into it. My knife, maybe ... except I didn't have my knife.

What I did have were the five jade stones I'd fished out of the river. The natural magic of the jade glimmered faintly in the pocket of my jacket. Kett always swore he could feel nothing magical about these bits of things that called so brightly to me. Supposedly, sensing magic was one of the talents the vampire retained from his previous life, before his death and transformation.

Were the stones large enough to hold the magic of the bindings on my hands? Magic had no mass or weight, really. Only my inability to perceive it as possible or impossible really mattered. Technically, I was touching the stones, or they were touching me, but could I combine magic through Gore-tex and jean fabric?

"Dowser," Kett whispered. His voice wasn't so cool anymore. The native grouping had splintered. Two magical signatures were heading toward us. Plus Desmond's breathing had changed, not so deep now.

Just focus. Focus.

I thought about the magic binding my hands. I felt the way it coated the rope beneath it. I thought about the glimmer of magic in the stones. I remembered the way I had taken the residual magic from Sienna's hair and the wedding ring from my necklace. How I had smoothed those together, using my own magic as a solder of sorts. I'd created a tracking device from those two glimmers. I hadn't known it would work then, but it had. So it could work now.

I imagined the magic from the bindings moving through my skin, sinking in, riding my own magic through my body, through my jeans, into my jacket pocket to mix with the natural magic of the jade stones. Then I imagined the jade holding the binding magic at bay, containing it as I wished I could contain the thoughts of my sister.

The two native magical signatures grabbed Kett and began to drag him around me, toward the fire at my back. Kett fought, but — now that I had intimate knowledge of the binding magic — I could feel how much imbued rope they'd wrapped him in. Which was okay, because they'd underestimated me.

I opened my eyes. Two more of our captors had rushed to help with Kett. He was twisting and writhing, knocking them off their feet, but they were still managing to get him closer, bit by bit, to the fire.

I imagined myself ripping through the plain rope now binding my wrists, like opening a bag of chips. Then I did so.

I sat up. All eyes were on Kett, including an older woman and a teenager — a girl, barely old enough to be called a teen — who'd chosen to not participate in the vampire torching.

I wrapped my hands around the rope at my ankles, and with the briefest of thoughts, channeled the binding magic into the stones in my pocket. Yeah, it was easier the second time.

The older woman was frowning at the group struggling with Kett. She was also holding my knife.

I stood and broke the rope around my ankles at the same time. This movement drew the attention of the older woman. I could see even by firelight — it was indeed after dark — the silver that shot through her glossy, straight black hair. As far as I could tell, without focusing too far away from my captors, we were still in the middle of the forest, nestled between looming mountains. I couldn't hear the river.

"I don't like people touching my things," I said.

The teen turned to me, her eyes widening. The four others, only a few feet away from me, dropped Kett and turned toward me, fumbling in their pockets for blow pipes, I guessed.

The teenager grabbed my knife from the woman, stepping in front of the elder to brandish it before her. Brave but stupid. We were probably kindred souls.

47

"I was pretty clear. That's mine." I pointed to the knife, only to have it appear in my raised hand.

Well, that was new, and completely unintentional. Super cool move, though.

The four who'd been wrestling with Kett, rushed me, but they hadn't noticed that Desmond had woken. He was back in human form, though I tried to not notice how sexy all that skin looked by firelight. He kicked out his legs and took two of them down. Then he spun his bound hands toward me.

I slashed through his bindings, hands and then feet, even as I pivoted away from the tackling move of the two other Native Americans.

Desmond grabbed Kandy, who'd been lying beside him. He swung her by me — she was still knocked out — and I slashed through her bindings.

One of the guys that Desmond had knocked off his feet leaped and tackled me below the knees. The alpha dashed off into the dark woods with Kandy in his arms. His priorities were always straight.

I fell, three sets of hands on me now, but managed to do so over top of Kett, who had rolled back toward me.

They'd wrapped the rope from his shoulders to his knees. Someone tried to grab the knife out of my hand as I awkwardly tried to cut the vampire's bonds. The would-be thief screamed as the knife burned him.

"Do I have to keep repeating myself?" I asked as I drove my elbow back into his sternum. "Don't. Touch. My. Things. Or my friends."

I freed Kett, slashing through his clothing and skin in my rush. He barely bled. He did that quick-moving thing that vamps were apparently able to do, and suddenly no one was holding me down any longer.

I gained my feet. Kett stood to my left. I turned back to the older woman and the teenager. The other four were recovering from being tossed away like a child's candy wrappers.

I locked my gaze to the older woman's. It was obvious by the way the others gathered to her that she was their leader. Not that she'd managed to stop them from attempting to burn Kett — though maybe it had been her idea and she didn't like to get her hands dirty.

My eyes flicked to the teenager who was attempting to not tremble. She had feathers woven into her hair.

Desmond, still in naked human form, stepped out of the forest behind me and stood to my right.

"Nice feathers," I said. I always paid compliments where they were due.

The four other adults — three men and a younger woman — grasped the necklaces they wore. Necklaces of teeth, which was just creepy. The tart but spicy huckleberry and onion magic rose up around them like a cloak. Then suddenly, the four had become the animals I'd encountered in the woods. A grizzly, a black bear, a coyote, and a red fox.

"Not shapeshifters," I said. "The magic is wrong, and they didn't transform."

"Skinwalkers," Kett said. His voice was as cool and unruffled as always. Not that that was any indication of whether he was pissed off or not. I'd figured that out the hard way a couple of times.

"This wouldn't be the treasure we've been hunting, would it?" Even as I asked, I was really hoping I was wrong, and that we hadn't been tracking a rare breed of Adepts this entire time.

Kett didn't answer.

Damn it. Maybe I was willfully ignorant, because I hated it when I was on the wrong side. Completely wrong. As in, not only were we most likely trespassing on First Nations land, but our treasure hunt — led by a vampire — probably looked way aggressive.

"Damn you, vampire," Desmond said under his breath.

The teenager and the elder hadn't transformed. I easily guessed that the woman was the raven, and that the teen hadn't been chosen by an animal yet. That's how most Native American legend worked, wasn't it?

"I get that our being here, on your land, is not cool. That you might have thought we wished you harm. But really, who brings a child to a monster party anyway?" I said, addressing the elder. Yeah, probably a little overly aggressive. But hell, they just kidnapped us all and tried to throw Kett in the fire.

"It is her right to confront the strangers trespassing on her land," the elder answered.

"Well, it's a hard lesson you've set her up to learn today. My own Gran opted to keep me safe and sheltered instead."

The grizzly stepped forward with a growl, but the elder held him off with a terse command in a language I didn't understand.

"Your Gran should have taught you the proper way to enter the territory of another."

"That is my error," Kett said. "The Conclave was unaware that the skinwalkers were ... resurfacing."

"Vampires," the elder spat, but didn't elaborate her distaste. She didn't need to. None of the Adept liked vampires, and it wasn't just the blood drinking. The immortality, invulnerability, and insular nature pissed them off as well.

"Here's the thing," I said, interrupting the staring match between the elder and the vampire. I'd noted the other skinwalkers getting impatient.

"You transgressed," the teenager said with a snarl. "We have every right to retaliate."

I ignored her. "My friends here — the all-powerful vampire and the two vicious shapeshifters — don't take kindly to being hunted and tied up."

"And you, witch? If that is what you are. Do the vampire and the shifters follow or lead you?" the elder asked. She wasn't being sarcastic or nasty. She sounded truly curious.

"Neither. And that's a problem. Because we're in the middle of the forest, and none of the magical community knows you exist. Right? So if you try to stop us from leaving and the slaughter and bloodletting happens, there won't be any tribunal stepping in to sort out punishment. I know. I've been through one before."

The skinwalkers in animal form shifted impatiently again, but the elder appeared to be listening to me.

"My name is Jade Godfrey. I own a bakery in Vancouver called Cake in a Cup," I continued. "Let's just part ways now without more violence and I'll treat us all to cupcakes. You name the date. My Gran would probably love to meet you." I let my offer hang in the smoky air between us, hoping the skinwalkers would back down, and marveling at the self-control that Desmond and Kett were exhibiting.

"Just to be clear. The sleep spells won't work a second time. Will they?" I asked Kett.

"No," he answered, turning his head slightly toward me. The firelight flared in his eyes, turning them momentarily red. I shuddered. I was more afraid of the monsters beside me than the ones in front.

"The skinwalking is an amazing ability. But you are still just human underneath, aren't you?"

The elder didn't answer, but I'd kicked the grizzly and seen his reaction. He was also still favoring the shoulder I'd stabbed when he took Kandy. They cloaked themselves in the animal forms, and possibly gained some strength as well as the teeth and claws, but they could be hurt ... badly.

"You understand that we ... well, my companions, at least, are not human?"

Again the elder nodded.

"Your magic is unique. And if I understood Kett's statement, thought to be extinct."

The elder nodded.

"Please don't do this." I said, turning to include Kett and Desmond in this appeal. "Please, we transgressed and for that we are sorry. Please don't make us fight."

The teenager turned to look up at the elder. Her grandmother, I guessed. The elder sighed. If they tried to detain us again, and Desmond and Kett killed them all, the teenager would never come into her powers. She would never understand her connection to the energy or spirit, as Gran called it, of the earth.

When the hell did I become the freaking wise diplomat of the group? And since when did Desmond and Kett stand quietly — though alertly — by while I chatted about the possibility of them slaughtering people. I guess they agreed. I felt old and jaded.

I sheathed my knife, shoved my other hand in my pocket, and brushed my fingers across the jade stones. The skinwalker magic they held was precious, but I didn't have any more words with which to convince the elder.

The teenager was correct — it was their right to retaliate against our trespassing. But they would likely die defending that right. Yeah, perhaps I was being a little melodramatic. But I'd seen Kett and Desmond in action. They'd defend themselves then exact their own revenge as was their right ... even though we were in the wrong first. My head was going to explode.

"Go get Kandy," Desmond said. And despite the command in his voice — and the fact that I usually chafed at it — I turned and walked away into the forest.

Kandy found me, actually. I was still stumbling around in the dark, attempting to track her werewolf magic, when a gray wolf with green-glowing eyes appeared in a shaft of moonlight between the trees. Deliberately showing herself to me, I assumed, so as to not freak me out further.

I held my hand out to her and she put her head underneath my palm and pressed up. Her potent werewolf magic was more concentrated in her animal form, and I could sense no further trace of the skinwalker sleep spell on her.

I knew how Kandy took her steak — blue rare — her preferred movies — horror or teen sex comedy — and that she was a fiercely loyal pack member. But I'd never seen her in her wolf form before.

I wondered if it was an intimate thing for this normally brash, outspoken, and slightly kinky woman. I also wondered if the transformation helped her burn off the skinwalkers' impressive magic. Impressive in that it took down a vampire, two shapeshifters, and whatever the hell I was.

Kandy whined and circled me to face back the way I'd come.

"You know he won't want us to go back," I said, guessing at her thoughts. She just continued to stare off into the trees.

I brushed my fingers in the fur of Kandy's neck, aware I would never take such liberties if she was in human form, but wanting to comfort her somehow. Her coat was silky and smooth underneath the guard hairs, and practically silver in the moonlight. I estimated that she was the same weight in both of her forms, about a hundred and twenty-five pounds of pure lean muscle. When we did yoga together, she put me to shame, though I was a fan of having all the right curves in all the right places.

I could still taste Desmond's magic behind me — so similar to Kandy's, though she was more berry than his citrusy dark chocolate. Her magic came with a refined but bitter finish. Delicious, but edgy. Not the kind of chocolate you bake with, but better paired with wine or even strong cheese. Kett's presence as well — all his cool peppermint magic — was still strong behind me.

But I wasn't too sure about the skinwalkers. The farther away I got, the more their magic collected into a grouping rather than individual signatures. Perhaps this meant they were all blood-related, or perhaps it was an adaptive evolution thing to better hide their nature. It could also mean that Kett and Desmond were hunting and slaughtering them one by one in the dark woods of their ancestral land.

Yeah, I got the irony.

Kandy whined again. Then she turned and began to lead me through the forest. I could still barely make out the shapes of the trees, but, when the growth got too thick, there was nothing at all.

I stumbled and fell three times before we came within hearing range of the river and hit the slightly smoother ground of the logging road.

Kandy headed in the direction the river ran, so I guess I'd been correct about it being the Squamish and flowing toward Vancouver — or specifically, Howe Sound. I didn't praise myself too much. The choice had really just been a coin toss ... if I'd had a coin.

We'd parked at Alice Lake Park and walked at least three hours before getting attacked. I wasn't sure how far away we were now, but I really wished I could turn into a wolf and run the entire way home.

There would be cupcakes left over from the bakery. Hopefully, we hadn't sold out of all the chocolate options while I was wandering lost in the forest and besieged by skinwalkers. I kept that thought in the forefront of my mind and followed Kandy's wolf without complaining out loud. My voice wasn't at all pretty in the whiny octaves.

We made it to the SUV in the Alice Lake parking lot where we'd left it. We had a ticket, of course, for illegal overnight parking. Delightful. Kett could pay it. I was just pleased they hadn't towed us. We were the only car in the lot. I wondered where Desmond had parked. Certainly, he hadn't run all the way from Vancouver in mountain lion form? Then I decided I was really too tired to worry about it.

I found the emergency key magnetically attached inside the rear wheel well, but only after Kandy scratched there repeatedly, tilting her head like I was an idiot when I didn't catch on right away. Werewolves were nasty creatures who didn't believe that trauma could affect your brain capacity. Actually, I had an idea that werewolves didn't believe in trauma at all, unless they were inflicting it.

Kandy then made me open the passenger door so she could leap gracefully up into the seat. I wasn't sure why she didn't just transform. Kandy certainly wasn't the shy type, so it couldn't be the nudity. I imagined that shapeshifters got over that quickly if it was ever even an issue to begin with. I could understand the idea of feeling more comfortable behind a predator guise, a more deadly form. Not that I had a more deadly form, but I could bake a brownie that made you think you'd died and gone straight to taste bud heaven.

Yes, I was completely aware I used chocolate as a sex substitute. So what?

I climbed into the driver's seat and started the car. My mind wandered to the idea of collecting huckleberries by moonlight and whether or not that would make them more potent, or if collecting things at different times of day was just a witch myth.

I put the SUV in gear and almost ran over Desmond, who suddenly appeared in the twin beams of the vehicle's headlights.

Jesus! That would have caused a ton of damage — to the SUV. Desmond would probably just shake it off his still utterly naked — and, thankfully, not blood covered — body. Yes, I get that I kept noticing the naked part, but I was out of chocolate. Actually, there wasn't enough chocolate in the western hemisphere to stop me from noticing.

I put the SUV in park and loosened my seat belt, thinking that Desmond would want to drive. But after scowling at me for a beat, he simply crossed around to the door behind me. I checked out his backside in my mirror. What? I hadn't seen him naked from behind. I was just checking to see that he was okay, but also noted he had a fine ass. Completely muscled. My ass was completely unmuscled, not that Desmond seemed to find it at all lacking during our make-out session a few hours ago.

He yanked open the door and climbed in. The obscenely large SUV sagged in response to his weight, but leveled out once he was seated. "You looked at me like you were thinking of running me over, dowser," he said. "What have I done to piss you off now?"

Kandy leaped into the backseat as Desmond slammed his door shut.

I most certainly hadn't been thinking about running him over. At least not with the car. I was relieved he was completely dense when it came to reading my face.

Kandy was nosing around Desmond as if making sure he was unharmed. Either that or she was thinking of eating him. Hard to tell with a werewolf.

"Okay, okay," Desmond said to the wolf. His tender tone hooked me somewhere painful behind my ribcage and I looked away from the rearview mirror.

"Are we waiting for Kett?" I asked.

"The vampire can get his own ride," Desmond answered. "Enough, Kandy."

The wolf settled down on the seat beside Desmond with her head resting on her paws. Submissive, I guessed.

Desmond reached into the back of the SUV and found — to my disappointment — a pair of sweatpants. It was Kandy's car, so it made sense there'd be extra clothing.

I tapped the gas and eased the vehicle out of the parking lot.

"It's going to be a long ride without chocolate," I said.

"Yeah," Desmond said. "Let's not talk about you and the vampire getting one of my wolves mixed up in your treasure hunting shit, putting a rare magical species in the unfortunate situation of kidnapping an alpha shifter, and triggering a life debt you still owe me. You owe me. Not the other way around. And yet here I am, at your beck and fucking call."

The life debt, which compelled me to help bring Hudson's killer to justice — and yes, should have been nullified with Sienna's death — shouldn't hold any sway over Desmond. So ... yeah, it was going to be a really long ride.

Chapter Five

I hit Highway 99 and wanted to speed all the way home. If my foot was heavy enough, I could turn the hour drive into forty-five minutes easily. And trust me, with the amount of angry magic sparking off Desmond in the back seat, that still wasn't going to be quick enough.

Yeah, I could taste emotional nuances in magic now. Fantastic. But that pleased me way less than it should have, because none of this was a game. Magic with Sienna had always been like a game, until it really wasn't anymore.

Unfortunately, we needed gas. So seven minutes later, I was pulling into a deserted gas station in Squamish. I must have driven through Squamish a dozen times as an adult headed to a party or dinner in Whistler. Or on a hiking trip to collect jade just outside of Lillooet. Actually, Gran had initiated those trips when I was a child as a way — I now knew — to distract and satiate my dowser magic. However, I'd never strayed more than a hundred feet from the highway. Squamish, caught between urban Vancouver and posh ski village Whistler, was a place to grab gas or ice cream. It also happened to be the name of the largest First Nations band in British Columbia. Yeah, that was a hard lesson learned. I knew I was thick about things, but I preferred to not have to get kidnapped and then nasty before I figured stuff out.

Magical etiquette and history were not my strong suits. They weren't even my weak suits ... bathing suit maybe, as opposed to an eighties power suit. All right, now I was just being insane in my head. At least my chocolate-obsessed thoughts kept me grounded. This other garbage wasn't helping at all.

Desmond actually grabbed the back of my seat and leaned forward to check the gas gauge when I slowed to pull off the highway. Yeah, jerk. As if I'd lengthen the trip if I didn't need to. Plus, I wasn't too pleased that the delicious taste of his magic grew more potent the nearer he got. It actually brushed over my right shoulder and neck when he exhaled his grumpiness in a huff.

I pulled up to the pumps, making a guess of the location of the gas tank. Desmond was out of the SUV and at the pump before I'd even shifted into park.

"Well, I hope he has a credit card," I said under my breath. "He wasn't wearing pockets earlier." I turned to Kandy in the back seat. She was still in wolf form and watching Desmond alertly through the side window. "I gather you aren't going to join me in the bathroom?"

Kandy flicked an ear at me in response. For the werewolf, duty came first and foremost. Now, with her alpha so near, that duty was firmly focused on McGrowly.

I wished my life — boundaries and all — was so clear for me. I thought it had been, but now I understood I'd been building a life on half-truths and guesses for a long time.

I slid out of the SUV and glanced around. The car stereo had declared the time to be 11:47 P.M., but I couldn't believe that I'd been lost, and then unconscious, for so much of the day until I saw how dead the gas station and highway were. Traffic came and went from Whistler all night long, but we were currently the only vehicle in the place. It was so well lit that most of the stars were obscured in the dark sky. I found myself wishing that I'd glanced up while we were in the forest. Granted, I hadn't wanted to be there in the dead of night, but the stars would have been spectacular.

"Dowser."

McGrowly had some speech or warning ready for me, but I cut him off with a snapped, "Bathroom." Then I crossed toward the minimart. I could see the cashier inside texting or playing a game on his phone. I wasn't sure if the bathrooms were inside or not. They weren't, but I needed a key.

The clerk's wide-eyed look was self-explanatory once I got a glance at myself in the bathroom mirror. Jesus. I had dirt and fir needles — or whatever — practically embedded in my curly blond hair. The word 'bedraggled' was coined for this look.

I — vainly, I know — really, really hoped I hadn't looked this bad when I'd plastered myself to Desmond in the forest.

And now that I'd opened that floodgate ... what the hell was up with that? I couldn't stand McGrowly. Granted, I hadn't laid eyes on him since he'd cut some sort of protection deal with Gran after Sienna died.

Maybe Sienna wasn't dead.

Hope bloomed as it always did when I considered this option, but I stuffed it back down deep into my heart. Yeah, and maybe she hadn't murdered all the people she'd admitted to killing. And maybe we could play Barbies, and steal cigarettes from her mom, and everything would be idyllic again.

Right.

Sienna was dead. I'd seen and felt her dissolve in the magic of the portal. And I was left here, not only practically friendless, but also utterly disgusted by my own willful ignorance.

Maybe that was why I'd kissed McGrowly. I wanted to be willful in a deliberate direction. I wanted some sort of control over my life again.

It had nothing to do with his delicious magic or his muscles or his extreme manliness. In fact, he was too muscled, too in-your-face manly —

Kett, with nary a pine needle or smudge of dirt in his white blond hair, opened the bathroom door and walked in.

I was damn sure I'd locked it behind me.

My brain did the automatic check it did every time I saw Kett now.

Skin? Pale, but normally so.

Eyes? Ice blue, not tinged with or fully blood red.

Teeth? Straight, white, but not pointy.

So this was a friendly bathroom-barge, not a dinner visit. The vampire had a thing for following me into bathrooms. He liked to intimidate on an intimate level.

"The men's is next door," I said. I'd brushed all the leaves and dirt from my hair while wallowing, so that now I was leaning over the sink and trying to splash some water on my face. The automatic taps made this simple task a slapstick joke. I never liked that kind of humor, and I certainly didn't like it happening to me.

"I can break the bond," Kett said.

I looked up. My face was dripping with cold water. "Excuse me?" A vampire breaking a life debt bond sounded like bad news, not good. I always needed bad news repeated. I was a glutton for punishment that way.

"I can break the life debt bond between you and the shifter."

I straightened very slowly, though whether that was to not startle the vampire or because my brain was working overtime, I didn't know.

Three months ago — after conversations that had taken place while I was sleeping and dreaming of returning to a peaceful life at my bakery — my grandmother made a deal with McGrowly. Gran was royally pissed that Desmond had extracted a life debt from me because he blamed me for Hudson's death. This magic, I had gathered since, was at his command because of how pack structure functioned for an alpha.

Problem was, the life debt hadn't dissolved like it should have after Sienna's death, and the reasons for that were still up for interpretation. Now that we were slowly figuring out how my magic worked, it seemed likely that the debt had been inadvertently sealed by both of us — not just by Desmond, as was usual. And my magic was an unknown quantity. As was my literal interpretation of what exactly I owed Desmond.

Yes, my guilt might be maintaining the bond.

The thing was, while Gran was extracting promises from the Alpha of the West Coast North American Pack, my mother was forging a relationship with a vampire — namely Kett. Yes, my mother loved to defy Gran. And Gran, like all witches — actually, like all other Adepts in general — loathed vampires. But Kett knew about my magic. And my magic — focused and refined — could make powerful people more powerful than anyone should be, according to Gran. Vampires were big on accumulating power and knowledge.

So, short of killing him — which I'm sure Gran decided would draw too much attention from the Conclave — a bargain had to be forged with Kett. My mother's solution had been to make him my mentor. Gran didn't talk to her daughter for two weeks after she found out

Scarlett had made this deal. In fact, my mother was currently living in my second bedroom rather than staying at Gran's as she usually did. Their estrangement dated back to before I was born, the reasons for which I wasn't entirely sure. But giving birth to me at sixteen — a child of unknown magical origins — had certainly cemented the divide between mother and daughter.

"You have remained silent for three minutes, dowser," Kett said. "I believe that might be a record of some sort."

Great, the vampire was attempting a joke. I was fairly certain that was one of the signs of the apocalypse.

"I'm thinking."

"That is obvious."

"Well, then, just leave me to it."

Kett inclined his head in the way he did when he was only pretending to acquiesce.

Gran had forbidden me to associate with the vampire. She'd been very clear that vampires held no loyalty, not even to their own kind. That vampires' morals were muddy, and their code of conduct indecipherable. This argument only escalated when I told Gran that I had saved Kett's undead life.

She had warned me then to forget what she called my error in judgement. "You don't know what a vampire would do to fulfill a life debt like that," she said. "He might decide that your very life is endangering you. That you're better off dead. Or worse than dead, if it's in his power to turn you."

So, piece that all together with the vampire's offer, and the fact that all — all — vampire magic was based in blood, and what did I get? Well, clammy hands and a racing heart for one.

I washed those clammy hands. That gave me an excuse to turn away from Kett. The water had dried on my face, making my skin tight, so I washed it a second time. Then I patted everything dry, including the counter — more stalling — with a paper towel.

Kett was doing his ice statue impression. He could stay like that for hours, never taking his eyes off me.

I cleared my throat, which was a bad opening because it drew his attention to my neck. "That is a generous offer —"

"I'm not attempting to gain permission to bite you."

"Ah, so biting would be involved."

"An exchange of blood, yes."

A spike of fear ricocheted up my spine as I ignored the impulse to run. He was effectively blocking the door, and I'd already broken my nose running into him once today.

"A bond with me would be nothing to fear, dowser." Kett's voice dropped into the soothing tones he sometimes used to get me to perform magic. I actually hated it when he acted so human. It blurred all the wrong lines for me.

"You want me to exchange a bond with McGrowly for one with you?"

"The bond with the shifter is malfunctioning. He is young and ill equipped to deal with it."

Okay, if he was referring to the kiss, how the hell did he know about it? Had he and Desmond been exchanging conquest stories while I was freaking out about them possibly slaughtering skinwalkers?

Kett didn't step closer. That was good, seeing as I was already gripping the sink so tightly I might rip it out of the wall. His tone became more intimate, though. "It would be pleasurable if you wished, Jade. And the blood would be only a drop or two."

My gaze dropped to his neck. I remembered Sienna slashing his skin open, his blood spurting into my stainless steel mixing bowl. Then my sister had gulped that blood like it was cold chocolate milk on a summer day.

I squeezed my eyes shut and shook my head. I was haunted from within — haunted by everything my sister did, and everything I didn't stop her from doing.

Cool fingers brushed across my cheekbone. "It is not a one-time offer, dowser. When you want the bond broken, I believe my magic can break it."

I nodded and opened my eyes. He was standing so close that I could see flecks of red in his eyes like bloody ice shards. I blinked and the red was gone, leaving only pure blue behind. The bathroom air was thick with his pepperminty magic.

"You're not trying to influence me, are you Kett?" I asked.

A frown creased his brow, replaced microseconds later with his cool demeanor. "You know that type of magic doesn't work with you, dowser."

"And if I let you bite me …"

"Yes?"

"You could tell me who my father is? Or at least what his magic is?"

"If I have tasted it before."

"Are there many of the Adept you haven't tasted?" Was I really having this conversation? As if blood was fine wine?

"Not many. And those of power who I haven't tasted, aren't likely to be your biological father. The Adept do not interbreed across species very successfully."

"You've made a list and checked it twice?"

"Yes."

"And who are the likely candidates? For father of the year?"

Kett fell silent as he always did when confronted with a question he either didn't want to answer or — heaven forbid — didn't know the answer to. And there was the itchy rub. If Gran and Scarlett hadn't figured out what kind of Adept my father was in all these years, then how the hell was a vampire going to know?

"You overplayed your hand, vampire," I said. Then I very deliberately stepped to the side, around Kett, and walked to the exit.

"You upped the ante yourself, dowser. Not I," Kett's cool tone was firmly in place again.

The door banged open and nearly hit me. I jumped back a step.

Desmond filled — literally — the frame of the doorway. He was doing a scowling-but-inscrutable thing with his face. He glanced from me to Kett over my shoulder and raised his eyebrows. "Caught up to us, vamp?"

"Apparently," Kett replied.

Completely blocked by Desmond and all but trapped in the bathroom, I noticed the way the magic built between the shifter and the vampire. I supposed my magic must be somewhere in the middle, but all I could taste was dark chocolate and peppermint on either side of me. One pressed from the front and the other from the back, never touching, never mixing as the magic continued to build. The shifter and the vampire just stared at each other with me caught in between, like, like ... oh, God. This was awkward and uncomfortable, but so ... so ... tasty.

I twined my fingers into the wedding ring charms on my necklace and tried to center myself within its magic. It helped. Problem was, magic was about intention, and my body didn't intend the same as my mind.

"Do you really want a broken life debt hanging over you?" I blurted.

"No," McGrowly answered. "But it's not the vampire's place to fix it."

I frowned. Had he been listening in to my bathroom conversation? That wasn't creepy at all.

"Nor," Desmond continued, "can he tell you who your father is. We've had this conversation, vampire."

"We disagreed," Kett said. He stepped closer to me. I couldn't see him, but I could feel his magic move.

Desmond's mouth twitched as if he was fighting the urge to speak. Then he said, "We will settle the bond, dowser. I wouldn't have come back to Vancouver without that intention. I was simply unaware you'd be in peril at the time of my arrival." This last bit was glared at Kett, but the vampire didn't respond.

"I'll drive," Desmond said as he turned away. He'd bought a 'Super, Natural BC' T-shirt from the minimart. On anyone else, it would have been a vast source of amusement, but my eyes mourned the sight of his naked backside. I'd never seen an ass like that before. It suited him, since he was such a colossal ass himself.

"I still need to use the washroom," I said to Desmond's too-wide back. Then I turned to glare at the vampire. I wasn't peeing in front of him.

A smile ghosted over Kett's face as he slid by me out of the bathroom. "The offer still stands, dowser."

"Yeah, I get it. My blood will always be a rare treat."

"Indeed," Kett laughed. His voice was soft and so, so human, emanating from the darkness between the light of the bathroom and the overhead lights at the pumps. "You will find I have endless patience and endless time."

I wasn't sure if that was a warning or a promise, so I just shut and locked the door on both possibilities.

Freaking vampires and shapeshifters with their tasty magic and arrogant pissing contests. I wasn't some prize. Okay, I was a prize, but I wasn't some toy. Not for either of them, at least.

By the time I climbed into the back seat of the SUV, things between Kett in the front passenger seat and Desmond in the driver's seat had cooled to glacial levels. I didn't mind at all. Kandy, still in wolf form, snuggled next to me and radiated the heat of a small volcano. The iciness between the two predators in the front somehow dampened their magical aura. So things were better all around.

The werewolf nosed something against my hand. A chocolate bar. A 70-percent single-origin chocolate bar from Venezuela, to be exact. The packaging was a bit battered by tooth and claw, but it was chocolate and I was in desperate need.

"Ha," I whispered. "You've been holding out on me. And developing expensive habits."

The wolf rested her head on my thigh as I tried to not simply tear off the wrapper and inhale the slightly melted bar whole. This kind of chocolate was meant to be savored, and the act of eating it should help calm me down. I broke off a piece and just let it sit on my tongue. It was smooth and creamy, with a cashew undertone that was divine and addictive.

Wary of her inch-and-a-half long canine teeth, I offered Kandy a square. She took it from me delicately. I figured if her werewolf metabolism could burn off skinwalker spells then a little chocolate wouldn't kill her. I wondered again why she didn't change back. Maybe the transformation was exhausting?

"Maybe you just helped yourself to this bar out of my personal stash, hey wolf?"

Kandy pawed at me and I laughed. Then I gave her a second piece.

Desmond caught my gaze in the rearview mirror while I was still smiling. "You going to share that?" he asked. "Or is there some sort of BFF club going on in the back seat?"

My smile fell, and not because McGrowly saying 'BFF' was ridiculous. Sienna was — had been — my BFF. Sienna who had tried to kill every single person in this car.

Desmond actually looked concerned for me. His green-flecked eyes reflected ... what? Pity? Because I was walking around completely and utterly aware that the object of my pain was — according to the rational world — utterly undeserving of my love?

He shouldn't be looking at me. He should be paying attention to the road. I dropped my gaze, snapped another piece off the bar, and passed it over his shoulder. He took it, and thankfully didn't try to engage me further.

"The Grand Council," Kett said. His cool voice was a balm to my aching soul. "Which, as you noted correctly in the forest, is comprised of representatives from all the major species of the Adept, is overseen by what governing body?"

"There is no higher authority," Desmond snapped. "The Grand Council itself barely exists."

I could actually hear the way the chocolate coated McGrowly's tone. Which would have been cool, except for the fact that it meant I was far too intimate with the sound of his voice.

"The question was for the dowser, shifter," Kett replied. "Your ignorance is well earned. Hers can be rectified."

I snapped off another piece of chocolate and wished I could see beyond the headlights of the SUV. This was a beautiful drive in the daylight or at sunset.

"Teach her something useful, vampire. Like how to fight or focus her alchemist powers."

"Everything has a time and place. The dowser already had a lesson in both those disciplines today."

Desmond's gaze returned to the rearview. I kept mine pointed out the side window. "You made a magical object today?" he asked.

I didn't like the almost imperceptible eager edge to his question.

"She rescued you, didn't she, shifter? Did you find the bindings of the skinwalkers easy to break?"

"I didn't bother testing them," Desmond said, a growl on the edges of his tone. "The dowser was handy with the knife. That was simple and quick."

Kett — his point made, I imagine — dropped the conversation. Or he just lapsed into one of his fugue states. I got the feeling that we all bored the hell out of him most of the time. We moved and thought too slowly, ponderously. I know I did.

"Has Kandy's magic been affected by the skinwalkers?" I directed the question to whoever would answer, lightly petting the short hairs on Kandy's forehead and nose.

"No," Desmond answered. For a moment, I thought he wasn't going to elaborate. He cast a look at Kett, who didn't stir, then shook his head as if in disbelief that a vampire was sitting next to him. Like I said, the Adept didn't like sharing information. And they really didn't like sharing information with vampires. "She's demoralized. The wolf form makes her feel more powerful, and it's ... simpler."

Ah. I wouldn't mind that kind of escape from everything going on right now. "It's that way for you all? Powerful yet simpler?" I wasn't really expecting an answer. I usually only got one at a time with the vampire.

" 'More focused,' might be a better way to phrase it. Hunt, eat, care for your pack, fight ... mate." His gaze lifted to mine in the rearview again. Yeah, so I was watching him. Having practically mauled him in the forest, I decided I was allowed to look at him now.

"Clarity. I wouldn't mind some of that."

"You got more of that chocolate?"

"Yeah." I passed him another piece. I was probably supposed to just give him the whole bar — pack status and all — but I wasn't in his pack. I also had a feeling that Kandy might have been withholding from her alpha in the first place. But, if she was going to transgress for me, and Desmond was going to let it slide, I'd be a moron to point it out.

I sucked on another square. At this rate, the bar would be gone by Britannia Beach, with thirty more minutes of chocolate-free drive ahead of us.

"Who oversees the Grand Council?" Kett asked again. His voice was cool through the darkness that had warmed between the shifters and me.

"The Guardian Council," I answered by rote. We'd gone over all this earlier today.

"And who are the Guardians?"

"Dragons," I answered.

Desmond laughed just once, but sharp enough that I flinched. The ride and the chocolate had relaxed me more than I thought. "Myth," McGrowly sneered.

"There are no such things as dragons or elves or leprechauns. Pure myth."

Yeah, I was familiar with having a narrow understanding of the Adept world. I'd thought that all shapeshifters were werewolves, that I was half-human, half-witch, and that my Gran would never, ever hide the truth from me.

"The west coast of North America is a very small territory, Desmond Llewelyn." I was pretty sure that was the first time I'd ever heard Kett refer to McGrowly by name. Oddly, I think he was trying to be kind.

"My father is a lord of the North American Assembly. I'm not just some ignorant hick born in the woods and raised to be the strongest," Desmond said. "Dragons are mythical creatures, as are elves and fairies and angels."

"And demons?" I asked. I'd hoped — ever so briefly — that it had been a demon, called up by Rusty, that had eaten him, and not as it turned out, my sister, Sienna. I was still attempting to bury that same hope underneath cupcakes, yoga classes, and tedious lessons with the vampire.

"Demon's exist," Desmond answered, before Kett could elaborate. "Possession and all that. Sorcerers getting into places they —"

"Dragons of tooth and claw and scales are indeed mythical, but Guardians who derive their powers from —"

"Bedtime stories for children. There are no all-powerful guardians watching over the world, human or magical. Protecting us from all the things we don't see, all the epic disasters that don't kill us."

"The nine make up the Guardian Council. Yes, they are rare, but they are a race, just like you and —"

"Have you ever met one, vampire?"

Kett went quiet. So that was a 'no,' then.

Desmond snorted, and returned his full attention to the road.

I was so going to run out of chocolate before Britannia Beach. No wonder Kandy stayed in wolf form. That way, she had a major excuse for not participating in what masqueraded as a conversation, but which was really just a sausage swing-and-measure.

I didn't know if vampires even had functional genitals, but I was damn sure that Desmond had Kett beat in girth alone.

And with that not at all unpleasant thought in my head, I attempted to sleep.

Chapter Six

A necromancer was sitting on my front stoop. Okay, I didn't have a front stoop. A necromancer was sitting on the front steps of my apartment building. A fledgling necromancer, to be more exact. Morana Novak, aka Rusty's sister, to be very specific. I hadn't known Rusty even had a sister, not until after he died. She didn't know me well enough to know I always entered my apartment through the bakery alley exit. But, neither did Desmond, seeing as how he'd pulled up on West Fourth Avenue rather than around the back.

We had managed to not actually speak to each other for the remainder of the drive down the mountain from Squamish. Kett had hopped out at a stoplight in the middle of downtown, and Desmond had continued to drive Kandy and me into Kitsilano without missing a beat. He'd pulled up right in front of my bakery, Cake in a Cup. Since it was now north of midnight, West Fourth was dead quiet.

Having jumped out the moment Desmond slid the SUV to a stop at the curb, I now found myself staring at the young teen, who was glowering at me from the third stair to my and Kandy's apartments. Kandy — or rather Desmond, for Kandy — had rented the neighboring apartment from Gran when he'd installed the green-haired werewolf as my keeper.

"Ummm," I said, because I'm crazy articulate when confronted by the teenaged sister of the man my foster sister had dated, eaten, and then killed.

Morana's glower deepened. She needed to refresh her black eyeliner, which was currently creeping for her cheeks. Also her purple hair dye, which showed at least two inches of ash brown at the roots and was faded to lilac at the tips. Unless, of course, the look was intentional. Paired with the too-large combat boots, it might have been. I hadn't see the teen since the tribunal had found Rusty guilty — along with Sienna — of the murders of three werewolves, one of which was my could-have-been boyfriend and Kandy's packmate, Hudson. Ah, just thinking his name still stirred ... things better left unstirred.

"You okay?" I asked.

"No." Well, she spoke. That was good. Maybe.

"Are you looking for me?"

"Did your sister kill my brother after using his siphoned powers to kill werewolves?"

Um, yeah. But I couldn't bring myself to say it out loud.

I felt werewolf magic — all earthy dark chocolate with an edgy bitter nose — bloom behind me in the SUV, which was still idling at the curb. Kandy must be transforming. It was too much of a risk to stay in wolf form, even if the streets were dead quiet. No one was going to mistake a hundred-and-twenty-five-pound werewolf for a dog.

I really wasn't sure it was a good idea for Kandy to meet Morana.

"It's late, Morana —"

"That's Novak to you."

"You go by your last name? What are you, twelve?"

"Fifteen." Morana spat. Literally. I guessed this was an attempt to be tough, but it was really just gross. I'd have to hose that spot down before I opened the bakery in the morning.

"How about I call you Mort? Or Mory?"

"Lame much?"

Yes, often. But I needed to speed up this insanely awkward bonding session, and the necromancer's own name felt too heavy for her tiny frame. "Right. It's, like, after one in the morning, Mory." I also needed to hurry the conversation along before —

Kandy, clad in Lycra shorts and a tank top, stepped out from the rear passenger seat of the SUV. The glower was wiped from Mory's face and replaced by fear.

"Who's this?" Kandy asked. Her voice was crackly from lack of use.

"This is Mory, Kandy. Mory, this is Kandy."

The teen opened her mouth — brave when faced with a pack member of the werewolves her brother had murdered — probably to protest my use of her first name. I neatly interrupted by actually looking at Kandy.

"What the hell happened to your hair?" I said. My voice was stupidly loud on the deserted street.

Kandy narrowed her eyes, and showed me the tips of her teeth. This was not a smile.

Mory snapped her mouth shut, her face actually blanching. Yeah, werewolves were scary even in human form. Especially this one.

Kandy's normally vibrant green hair was dull brown. Her short pixie cut had grown out, but she usually kept it gelled or moussed. It was now hanging limp around her eyes and ears.

"Stop staring," the werewolf said with a snap of her teeth.

I looked away.

Mory's eyes were saucers. She had that sort of face I associated with cherubs or fairies — large eyes, rounded cheeks —

"It doesn't stick. The dye. When I change." Kandy ground this information out through clenched teeth. "Is there a problem here?" She looked pointedly at Mory.

Mory turned and looked at me. Kandy didn't appear to recognize the fledgling necromancer.

"No problem. Except your hair," I answered.

Kandy snorted and crossed to say something to Desmond, who hadn't pulled away from the curb yet.

I stepped closer to Mory and she rose from her sitting position on the stair. Two steps up, and she was barely two inches taller than me. The fairy description held. She was having a difficult time keeping her eyes off Kandy.

"Is that," the necromancer whispered, "one of your witchy friends?"

"I have no witchy friends. And does she look like a witch?" I followed Mory's rapt gaze. Kandy was now leaning through the passenger-side window of the SUV. The werewolf was as tall as me, heavily muscled, and lean. So lean that I sometimes joked about her waist being the size of my thigh. It wasn't much of a joke.

She stepped back from the SUV with a gray cellphone in her hand. Her phone was usually green. This was obviously a backup. The SUV pulled away.

Yeah, sweet goodbye McGrowly, old buddy, old kissing pal of mine.

"I need your number again," Kandy said as she approached. "Just until I get a proper replacement and sync it." She looked up. "Why is the kid still here?"

Mory shifted from foot to foot. Kandy's eyes narrowed into predator slits. She lifted her nose slightly in the necromancer's direction and sniffed.

I didn't know whether werewolves could smell the connection between blood relatives or not, but the underlying taste of Mory's magic was very similar to Rusty's. I wouldn't be surprised if the werewolf was putting two and two together, and getting pissed off by my casual introduction.

"Your hair," I mock-whispered, "is seriously freaking me out."

Kandy laughed, though it was more of a snicker than a guffaw. Then she shouldered by me, nearly knocking the teen off the stairs as she passed. Mory didn't have much bravado when faced with Kandy, the floppy-haired werewolf, but she seemed to be trying to stiffen her spine now that it was just me. Obviously, she didn't get that it was worse to have a werewolf behind her than in her face.

"You should call your mom, Mory." I cast my voice low, even though Kandy could probably have heard me from a block over and down.

"My mom probably hasn't even noticed I'm gone," Mory said, managing to sneer and sound pitiful at the same time.

"Let's go upstairs —"

"Don't pretend to care."

Kandy stopped two steps from the top of the staircase.

"Listen —"

"I want you to take me to where my brother died," Mory blurted.

Kandy slowly pivoted. She stood in the shadows between the streetlight and the outdoor apartment light. Green rolled over her eyes. She was accessing some of her werewolf powers ... hopefully not claws.

"Mory," I said, trying to be as kind as possible. "I'm not going to do that."

Mory glowered and crossed her arms. Kandy took a step down. I looked up to try to catch her eye, but the werewolf was fixed on Mory — probably specifically at the soft tissue where her neck met her skull.

"I just want to speak to his ghost." Mory was on the edge of pleading. I wasn't sure I had it in me to resist that.

"Necromancer," Kandy growled from her perch seven or so steps above us.

Mory stiffened but didn't turn around. I wasn't sure that was the correct way to deal with a werewolf. But then, my dealings hadn't been all that smooth lately, so maybe I was completely wrong.

"Yeah, what?" Mory sneered, directing her answer to Kandy's question at me.

"Fledgling," I corrected.

Kandy's eyes blazed green again. Mory must have seen something in my face because she bit her lip, dropped her eyes, and hunched her shoulders.

"Fledgling," Kandy repeated. "There aren't any ghosts around here. Try a graveyard."

"You'd be surprised," Mory snipped back, still not making eye contact with the werewolf above and behind her.

Kandy slid two steps closer, her body still in shadow but her fully clawed hand visible in a pool of light on the railing.

"Okay," I said, "let's …" What? Calm down? It wasn't a good idea to tell a werewolf to take it easy. Kandy could be brusque and edgy, but I'd never really worried about her bestial nature, not since it felt like we'd become friends, not until confronted by a fifteen-year-old lavender-haired necromancer —

"Raise any werewolf corpses lately, fledgling?" Kandy asked. Her voice was molten steel.

Mory finally raised her gaze to mine.

"You understand who Kandy is?" I asked her gently.

"I had to come," the fledgling answered, her voice hanging on the edge of a sob. Her life was obviously a balancing act along that edge as well. "I have to know … if he … if he did those things."

"If," Kandy sneered, but she didn't move closer. "The tribunal sent investigators to the crime scenes."

"Witches," Mory said. Her tone made it clear that witches ranked somewhere above pond scum but below slugs in her estimation.

"Impartial investigators," I said. "Including a necromancer sensitive to —"

"On the payroll of witches."

I sighed, but noted that Kandy's hand looked totally human again. Perhaps even the wolf in her recognized the pain in this girl.

"I have the right to face my brother's accuser. I have first-blood-right to challenge my brother's killer."

"Mory," I said, and then faltered. The pain that laced suddenly through my voice matched that in hers. She had an actual blood connection to Rusty, but we'd both loved our siblings just the same. "Sienna is dead."

"She's not dead." Mory was back to her glower face. I would have thought that someone who looked so much like a fairy would be less belligerent.

"You know the investigators assessed that no one could survive —" Err … wait. The portal wasn't common knowledge. Its existence below the bakery had been shared only with a few key people — the investigators and a couple of Convocation members — in order to clear Kandy, Desmond, Kett, and me of any wrongdoing. "No one could survive," I said in an awkward and lame attempt to cover myself, "what happened to Sienna ... magically."

Kandy smirked. Mory glowered more. So, yeah, I was a bad liar. So what?

"Oh, that bitch is alive."

I shook my head and looked up to Kandy for help. The werewolf shrugged and, affecting boredom, looked away. Ah, inscrutable shapeshifter games. My favorite. Ranked right below getting knifed by my sister and chased by a vampire.

"Mory, come upstairs." I was really tired of standing on the sidewalk, and I had to be up in less than three hours to bake.

"She's alive," Mory insisted, not budging from her step.

"Yeah, fledgling? Did Casper tell you so?"

Great, now the werewolf was attempting to be witty.

"I have no frigging idea who Casper is. But, yeah, a shade told me."

"And ghosts can't lie?" I asked, already knowing the answer.

Ghosts, or shades, or spiritual energy — whatever you wanted to call it/them — could lie just as much as the person they used to be. Mory's shoulders slumped. She looked as pitiful as I felt.

"Come upstairs," I coaxed.

"Your mother is up there," Mory said. "I don't much like mothers right now."

Point taken. "She's not that kind of mother," I answered, and brushed by Mory to climb the stairs. Either the necromancer would follow or I was about to spend the remainder of my allotted shut-eye attempting to dig up her mother's phone number. I knew that I was the very last person Rusty's mother wanted to speak to.

However, Mory was probably the very first, so hopefully Rusty's mom wasn't proficient in death curses.

Kandy preceded me up the stairs, both of us stopping at the landing that branched off east and west to our neighboring apartments. Our floor plans were identical, but Kandy had no actual furniture except for a huge fridge in the living room. Yeah, it didn't fit in the kitchen. I tripped over the freaking cords every time I ventured in, which was only rarely because Kandy spent all her noneating and nonsleeping hours at my place or in the bakery. She refused to touch anything remotely resembling work, though.

"Do you just stock up on hair dye?" I asked the werewolf, pausing to give Mory time to make up her mind whether to follow me or not.

"Yeah. You think it's easy to maintain that perfect color?"

I wouldn't call green the perfect hair color, but now I knew why Kandy's green always looked perfectly fresh. She had to dye it every time she transformed.

"Yoga tomorrow?" I asked, keenly aware of Mory slowly climbing the stairs behind me. Her magic was much stronger than her brother's had been. But then, necromancer powers usually followed the female line. She had that same candied-violet undertone I associated with Rusty, layered with toasted marshmallow and buttercream icing. Which gave me an idea...

"All right," Kandy answered. "But power. Not that wimpy hatha shit. You don't push yourself enough."

That was a nice summing up of my life story in one snarly sentence. I nodded. "Sleep well."

Kandy snorted. "Going to have to wax my legs. The bloody hair grows back there every time, too, and I can't sleep with hairy legs."

"Didn't seem to bother you a couple of hours ago."

Kandy flashed her nonsmile at me. Her teeth were very white in the deep shadows of the landing. I really needed to get more lights installed. The werewolf lifted and tilted the large ceramic pot by her front door. It must have weighed at least seventy-five pounds including dirt and dying bush, but she hefted it as if it was nothing. Apparently, that was where she kept her spare key. I guessed werewolves needed a lot of spares ... keys, phones, clothes, and hair dye at least.

Mory sidled up, placing me between her and Kandy. The werewolf noticed and offered another spine-tingling grin. "Don't let the blondness fool you, fledgling. The witch stabbed a nine-hundred-pound grizzly in the ass today. She just keeps her claws better hidden and painted pink."

I raked my bright, dark pink Opi-lacquered nails at Kandy. The color — lyrically named *Feelin' Hot Hot Hot* — needed a touch up, actually, before I served any customers tomorrow.

Kandy snorted and let herself into her apartment. I noted that she didn't close the door behind her. Still keeping an eye on the necromancer, I guessed. Or maybe Desmond was staying the night with her, rather than at a hotel as I'd assumed, and was currently looking for long-term parking. I wasn't sure how I felt about having him easily accessible in the middle of the night.

I turned to let Mory through the wards that protected my apartment. I'd been doing a lot of that lately, letting potentially dangerous people get way too close to me.

"My cat Lester loved marshmallows, even untoasted," I said as I reached out to the magic surrounding the door, walls, and windows of my home. "If you accidentally left a bag out, he'd totally molest it."

"What?"

"Your magic tastes like toasted marshmallows."

"And, so? Your cat is going to molest me?"

"I don't have a cat," I said. My mind eagerly flashed back to the vision of Desmond in the forest. His green-flecked eyes, his powerful body, his long hard —

"You're really weird for a witch," Mory said, interrupting a train of thought that was going nowhere psychologically healthy. "Aren't you supposed to be all earthy and shit?"

I sighed. "I'm not that kind of witch."

I pulled the magic of the wards to me and over Mory. This effectively let her into my apartment, though it didn't fully key her to the wards. She could enter now accompanied by me, but not later or again on her own. Yeah, I was full of new tricks these days.

My place looked very different than it had three months ago. Then, when I'd arrived home after 2:00 A.M., all blurry-eyed and dragging a practically nameless dance partner with me, the two-bedroom apartment was ... well, pretty unlived in. Maybe even uninviting. Not intentionally, but I'd spent the two previous years of my life devoted to opening and running a successful cupcake bakery on one of the busiest streets in Vancouver. My apartment — and life in general — had taken a back seat.

Then, after everything that had happened with Sienna and Rusty, Scarlett had moved in. And my mother never did anything in half measures.

The changes to the space had been subtle at first. A new silk or linen couch pillow and an orchid on the kitchen island. Then I suddenly had matching glassware, and the dining set I'd been slowly collecting from a local potter became a full set of ten. No matter that I had no dining room table capable of seating ten dinner guests.

The table showed up a week later.

Everything Scarlett added fit my handmade, local esthetic perfectly. The table, for instance, was made from hundred-year-old reclaimed fir. And, oddly, I never saw anything delivered or a single bill.

Tonight, the lamp hanging over the dining table dimly illuminated a gorgeous handblown glass vase ... or maybe it was a large misshapen bowl. The colors swirled around in it — golds, blues, and greens — in a way similar to how I saw magic. I wondered if my mother knew that when she picked it out. And yes, there was now a dimmer switch for the hanging lamp — which itself was crafted out of some sort of old steel box — where there'd once been no lamp at all.

"Nice place," Mory said. Even her compliments came out dour and angsty. Oh, to be a teenager again ... not.

I instantly felt bad for generalizing the fledgling necromancer. I'd never lost a brother at fifteen. Sienna had lost her dad at thirteen, and that had been difficult for her. But honestly, not for me. Actually, I'd lucked into a fulltime sister after that, so in a purely selfish way, her father's death and her mother's abandonment had been a bonus for me. I certainly hadn't wished them dead or anything, but ... never mind.

"My mom has been staying," I said as I crossed to the kitchen. The fridge was full of food. Also a new development, courtesy of Scarlett.

I pulled out fixings for a turkey sandwich and watched Mory slowly wander around the living room. The door to the craft room, aka the second bedroom, was slightly ajar, but it was dark within. I guessed that Scarlett was asleep. I could feel her magic — the base of fresh-cut grass and lilac that she shared with Gran, topped with strawberries and white chocolate.

I spread mayo on a slice of whole wheat bread.

"I'm not lying," Mory said as she settled onto one of the stools at the island situated between the living room and the kitchen. The grand room was open concept. I'd renovated the kitchen when I moved in — gray granite counters, stainless steel appliances, and the kitchen island — as it was the only room that really mattered to me. Scarlett had replaced the cheap stools. They'd been so badly weighted that they were constantly being knocked down.

"I know," I answered, trying to push thoughts of falling stools, broken bowls, and murdered werewolves out of my head.

I sliced tomato and placed it on top of Havarti cheese. I salted and peppered the turkey on the opposite side of the sandwich, flipped it closed, plated it, and slid it across the counter to Mory. The necromancer eyed it distrustfully while I put together another for myself.

"How do you know I eat meat?"

"You're a necromancer."

"What? Eww."

I laughed quietly. I never felt much like laughing these days. Mory's presence in my apartment didn't make that any easier.

"I thought there'd be cupcakes," she said, though she didn't look up from her sandwich.

I felt tears well up, quickly turning to the sink to wash and dry my hands before Mory saw them in my eyes.

Then I crossed to the fridge, pulled out three cupcakes, and put them on one of my jadeite plates. I put the plate on the counter. "For dessert." Then I crossed with my sandwich to sit beside Mory.

She finally took a bite of her sandwich. After this went down okay, she inhaled the rest.

I didn't feel much like eating, but I made an effort. I passed the second half of my sandwich to the fledgling necromancer and she ate it without comment.

"What kind are these?" she asked, her mouth full of partially chewed sandwich. She meant the cupcakes.

"Solace in a Cup," I answered. My voice only cracked a little. "Chocolate carrot cake with chocolate cream-cheese icing."

Mory, her sandwich finished, reached for a cupcake. She swiped a bit of icing from the top of one and sucked it off her finger. "Did Rusty like these ones?"

Ah, there it was ... I fought past the tight space in my chest. I spent so much time mourning Sienna, trying to not mourn Hudson, and distracting myself with magic theory that I hadn't really thought about the kind man who I'd hoped was a monster underneath for my sister's sake. I wanted Rusty to be the evil, perverted one, so that Sienna could be innocent. But even now — though the tribunal had convicted Rusty posthumously as Sienna's conspirator largely based on my hearsay testimony — I still wasn't a hundred percent sure he'd ever killed anyone.

I cleared the clog of emotion out of my throat and tried to answer calmly. "Rusty never tried these ones."

"Oh," Mory said. She peeled the paper off her cupcake and tried a bite. "Mmm. Good."

My heart constricted in my chest even tighter. I abandoned the uneaten eighth of my sandwich and reached for a cupcake.

"So ... Solace in a Cup, eh?" Mory asked, still chewing her second bite.

"Yes."

"Because ... you're sad, right?"

"Yeah."

"There aren't any shades here."

"No?" I answered. "But they wouldn't be able to get through the wards, would they?"

"Oh. Maybe not."

"You thought someone died here recently?" I was practically shoving the cupcake down my throat in an attempt to steady myself, once again smothering my emotions in chocolate and icing.

"Um, yeah."

"Downstairs. Sienna. Downstairs."

"In the bakery? I was in there today and I didn't see any shades in there either."

"Who let you through the wards?" Different protections warded the bakery, keeping out anyone magically inclined. Once invited, however, an Adept could buy as many of my cupcakes as he or she pleased. Humans could pass without issue, of course.

"Your Gran."

"Did you speak with her?"

Mory shrugged and went for a second cupcake.

"Did you expect to see Sienna's ghost in the bakery? Is that why you think she's alive?" Even as I said it, I attempted to ignore the completely inappropriate bloom of hope in my heart.

"No." The edge of finality in Mory's tone made me suspect the conversation was over.

Chapter Seven

I was exhausted, but I dreaded calling Rusty's mother — if I could get her number off Mory — so I was dilly-dallying with the food.

Obviously, the skinwalker's spell didn't come with a restful sleep side effect. God, that was yet another thing Gran was going to hold against me. Maybe I just wouldn't mention it. Thankfully, there was no way the vampire or shifters would be forthcoming about me kind of saving their asses.

Mory had rolled the cake-crusted paper cups into rolls. She fished her phone out of her pocket and opened her messaging app. Then she slid the phone over to me.

I tried to ignore the multiple instances of *where are you* and *come home please* that spanned back days, just focusing on the last two entries.

@Amy's 2nite
Okay, Mory. Have fun.

"This is not Amy's," I said, secretly pleased I'd correctly guessed the fledgling necromancer's nickname.

Mory sighed and tapped her screen to open another set of messages. These were addressed to an Amy.

Waiting 4 Jade.
Cupcake Witch?
Yeah
That ok?

Fine

Ok. Text me

Cupcake Witch? If the Adept world only knew the truth about me ... well, then — according to Gran, Scarlett, and Kett — I'd be sold off to the highest bidder. Honestly, I already felt a little like that when Desmond and Kett fought. Though I wasn't completely sure they were actually fighting over the possession of my fledgling alchemist powers, or whether they just really loathed each other in that interspecies way.

"So text her, then," I finally said as I stood to clear the dishes to the sink.

"Am I sleeping here?"

"The couch is available."

"The couch looks okay." Mory bent over her phone to text her friend.

"What sort of Adept is Amy?" I asked, because I really hoped a human wasn't referring to me as a witch. I was still a little fuzzy on the exact ways that other powerful Adept kept their identities secret from the human world — such things were the purview of the various Councils, Conclaves, and Convocations. But I still knew that Mory could be in a lot of trouble if she was showing off to humans. It helped that people didn't see magic when they didn't want to see magic. Miracles, disasters, and the unexplained, yes — but not magic. Children, human or otherwise, saw more, of course. A teenager might believe Mory if told that things such as witches and necromancers existed.

"Like a quarter witch or something," Mory answered. Vancouver boasted a relatively tiny Adept community. Hardly anyone was full-blood around here. I used to think that included me. Technically Mory was half-witch, half-necromancer — as her brother Rusty had been. The necromancy usually only manifested fully in the female line, though the magic was latent in the male members of the species, who often could see or feel ghosts, but not communicate with them. Rusty had inherited a slight spell casting ability from his father along with a talent for reviving neglected plants and such. Necromancers and witches didn't usually mix, but within such a small community, it was bound to happen.

I turned the lights off in the kitchen, keeping the oven hood light on as I used to do for Sienna when she crashed here. The bed in the second bedroom had been Scarlett's first addition to the apartment. Before the bed showed up, I hadn't even known my mother was planning to stay.

I skirted the island and offered Mory a throw pillow and a hand-knit blanket. The pillow was new. The blanket was a gift from Gran.

She tossed the pillow to one end of the couch and held the blanket to her chest. Her gaze was fixed on my feet. "You'll take me tomorrow? To the place that Rusty died?" she asked quietly.

"I really don't want to."

"But you will? You don't have to stay ... or even come in."

"I wouldn't leave you there alone. Maybe your mother —"

"She doesn't want to talk to him."

Jesus. I didn't want to talk to him — or be in the same room while his sister talked to him — either. The very idea of ghosts freaked me out. And a ghost of someone I knew? Freaky as hell.

"So you'll take me?"

"I have to bake tomorrow. If you wake up and I'm not here, you can find me down there." I pointed to a closed door off the living area that led downstairs to the bakery kitchen. "Don't leave from the front door, unless you don't want to come back."

"The wards will still keep me out? I thought ..."

"Yeah. I'm not that kind of witch." I turned toward the hall that led to my bedroom. "Bathroom is here. New toothbrushes under the sink."

"You'll take me, won't you, Jade?" Mory whispered behind me. It was a whisper I shouldn't have been able to hear so clearly. But ever since I'd opened the portal and connected to the magic that flowed through it, I could do lots of new things. I almost didn't turn back, but guilt was a whip-snapping motivator.

"I'll think about it," I said over my shoulder. I could barely see Mory's face in the dimness of the living room. Her eyes were two dark holes.

She nodded her chin, then curled up on the couch.

I restrained myself from going back to tuck her in. My sister had killed her brother. After she ate parts of him to access his latent necromancer power. Tucking in wasn't on the list of things Mory was likely to accept from me.

I was surprised she'd let me feed her, except the cupcakes were always a draw. Not many people were capable of refusing one after they'd laid eyes on it. Hence, the popularity of my bakery.

Attempting to ignore — as I always was these days — the whirling, unanswered questions and lingering heartbreak that was always on my mind, I climbed into bed without changing or brushing my teeth.

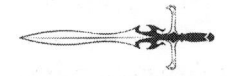

If I slept, I didn't notice. True, I didn't need much sleep these days — but no sleep at all was ridiculous.

Perhaps I didn't sleep because I didn't want to dream.

I rose before my 5:00 A.M. alarm and padded out to check on Mory. She was sprawled with utter abandon across my couch and snoring in short bursts like a puppy. But she's not a puppy, I warned myself as I pulled my hair into a ponytail. Then I looked up to meet Scarlett's gaze.

I'd felt my mother's magic approach before I saw her in the doorway of the second bedroom. Wrapped in a navy silk dressing gown, she smiled at me as she always did ... a tender smile just for me, as far as I'd ever seen. Not the blazing one she used to discombobulate her prey. Though perhaps 'prey' was an erroneous and uncharitable word, because everyone always felt special in Scarlett's presence. I'd never once heard of any of her lovers referred to as jilted.

"Rusty's sister," she murmured as she approached. Her strawberry blond hair always looked as if she spent hours in hair rollers that I'd never once actually seen. Maybe it was some sort of hair spell?

"Yes," I murmured back.

"She wouldn't come in earlier."

I nodded and moved into the kitchen for a banana, aka my breakfast.

Scarlett followed me. I knew our eyes were the same color, but on her, the blue looked endless and deep. On me, they looked just like blue eyes. She was wearing multicolored hand-knit socks that completely clashed with the silk gown. Gran's handiwork.

"You were home late and are up early," Scarlett said.

"Yes." I didn't elaborate and she didn't question me further. She just brushed her fingers along my forearm, leaving her magic tingling on my skin, then retreated back toward her bedroom. This had been going on for months now, but the silence between us wasn't uncomfortable, just years deep.

I crossed to the bakery exit and looked back to see Scarlett lean over to tuck the blanket around Mory's feet. True, my mother didn't feel like I did about Sienna, but no one defined what behavior was appropriate for her. If she wanted to tuck a wounded teenager in, she would. I'd never aspired to be anything like Scarlett, and had actually strived to be her complete opposite — stable, homey, and focused. But now I wondered if that might have been the wrong path all along.

Even after losing Sienna in more ways than one only a floor below, the bakery was my haven — one that Scarlett and Kandy and Kett kept coaxing me out of. The kitchen was swathed in stainless steel, including the two long tables that I'd had custom built slightly higher than normal. That way I didn't lean quite so far over for so many hours every day. Though my apartment cleaning might be considered neglectful, I kept my bakery spotless. Sometimes I stood in the walk-in pantry — loaded full of chocolate, sugars, and spices — and just breathed. I once considered hauling my yoga mat in there, but I figured I didn't quite have enough space between shelves. Though, lately, I came and went from the pantry as quickly as possible, because I didn't like to lay eyes on the door to the basement. Yeah, my sister had almost ruined one of my favorite spots in the world. Almost.

Since Sienna had died, I'd expanded my cupcake bases to include carrot and banana cake, as well as tested out a bunch of new frostings based on seasonal berries. Strawberry was still my personal favorite, with or without a chocolate cake base — which was a bit surprising, as I was a chocolate fiend.

We didn't open until 10 A.M. on the weekdays, the same as all the other retail stores along West Fourth Avenue in Kitsilano. I wasn't a coffee or breakfast place. I was Cake in a Cup, with a few cookies on the side.

To that end, I softened extra butter and zested some lemon for Citrus Chipsters. I was hoping Mory would like them. Yeah, I knew the fledging necromancer wasn't a puppy. Would I feed chocolate to a dog? Ignore the fact that I fed chocolate to a werewolf last night. That's not the same thing at all.

So I baked.

As I worked, I tried to keep my thoughts away from the events of the day before ... it was more of a struggle than usual. Usually, just being in the bakery soothed me.

Around eight o'clock I became aware of Gran arriving through the back alley door. She was magically keyed to the lock, of course, and her magic — the taste of my childhood — was instantly familiar. She paused, without speaking, to watch me bake.

I looked up and she smiled but shooed me back to my icing with a wave of her hand. Her long silver hair was only half pulled back from her forehead this morning. The rest of it cascaded down her back in a frothy river that was reminiscent of Scarlett's perfect hair. My own curls were tight and more unruly. The Godfrey hair was yet another thing I hadn't inherited.

Gran hadn't watched me bake since she came back from her annual surfing vacation and found the bakery basement full of shapeshifters, a vampire, and putrid blood magic. The fact that the surfing trip was actually an annual meeting of the witches Convocation — of which Gran was the chair — and that this knowledge had been withheld from me hadn't helped our strained relationship.

She was wearing a necklace I was making for her. It was a work in progress, just like the one I wore, but with silver charm-bracelet charms rather than the wedding rings I collected. I hadn't added to it for months.

Now that I vaguely understood how my alchemist powers worked, I'd begun to wonder what I was weaving into Gran's necklace as I constructed it. Mine was a shield against magic, an extra layer of protection. The glimmers of the residual magic in the wedding rings were brought together and mortared with my own magic to create an extrapolation of marriage. Obviously, I believed that marriage offered some kind of heightened protection from the world, and I'd brought that intention to my work. Could I take Gran's necklace and work on it with the same open heart as I had before? Or would I alter it if I tried to work on it now? Even weaken it?

Would we even forgive each other ... ever? Would I forgive her for the half-truths I'd built my life on? Would she forgive me for ... for what? I still wasn't sure what I could have done differently about my parentage, or my sister, or whatever else I was currently doing wrong in her eyes.

I silently offered Gran a partly cooled tray of cookies as I stepped by her to wash my hands. I always got egg whites all over my fingers. She smiled at me in a way that made me think we might actually be able to make it through this rocky part.

Then Scarlett showed up. She'd been doing a lot of that lately. Of course, I was the one who started it three months ago. The one who'd reached out for help, to which she'd responded willingly and overwhelmingly.

"Jade," she said as she stepped from the doorway to the upstairs apartment. "A courier came for you but wouldn't leave the letter with me."

"Really?" I checked my phone. It was 8:36 A.M. Did courier services usually deliver so early?

"I told him to come around the bakery after ten. Good morning, Pearl." Scarlett offered Gran one of the blinding smiles that made people beg to do things for her.

Gran raised an eyebrow and regarded her daughter coolly with eyes the blue of deep water. "Good morning, Scarlett. I hope you slept well?"

"Indeed, thank you. Jade keeps a comfortable home."

"You're blessed she invited you into it."

Oh, God. They were going to do that sickeningly polite thing that they did whenever I got stuck between them. Usually they just avoided each other, which I much preferred.

"Yes, she has a big heart. But I'm not her only stray today."

Gran's eyes flicked to me, her expression ready to turn to disapproval. I groaned inwardly. I really didn't need Mory — or Mory's request — brought into this mix.

I lamely attempted to change the subject. "Do you want a cookie, Mom?"

"No, my Jade. Thank you. After breakfast, perhaps, with my coffee. Pearl and I are going out."

Oh? That was news. I was sure they hadn't been alone together in three months. Yeah, it seemed my other hidden talent was driving wedges between people. Only in this case, I might have just shifted the wedge more firmly into place.

"Yes. We have things to discuss," Gran said. She reached up to touch her necklace.

Scarlett's gaze dropped to follow this gesture. Then she offered me a smile that might have been a little sad around the edges. Had she not seen the necklace before?

I felt pleased whenever I saw Gran wearing it, but now I wondered if it was just another symbol of power and hierarchy. A visual reminder that Pearl had been the one to raise me. But thinking of how young Mory had seemed last night, who would ever think a sixteen-year-old had the capacity to raise a child of unknown magical origins on her own? Not me.

Gran turned to exit through the alley door — locking the front bakery door required a key — and Scarlett followed. My mother was wearing a hand-painted skirt — a swirl of pinks, purples, and blues around her knees — that I had instantly coveted the first time I saw it. Of course, I would have paired it with a T-shirt and not looked anywhere near the polished perfection that Scarlett did.

My mother took a cookie as she passed my workstation. For some reason seeing her second guess something as small as an offered cookie upset me. It didn't meld with the fun and flighty image I had of my mother.

"Mom?"

"Yes, my Jade?"

"Enjoy breakfast."

Scarlett laughed. Her magic turned this everyday sound into an orchestra of joy and harmony.

Then she left.

I wondered if I could make a cupcake to match my mother's laugh.

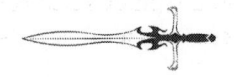

Bryn arrived at nine to set up the bakery, fill the display case, and start the coffee. She was my full-time employee/part-time baker, taking the Sunday and Tuesday early-morning shifts. She had enrolled in a pastry chef course in the fall, though, so I might lose her Tuesday mornings. My other full-time employee, Todd, knew more about coffee than all of us put together. He usually covered Bryn's days off and worked on his comic book series in the evenings. Tima, my part-timer, was still in high school and usually worked weekends.

"What pretty bits have you got there?" Bryn asked, as she crossed by me to pull a tray of *Comfort in a Cup*, a banana cake topped with buttercream, off the stacking shelf.

I followed Bryn's gaze and noted I was — completely unconsciously — rolling the jade stones now imbued with the skinwalker binding magic in the palm of my left hand. I'd dug the stones out of my trashed Gore-Tex this morning and transferred them to my left jean pocket. I didn't like the idea of leaving them lying around, even within my heavily-warded apartment.

"Trinket fodder," I answered.

Bryn smiled. "Oh, good. We need a new one for that space in the window."

I tried to return the smile as Bryn crossed back out to the store, but I was unsuccessful. I stuffed the stones back in my pocket and turned my full attention to the dark-chocolate buttercream icing I was supposed to be mixing. The bakery window was missing a trinket because my sister had used it to slaughter werewolves last spring.

Not that Bryn knew that, not that Bryn needed to know such things.

I hadn't made a trinket since then. Gran had told everyone — everyone not an Adept — that Sienna was grieving for her dead boyfriend while traveling the West Indies. I wasn't sure what we were supposed to say when she never came back. Gran probably had it worked out with a timetable and everything.

Bryn's dark, thick hair was lightly wavy and currently chopped into a short bob for the summer, which was probably super smart given the heat in the bakery. I was suddenly struck by a vague sense of similarity between her and the teenage girl who had been with the skinwalkers. I hadn't thought about it the previous day — being kidnapped was a little distracting — but Bryn was also First Nations from the North Shore. She was purely human, though. Not a hint of magical taste about her.

"Is your family from the Squamish band, Bryn?" I asked as she grabbed a tray of *Serenity in a Cup*, a carrot cake with cream cheese icing. A very basic, very solid-selling cupcake. It was the cinnamon that made the difference. I freshly grated the bark rather than using it bottled and already ground.

"Hmm? Yes. On my grandmother's side. Why? You're not thinking of doing something themed, are you?"

"No."

"Oh, good. Native American art is so appropriated and overdone right now." She crossed back to the store front.

Coincidence, right?

Or ... had the skinwalker elder known me? The group had been debating something for hours while my body worked through the magic of the sleep spell. They could have killed us and burned the bodies in that time.

Unless.

Unless what?

Unless Bryn was a plant or something? That was insane.

I opened my mouth to question her. I opened my mouth to accuse her ... of what? I'd hired her. We'd been in the same cake-decorating class, which I'd taken on a whim of Sienna's, who had only made it through the first half of the first session. I rarely did more than pipe frosting on my cupcakes, or on occasion sprinkle them with shaved chocolate or sugared violets, but I'd enjoyed the class.

It was just a coincidence. A connection my beleaguered brain was attempting to make, because of the magic I carried in my pocket. The magic I was now responsible for. A responsibility that actually scared me more than I liked to admit.

I shut my mouth and iced the final batch of *Cozy in a Cup*, a banana dark-chocolate chip cake with dark-chocolate buttercream frosting.

Kett walked in the back door from the alley just before we opened. It still freaked me out that he could just casually wander in and out of the bakery like that.

"Coffee?" I asked the vampire. Yeah, I hid behind sarcasm when rattled. Who didn't?

Kett ignored me and offered Bryn a smile. She blushed and bobbed her head like an idiotic plastic bird. Okay, it wasn't that bad, but I hated it when Kett played with the humans. Bryn appeared to find his icy blond looks irresistible. I briefly hoped he hadn't fed on her — vamps could compel and adjust the memories of their victims. However, I knew that Kett was too strict with his rules of etiquette to confuse sustenance and ... and what? His undead life? His responsibilities? Was I just a job to him or what?

Bryn retreated from the kitchen to open the French-paned front doors. My trinkets, which I hung liberally throughout the bakery, chimed. Though the glass cupcake display case took up three-quarters of the front of the shop, there was also just enough space for a small seating area. The mixture of high stools at round tables, wide-slat wood flooring, and paned front windows — everything painted white — was my attempt at a classy French provincial look. I hadn't quite pulled off the classy part, achieving more farmhouse than sleek old country.

I leaned sideways to look through the open pass-through doors to note — yes, a little smugly — that there was already a line outside. Bryn greeted a customer with a pleasant ring in her voice. He responded in baritone. I'd have to lay eyes on him, but by the sound of Bryn's voice, he was worth the effort.

"Hanging around the bakery today?" I said to Kett. Yeah, I was still feeling snippy. "Scarlett is having breakfast with Gran."

"I'm aware."

Of course he was. All-knowing stick-in-the-mud.

Kett cast his gaze to my hands and raised an eyebrow a sixteenth-of-an-inch. I was rolling the skinwalker magic-imbued jade stones through my fingers again. I had to stop doing that. The magic in the stones obviously rattled me. I wasn't sure of its purpose or what to do with it. Not like my necklace or my knife. The magic of those grounded me. I actually felt naked, incomplete without them. Even now, even while baking cupcakes, the blade was invisibly strapped over my right hip.

"There's a necromancer upstairs," I said.

Kett's growing look of interest left his face in an icy wave. Vampires really didn't get on with necromancers. Necro-controlled zombies were like vamp kryptonite, though it took a powerful necromancer to actually raise a body. Or a witch fueled by blood-magic and willing to eat her boyfriend's organs to steal his latent powers.

Hopefully — in both cases — such a person was a rarity.

"She's behind the wards of the apartment now," I said, "but I'd appreciate you not killing her if she happens to wander down into the bakery."

Kett looked affronted at this suggestion. Not that I knew so by his facial expression. It was the slight tightening of his shoulders that tipped me off. Yeah, I really was hanging out with him too much if I was actually starting to be able to read him. Now I felt bad about teasing him with the necromancer announcement.

"She's just a girl —"

"Rusty's sister."

Freaking vampire always knew everything. I don't know why I even bothered to talk to him. Oh, yeah, right. Because Gran had kept me ignorant half my life. That's why. Never mind that the information had been there for me to seek and I hadn't bothered to look. I was still pissy about it.

"I have customers," I said.

"So you do."

I thought about stabbing him in the stomach, but I'd done that once before and it hadn't fazed him any more than my sarcasm did. Or any more than the cold shoulder I turned his way now as I stomped into the bakery to help Bryn with the opening rush.

Chapter Eight

The courier showed up just after ten. I knew that because I actually looked up and saw him barrel into, then bounce right off, the wards protecting the bakery.

He stumbled back and rubbed his nose, affronted and perplexed. So he was magical enough that the wards excluded him from entry, but not enough to be able to feel the barrier before running into it.

Kett was up and moving — at human pace, because the bakery was currently full of the magically lacking — toward the front doors while my mouth was still hanging open in surprise. I'd never seen someone bounce off the wards like they were a screen door before. Any of the Adept in Vancouver could either already enter the bakery or knew to catch my eye and request entry with a wave. The wards on the bakery weren't as complex as on my apartment. I had always been able to invite people through verbally, or even with a nod of my head. Though now I was beginning to understand how that might have something to do with my ability to manipulate magic with subconscious intention.

The courier wasn't wearing a recognizable uniform, but he was carrying an official-looking bag and dressed in a generic blue top and gray pants. He also really needed to wash his thin hair, which might have been dirty blond if it was clean. He stepped back as

Kett loomed to block the door. Not that Kett physically needed to block a warded door. I gathered this display was for intimidation purposes. The vampire was an inch or so shorter than the courier.

I wiped my hands on a tea towel rather than my apron, which I liked to wear for show even though the pink ruffles clashed with my jeans and Converse sneakers. The bakery and yoga studio were pretty much the only places I didn't shoe myself exclusively with Fluevogs. My hands weren't dirty, just clammy. I didn't like the set of Kett's shoulders. I also didn't like that Kandy had just appeared behind the courier on the sidewalk. Like I said, the bakery was full of human customers. Humans didn't do well caught between Adepts at odds.

The werewolf's T-shirt was a slightly more lime version of her hair, which was back to its normal vibrant green.

"Hey," I heard the courier say to Kett as I rounded the corner of the display case. A breeze stirred my trinkets in the doorway and they tinkled. This sound was normally a comfort, but today it sent a shiver of worry down my spine. Why was this obviously magical person dressed like a courier? Not that the Adept didn't have jobs as I did, but like I said, Vancouver was a really small community. I might not know every magical person among the two-million-plus human residents of Greater Vancouver, but I should know anyone with enough magic to be bothered by the wards so much that they couldn't enter.

"Hey," Kett replied. The vampire's hands were in his pockets as if he was laid-back, easygoing. His voice was a welcoming drawl. I didn't like the look or sound of either.

Kandy wasn't any better. She was sporting that predator grin. Her eyes narrowed, maybe from the sun but probably because she was honed in on prey. Or, more specifically, imagining ripping the courier's spine free from the back of his neck.

"I ... that was weird, hey?" the courier asked.

Jesus, only seconds had passed. How had I noticed so much and moved so close to the door in seconds?

"What was weird?" Kett asked. He didn't step out from the bakery.

Kandy, outside, stepped closer to the courier and actually sniffed him. She wrinkled her nose with a frown and shook her head at Kett, who didn't react.

Oh, God they were working together. That wasn't good.

I stepped up behind Kett. He was actually only a couple of inches taller than my five feet nine inches, but he could make himself feel like he was blocking the entire door.

"Hey," the courier said again as he caught my eye. An admiring grin spread across his face. It was a look I was accustomed to. He wouldn't have even noticed me if Scarlett had been in the room, though, and she was double his age. He really needed to get his teeth whitened and straightened. "Jade Godfrey?"

Kandy shifted her stance, legs slightly apart, and arms ready. I was unconsciously playing with the stones in my left hand again. The skinwalker magic tingled in my palm.

"Yes," I answered.

"I have a letter for you," he said. He reached into his satchel and pulled out a thick, unusual-sized envelope. It was hand folded and sealed with wax. He wasn't wearing a name tag. I didn't recognize the logo on his bag.

My name was written on the envelope in pitch-black inked handwriting that borrowed heavily from calligraphy. The courier tried to pass the envelope to me. It met the ward and crumpled against it. His mouth dropped open again.

"Shit," I muttered, and tried to pass by Kett before one of my customers saw an envelope crushed against an invisible wall.

Except before I could move more than a step, Kandy grabbed the courier by the back of the shirt and began hauling him down the sidewalk.

"What the hell?" he yelled.

"Deliveries in the back," Kandy said with a cheerful chime I wouldn't have thought her vocal cords capable of.

I met the concerned gazes of a couple of pedestrians with a sunny smile. "She's just enthusiastic." Yeah, lame, but what the freaking hell? I cast my voice low and kept on smiling. "Manhandling couriers isn't great for business, vampire."

"Neither is accepting magically sealed correspondence. And he doesn't work for any local courier company."

Kett turned and crossed back through the bakery toward the kitchen.

I, dodging a couple of exiting customers less gracefully than the vampire, followed.

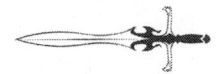

Kandy had the courier pressed against the building wall behind the dumpster. He looked more angry than freaked. His ears were red with it, actually. What regular courier wouldn't be freaked by a girl a third of his size pinning him against a wall? A courier well versed in the Adept world.

Had running into the ward just been for show? His magic was unfamiliar to me, but the magic radiating from the envelope in his hand was obvious.

"Sorcerer," I murmured to Kett. "The letter, anyway."

"Makes sense."

It did. Sorcerers derived their power from books and magical objects. The written word was — for the more powerful — potent for them as well. Among the Adept, sorcerers were almost as numerous as witches. But no sorcerer of power resided in Vancouver, which was witch territory because my grandmother deemed it to be.

The fact that my name was on the outside of a letter written by a sorcerer was definitely troubling. I was oddly glad it was Kett rather than Gran looming over the courier right now. I knew Gran would see the letter as a threat, whereas Kett would simply be mildly interested. Vampires got bored. A lot. Sometimes they went randomly rogue just to spice up their eternal lives.

The courier's face blanched at the sight of Kett. Or, rather, the sight of a vampire outside the bakery wards, as he'd already seen Kett but hadn't twigged to the vampire part yet. The wards kept magic in as well as out.

Kandy leaned in, her hand still on the courier's chest and pinning him to the wall. She gave the guy's neck a long sniff. "Spellcaster, low grade," she said, assessing the courier's magical power.

"All spellcasters are low grade," Kett replied mildly. He tilted his head in his very deliberate fashion to look at the envelope the guy still clutched at his side.

"What?" the courier sputtered. "I'm not —"

"You don't interest us, guy," Kandy said.

"Dowser?" Kett asked. "The envelope?"

I stepped to the vampire's side but not in front of him. It was always better to stay out of a predator's path. The courier looked at me as if in assessment. Normally, if an Adept of any power came to Vancouver, Gran would keep me behind wards. Not that I had any idea she'd been doing so for years. But it was rare that someone so low grade, as Kandy assessed the courier, could actually see magic. So he shouldn't be able to see that I had powers beyond that of a normal witch with a rare specialty, namely the dowsing.

Kett had known of my power the moment he saw me outside the wards of my apartment, of course. He'd known I was more. Same with Desmond.

I focused on the letter clutched in the courier's hand. It didn't feel malicious. But then, I didn't have much experience with that sort of thing. Glimmers of magic twinkled from my inked name. This could be evidence of a spell, or it might just be a trace embedded inadvertently in the ink. Whoever wrote it might just be powerful enough that such an effect was commonplace. I didn't mention out loud that though I could see similar glimmers in Gran's spellbooks, such residual energy didn't appear in her casually jotted notes.

"This isn't some big secret," the courier said. He attempted to hold the envelope out to me again. Kandy grabbed his arm by the wrist and twisted. He shrieked.

Jesus. Any neighbors along the alley with the day off were going to be making 911 calls soon.

"Drop it," Kandy said. She twisted the courier's wrist a second time.

The courier whimpered but didn't let go of the letter. "I can't," he said, choking through the pain. "I can't drop it. From my hand to hers. Get it?"

Ah, that made some sense.

"Who sent it?" Kett asked.

"Mot Blackwell. His instructions were explicit. He said there were other witches —"

Kandy twisted the courier's arm up until it was level with her nose. Then — careful not to come into contact with the paper — she sniffed the letter. She shrugged and stepped back from her hold on the courier.

"Who's Blackwell?" I asked. I had seen Kett go even more motionless than usual in response to the name. This usually meant he was thinking ... or bored.

The courier was rubbing his arm and massaging his wrist while casting baleful looks at Kandy. The green-haired werewolf ignored him as she prowled a ten-foot perimeter of sorts around us.

"Blackwell?" I asked again.

The courier shrugged. "A sorcerer I run errands for."

"And you? You're a spellcaster?"

His thin face stretched to accommodate an unusually wide grin. "Curser, actually. There ain't anything low grade about me."

Kandy sniffed. Kett was still zoned out, so I continued with my personal line of questioning.

"You write curses?"

"Not always. I've got some personal ones on my fingertips." He showed me his unremarkable fingers. The ones not holding the letter.

Spellcasters, sorcerers, and witches all shared the ability to cast or call up magic. Witches could access magic from natural power sources — namely the earth or their own reserves. Sorcerers, as the name seemed to suggest, needed a source for their magic such as a written spell or magical object. They could create these written spells through trial and error, but they couldn't simply draw a circle in the sand, light some candles, and make magic do their bidding as witches could.

Spellcasters were even more limited than sorcerers. They usually relied on spells written by others, unable to access magic beyond their own. So they were usually low on the power scale.

Curses were a specialty I'd never heard of, and I was hoping there was no demonstration scheduled in my future. The courier's magic didn't look powerful enough to kill anyone. It was rather tasteless, like hothouse cucumbers or day-old water.

"Don't worry," the courier said. "You're way too cute to curse."

"Moron," Kandy muttered to me as she passed behind in her pacing sequence. She appeared to delight in the courier's stupidity.

The courier ignored the werewolf. That was never a great idea, but I wasn't one to randomly give advice.

"So Jade, right? I'm Hoyt."

"Utter moron," Kandy said with more glee.

"You don't have to be such a bitch about it," Hoyt said with a sneer that suited his thin face a whole lot more than the smile had. Magic glimmered across his fingers, the bland cucumber taste resolving itself into something tinged with licorice.

I wrinkled my nose. "Fennel, ugh. Everyone is constantly cooking with fennel now, and I can't stand the taste. I'd keep that curse to yourself if I was you."

Hoyt stared at me. His mouth was actually hanging open. People did that a lot around me these days. I had a feeling I was speaking out loud a lot more than I used to, and most magic users didn't see or taste magic like I did.

"Oh, yeah?" Kandy said as she pivoted back. "I'm not a fan of licorice but I'd be happy to bite the moron's fingers off if he even wiggles them in the wrong direction."

"See? Drop the curse, spellcaster, or lose the fingers," I said. "And just hand me the damn letter."

He grimaced, shook the curse he'd been readying off his fingers, and held out the letter to me.

I reached for it, but right before I touched it, I felt cool fingers on my wrist. Kett had snapped out of his fugue state to touch me lightly. The tingly peppermint of his magic itched my skin, but I didn't shake him off. It was rare that he touched me. His fingers were lightly pressed to the pulse points of my wrist.

Hoyt flinched. His reaction time was purely on human levels. Unlike my own, obviously.

"Blackwell is well known to the Conclave," Kett said. "Your grandmother would not be pleased." His voice was barely a murmur, but this statement wasn't offered as a warning. And Gran being displeased was her currently natural state of being.

"The chances of the spell actually being keyed to me are slim," I said. To key a spell to that level, a witch would need the hair, blood, or saliva of her target. But I didn't think a sorcerer could even work magic on that level, not without a magical object. As far as I could tell without touching it, the envelope didn't contain such an object. Knowledgeable of me, hey? I couldn't claim natural intelligence though. Kett had me studying witch and sorcerer magic as a basis for the alchemy.

"True," Kett answered, but he kept his fingers on my wrist as I reached the last inch to take the letter from Hoyt.

The spell on the envelope dispersed as it transferred to my hand. Hoyt's reedy shoulders sagged in relief. The magic embedded in the letter had simply compelled him to hand it over to me, or at least to a person he thought to be me. I wondered if he'd even known what I looked like ahead of time.

"What are you still doing here?" Kandy snarled at the courier. The top of her head was level with his nose, and yet he stumbled back from her ferocity. Curse magic bloomed across all his fingertips before he seemingly reminded himself that Kandy didn't scare him. Yeah, right.

"I have to wait for an answer," Hoyt said.

I opened the envelope. The sorcerer's magic danced within the ink on the single sheet of card stock within. The paper was so thick it was practically fabric. Maybe it was woven linen?

The card read, *Jade Godfrey, Dowser. Granddaughter of Pearl Godfrey, Witch. Convocation Chair. Please accept my invitation to view —*

"Yes," Kett said.

Err, what?

"I need the answer from her," Hoyt said. "You know, the person the invitation is actually addressed to."

Kett rolled his shoulders. That was a whole lot of reaction from him. Kandy noticed as well. The werewolf paused her pacing to eye the vampire. I wasn't sure if either of us were quick enough to stop Kett from ripping Hoyt's throat out.

The courier shifted on his feet, aware he'd done something wrong or that something was happening, but not sure what.

"Continue," the vampire said. He didn't take his eyes off Hoyt.

I reluctantly dropped my gaze to the invitation. Man, I never knew what would insult the vampire. And here I was without an outside tap in the alley. Trying to clean up the blood would be really obvious by daylight.

Jade Godfrey, Dowser. Granddaughter of Pearl Godfrey, Witch. Convocation Chair.

Please accept my invitation to view
The North American Blackwell Collection

Your expertise as a dowser would be greatly appreciated.

Please reply as soon as possible.

— Mot Blackwell, Lord & Sorcerer

More power was poured into that signature than I saw in most of the Adept — face to face — in Vancouver. Mot Blackwell, Lord and Sorcerer, was not to be trifled with. Which was okay, because I really wasn't a fan of trifle. Too boozy. Too much mushy cake and not enough icing.

"The Blackwell Collection?" I asked.

"It is an unprecedented invitation," Kett said. This, obviously, didn't answer my question. "We accept."

"The invitation is for one," Hoyt replied. Then he stepped back with a swallow in reaction to whatever he saw on the vampire's face.

"A dowser of Jade Godfrey's ability does not travel unescorted. Blackwell would not be so foolish," Kett said. His tone was typically cool even though his shoulders were rigid. "Where does the collection currently reside?"

"I don't know, but Blackwell wishes to meet in Portland," Hoyt answered. His gaze flicked to Kandy.

The green-haired werewolf stiffened and bared her teeth. "Portland is the territory of the West Coast North American Pack. No sorcerer would dare take up residence there."

"I assume it is simply a rendezvous point." Kett was actually attempting to soothe the ruffled werewolf. I felt like my head might explode if I hadn't been distracted by other more seemingly important things.

"What?" I asked. "Like a treasure hunt?" I really wasn't a fan of those anymore.

"No. More like a neutral — patrolled — territory."

"None of the Adept would be stupid enough to start something in Portland," Kandy added.

"Yes," Kett said. "Far enough away from Pearl Godfrey's domain, but not too far from Vancouver. Neutral for witch and sorcerer, but not unrestricted."

"The sorcerer is seriously asking me to look at his collection? Isn't that the start of some olden-days, crappy pick-up line?"

Kandy smirked. I could always count on the werewolf to find me amusing.

"Blackwell's collection of magical artifacts is legendary," Kett answered, as put out as he had the ability to sound.

"For vampires," Kandy muttered. Kett ignored her.

"When does Blackwell expect us?" the vampire asked archly.

"At your leisure," Hoyt answered. His tone mocked Kett's. This guy really was a moron. Either that, or he mistakenly thought a curse would actually be a defense against a vampire. It was comforting to know there were Adepts even more ignorant than I was.

"You may tell him we will be traveling as a party of four. By auto. We will leave tomorrow morning."

"Kett," I hissed. The vampire almost imperceptibly shook his head. I clamped my mouth shut, but I wasn't happy about it.

"You may leave us now." Kett dismissed Hoyt and turned his back on him. The courier pulled a face behind the vampire's back and got a snicker from Kandy. I didn't pout at her finding Hoyt amusing, even though this diminished her sense of humor in my mind.

"I'm to accompany you. As your liaison," Hoyt said. "Though I assumed we would fly." This last bit was delivered as a barb to Kett's shoulder blades, but the vampire didn't even twitch.

"The bakery. 8:00 A.M.," Kett replied. "We will provide the transportation."

Hoyt backed away, moving as quickly as he could without actually running. Before he turned onto Yew Street, which ran perpendicular to West Fourth Avenue, he had a cellphone in his hand.

"I'm not going anywhere," I said. "And I'm certainly not going anywhere on your say so."

"Yeah, the dowser ain't leaving," Kandy added. "Not without permission."

"Hey," I said, affronted. "I'll go where I want to go."

"I will speak to Scarlett." Kett smoothly interrupted the argument brewing between Kandy and me. "May I see the invitation?"

I flipped the invite at him with a flick of my wrist. I wasn't going to be told where and when to go anywhere, not even by my freaking mother. "I have a bakery to run. Have a great trip." I yanked open the alley back door. "Some sorcerer guy powerful enough to leave traces of magic in his handwriting invites me to Portland, and that isn't a red flag for either of you? And you call me stupid."

Kandy shrugged. Her hands were in her pockets and her eyes downcast. "I like red," she said. The joke fell flat between us.

"And I like magical collections to which I have been denied access for decades," Kett said. His eyes were on the invitation. "I also never call you stupid, dowser. Just uninformed and untrained." The vampire briefly flicked his eyes at Kandy. "And shouldn't you be tracking someone?"

Kandy curled her lip in a snarl. But then, also pulling out her phone, she turned to follow Hoyt out of the alley.

I shook my head. When had I become the rational one?

Though it really was a pity, because I'd always wanted to spend a long weekend in Portland.

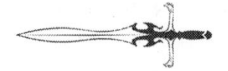

I slammed the alley door behind me, wondering if I could alter the wards to exclude a certain werewolf and vampire again. I turned around and literally ran into Mory, who'd apparently been loitering by the back door.

"Portland, huh?" the fledgling necromancer asked.

"You have icing on your face. Is that dark-chocolate buttercream?"

Mory wiped her face and observed the transferred streak of icing. "Yup." She licked the remnant off her hand.

I narrowed my eyes at her. "From a *Cozy in a Cup*?"

"Nope." Mory offered me a saucy grin. It was the first smile I'd seen from her. However, only two other options with dark-chocolate buttercream icing were currently available in the bakery. The ever-popular *Sex in a Cup*, a cocoa cake with a dash of cinnamon, and the *Desire in a Cup*, a chocolate raspberry cake. I was fairly certain Mory's mother would not be a fan of her daughter eating either of those for breakfast.

"I like Portland," Mory said. "Good shopping, big book store, and lots of bridges." Her grin widened. Someone slept well last night, at least.

"If books and bridges are all you're looking for," I answered, "then you should never have reason to leave home." Still pissed about Portland, and sorcerers, and vampires, I crossed back to my workstation and started to transfer cookies from a cooling rack to a tray, just to do something with my hands.

"Rusty took me. A year ago," Mory said behind me. It was a deliberate mention of her brother designed to tug at my heartstrings. It worked.

"During the beer festival," I whispered, more to the cookies than Mory. I remembered Rusty talking about it at a fireworks party last summer on the roof of his building. That had been the first time I'd met him. He'd just started dating Sienna, and had managed to stick around long enough for me to bother meeting him.

"Yeah." Mory continued chatting as if she wasn't stabbing me in the gut with every word. My guilt resided in my stomach, hence my need to constantly fill it with chocolate, and cookies, and cupcakes. "While he was at the festival, there was this camp thing I went to for two days. I met a bunch of werewolves and we practiced stuff."

A camp for Adept kids. Great. One more thing I'd never been to. Jesus, I was tired of my own whinging. I was freaking tired of trying to be the best granddaughter, the best dowser, and the best ... friend.

Well, I guess I didn't have to worry about the last one anymore.

"So you'll take me, then? To the warehouse? To Rusty?"

I turned around, knowing I needed to say no to her face. Knowing she needed to understand that the right thing for me to do was to take her home to her grieving mother. A mother who didn't need her daughter even more traumatized by my family than she already was.

Then I saw her face.

Mory didn't really look like Rusty. She was so tiny, but still gangly around the edges as if she wasn't finished growing yet. Her eyes were dark pools on her face, too large for her round cherub cheeks and pale lips.

"Tima is here," Mory rushed to add. "So she ... so you can leave now, yes?"

Tima came in part-time during the weekends, though with it being summer now, she'd picked up a few weekday shifts. She was only a year or so older than Mory, and had probably just been dropped off by her brother. Her not-dead brother.

I faltered. This wasn't a decision I should make ... but it was a decision I could make. When was the last time I'd chosen, I'd decided? Damn it. Tima covered me midday for yoga and paperwork, not ghost hunting.

"How do you know he'll be there?"

Mory chewed on her lip. "He'll come for me."

"Why?"

"It's a necromancer thing."

"You mean you can call any ghost to you from their ... from the site of their death?"

Mory hesitated. I folded my arms and stared her down. Necromancer secrets or not, she'd answer my questions or we wouldn't step one foot away from the bakery.

"No," Mory said. "Just a blood relative."

"Why doesn't your mom take you? You obviously know the location, or at least that it's a warehouse."

Mory ducked her head. She was playing with a bracelet on her left wrist. It was too big for her and too manly. Rusty's, I guessed. "She doesn't want me to do it. She doesn't want me to ... be tied to him."

"What do you mean?"

"He's my brother. If I call him, he can choose to stay. To use me as an anchor point."

My mind boggled at the idea. "I thought ghosts were just impressions of a person's energy left on this plane of existence?"

"That's shades."

"Shades and ghosts aren't the same thing?"

Mory squirmed uncomfortably.

I crossed my arms, raised my eyebrow, and remained quiet. A technique I was — rather unwillingly — learning from Kett.

"Shades are like ... like a photograph, like you said, impressions," Mory said. "Ghosts can talk, and even answer questions about their life. If you know the right thing to ask. But they don't ... they don't learn or, like, grow." Mory fell silent, and bit her lip.

"Then what are you saying about calling Rusty and him staying? How can a shade or ghost stay with you?"

Mory bowed her head further, fiddling with the edge of her blue T-shirt now. I could see the bones beneath the flesh of her wrists. She was skinnier than she should be.

"She means a necromancer can trap a soul with her, as a familiar," a cool voice said from behind us.

I'd felt the vampire's magical signature remain in the alley, but he moved swiftly enough through the back door that he almost startled me.

Mory jumped and spun around. "That is not what I mean —" Her retort died on her lips with a squeak. Yeah, if you knew what you were looking at, vampires were damn scary. A necromancer would know what she was looking at — not by his magic, as I did, but by his soul. Or the lack of one ...

"Kett," I said, matching his cool tone. "Eavesdropping is beneath you."

Kett stiffened, his icy blue eyes locking to mine rather than on the necromancer. He didn't like being given personal critiques, but it kept his attention on me and off Mory.

"Nor were you invited into this conversation," I added. "Please don't make me ask you to leave." Sometimes channeling my grandmother was the best defense against the vampire. Plus, I had a feeling we were both a little unsure of what would happen if I did actually ask him to leave and he refused.

The magic of the wards might back me and eject him — maybe even tear him apart if he fought. It would be an insult and an affront. Vampires liked to think of themselves as all powerful. They didn't like being trumped by magic — hence their hatred of necromancers. Ironically, death magic was their Achilles heel. Yeah, I was a slow learner, but I had started piecing things together.

"It's not like that," Mory said. Brave girl to find her voice in the presence of a vampire. "I would never trap a soul. I wouldn't. I couldn't. I'm not powerful enough. I doubt anyone is —"

"Someone was, once," Kett said. A chill ran down my spine. I had no idea what the hell he was talking about, but I didn't like the faraway tone of his voice.

I stepped around Mory, placing her behind me. I didn't like that this put the workstation between her and the bakery, but it was the quickest option.

"It would be his choice, Jade," Mory said. "Like my uncle."

"Excuse me?" I asked, distracted by the implications. "You have a ghost uncle who follows you around?"

"Eww, not me. My mom. It's her great uncle. He died when she was super young, and he chose without her asking. To stay with the family. Rusty could stay with me ... if he wanted."

I could hear Mory fighting tears behind me, but Kett's face remained like clear ice. "Your grandmother would not approve," he said.

"You going to run and tell her, vampire?" I asked, knowing that Kett was very careful to avoid contact with Gran. He wasn't scared of her, I don't think, but he was always wary of ramifications. Gran was well liked and highly ranked in the Adept community. Vampires were neither.

Kett smiled. I hated it when he did that. It was too human, softening everything about him. Making him almost accessible. Likeable. Sexy.

I felt his magic shift along with the smile. I wasn't sure what the shift meant, but I didn't like it. Or rather, I didn't like that I noticed and enjoyed the taste and feel of it.

I narrowed my eyes at him and glowered.

Kett's grin widened, as if he thought I was an adorable curmudgeon. I was, but I really had to stop being so around him.

He pulled out a cellphone and sauntered into the bakery. I wasn't impressed. I was certain he'd been practicing that walk.

"He has a cellphone," Mory said quietly.

"No point in whispering. He just heard our conversation through that steel door. Dog whistles must be a bitch for him. Which, now that I think about it ..."

"A vampire with a cellphone."

"Yeah, he's all twenty-first century."

"He's not twenty-first century."

"You can see that, huh?"

"He's ... he's ..."

I gave the fledgling necromancer a cookie, then slid the partly full tray onto the stock shelving unit.

"He would have killed me if you hadn't been here," Mory finally articulated.

"Nah. Vamps have a rep, but they're pretty anxious about bad press."

"All vampires hate necromancers."

"Yeah, I've seen why." First hand actually, when Sienna — after absorbing Rusty's latent necromancer powers — had raised Hudson in the morgue. The zombie werewolf had kicked Kett's ass. Mory didn't need to know that extra part of the saga though. "The immortal really don't like being mortal."

"I have no idea what you're talking about. All I know is my uncle was killed by a vampire that was hunting my mom."

"Wait, what? Creepy great uncle was drained by a vamp?"

"Well, not exactly," Mory answered. "My mom was young, like two, and she got out of the house at night. Her uncle found her in the graveyard —"

"Your mom grew up next to a graveyard?"

"It was a family plot. You know, on the estate. Mom probably went there to talk to the ghosts."

Okay. No sane vampire would be caught on the estate of a necromancer family. And definitely — whether sane or rogue — not in a graveyard. Actually, I guess it pays to be able to speak to the dead.

"Anyway," Mory continued. "They found them in the morning. My great uncle dead and my mom sleeping beside him."

"Okay, that isn't super creepy at all. He was drained?"

"Broken neck."

"Your family thinks a vampire would have killed without draining? And then didn't kill your mom?"

"The family thinks the ghosts drove the vampire off. They can do that, you know."

"And the ghosts confirmed the vampire's presence?"

"Well, my mom was the only full necromancer in the family at that point. Her mom died giving birth to her. So she was the only one who could communicate with them directly. And she was two."

A more likely scenario, I thought, was that the great uncle — left alone to tend baby necromancer — got drunk, passed out, and then woke to find baby gone. Stumbling out of the house, he found baby in the graveyard, tripped over an old headstone and broke his neck. Then dead, he forever after chose to stay with his great niece — the only person who could now see him — and tell her he saved her from a vampire.

Ah, families. So full of loyalty, love, and half-truths.

"So you'll take me? I'm not powerful enough to do any damage or hurt anyone. I just want … I want Rusty to have a chance to …"

"Redeem himself?" I asked gently. Mory didn't answer. "If he murdered those werewolves with Sienna, do you think he'll tell you?"

"My mom thinks he's guilty." Mory's whisper cut me right across the unhealed spot on my heart.

"There was a lot of evidence," I said, trying to somehow contain and control the emotion threatening my rational thought process. "Evidence collected by trained Adept investigators. People I didn't even know existed before the tribunal. They had that magical cube thing, like YouTube only with better camera work."

"I saw it."

The reconstructionist had somehow created a 'magical imprint' of Hudson's death. Even through my grief, I'd thought the magic was amazing. I could feel residual magic, of course, but I certainly couldn't reconstruct scenes from the past. Hell, I barely comprehended the present.

"And now what? You're hoping Sienna made him do it?"

"I don't care!" Mory cried. The sentiment drove straight into my soul. I, too, worried that some part of me didn't care one way or the other. That some part of me just wanted my sister back.

I remembered Sienna standing in the magic of the portal just a floor below where Mory and I stood. I remember how she dissolved into the magic — washed clean away. First her dark magic, then her very being. I'd held on to her as long as I could feel her fingers. I'd held on, wishing she could stay, wishing everything could go back …

"I have a purple lip gloss that looks terrible on me," I said. "It would look great on you."

"Yeah?" Hope flooded across Mory's face and out through her limbs. She'd been clenching her fists so tightly it was a good thing she obviously chewed her nails. Though it was hell on her fluorescent orange manicure.

"Yeah. Let's grab it. Along with some proper shoes. I can't go ghost hunting in sneakers."

Chapter Nine

A quick stop at the Godfrey Properties offices — and a dozen cupcakes — yielded the keys to the warehouse on West Sixth Avenue. Gran, aka Godfrey Properties, owned an entire block of West Fourth Avenue including the bakery and the apartments above. She also owned various commercial and residential properties in and around Greater Vancouver. She was a powerful witch and real estate mogul.

I asked Linda, Gran's office manager, for the keys to all the larger retail spaces that Godfrey Properties currently had available for lease to cover my tracks. If Linda told Gran I was looking to expand the bakery — cupcake bribe or no cupcake bribe — the gig would be up. But then, Mory and I wouldn't be hanging around just waiting to be caught anyway.

We cabbed it to the warehouse where I'd found Rusty half eaten inside a pentagram, with my sister hiding with her arms slashed in a protection circle close by. At the time, honestly, I'd just been happy that Sienna was alive. Beyond all the blood — and the vivid picture still imprinted on my mind — I hadn't really absorbed Rusty's death. I'd wanted him to be the bad guy so much that I didn't dig into — hell, I barely even listened to — Sienna's story. Only after she literally stabbed me in the gut with her duplicity did I finally wake up and figure it all out.

Now, here I was standing outside the same warehouse, on the same sidewalk, looking for Rusty. Or at least helping Mory find Rusty. The warehouse looked smaller in the midday sun than it had in the middle of the night, when I'd been surrounded by a vampire and four shapeshifters.

The building was empty and still in need of a coat of blue exterior paint. The 'For Lease' sign was gone. Other than Mory standing next to me, I couldn't feel any magic in the immediate vicinity. The witch cleanup crew had scoured the area.

Mory shifted beside me, shuffling her feet. I wasn't too sure how long I'd been staring up at the second floor of the east side of the building. The cab was long gone. I was desperately trying to not wallow in the memories of the night three months ago that changed the fabric of my life.

I'd never thought of myself as easily manipulated — not mentally or physically. But the path I'd seen so clearly stretched out before me had been a false construct based on Gran's half-truths, Sienna's lies, and my own willful ignorance. Now, whenever I stepped forward, I did so with no trusted guidance and no perception of the future.

The worn cement of the parking lot felt solid underneath my feet, and that was good enough for now.

I approached the side door, ghosting my footsteps from three months ago. Though the key ring held multiple options, the key for the eastern door was clearly marked, and I slipped it into the lock, very aware that I hadn't actually spoken to the young necromancer standing behind me for a number of minutes.

This field trip was turning out to be far more selfishly motivated than I'd thought, as if I was seeking some sort of cathartic release I hadn't known I needed.

"I'm sorry," I said. My voice cracked embarrassingly.

"What for?" Mory asked. Her voice was much more steady than mine, but her tone was remote, as if she might be steeling herself.

"I should have done more. I should have figured it out before ..."

"Yeah, everybody says that."

"I guess they probably all think so, but ... I was here. I should have been ... wiser, stronger."

"But you weren't."

"No."

"And neither was anyone else."

Jesus, now a fifteen-year-old was laying truths on me like they were plucked out of the air when I — the supposed adult — was still struggling to see them hanging there.

"Inside?" I asked.

Mory nodded. I turned the key. The lock was newly stiff. The original had been broken by Desmond ... no, Kandy, during my last break and enter.

The side door opened into the wide room I'd expected. Tables, chairs, and some cubicle dividers were stacked along the outer walls, but essentially the main floor was empty. Empty and very, very clean. I doubted it had been this clean three months ago. But then, I couldn't see in the dark so I could be wrong.

"I had two seeing-eye werewolves guiding me through here last time," I said as I crossed into the warehouse and shut the door behind Mory.

"Your friend whose hair freaked you out?"

"No. Two others."

"But she's a werewolf."

"Yeah."

"She's like your bodyguard, hey?"

"Why do you say that?"

"She was pretty pissy with the guy in the alley."

"Ah. Yes."

"Do you really need a bodyguard?"

I sighed. "It's stupidly complicated."

Mory snorted. "Yeah, I get it."

"We should grab some ice cream after this. Mario's Gelati. They have this black forest cake flavor I totally want to rip off, it's so good."

"Okay."

"Okay." I moved determinedly across the length of the warehouse, toward the stairs I knew to be in the back corner. "Upstairs."

Mory followed a pace behind.

No dark, sickly magic threatened to overwhelm me as it had the last time I'd crossed through the warehouse. I thought about how many people I was currently pissing off with each step I took and it actually buoyed me. We were crafted by our choices, after all. Even the ones that everyone else knew were wrong. As long as I wasn't leading Mory into any danger, I was perfectly happy being utterly wrong. Because it was my choice leading me this time.

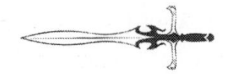

On the second floor, the door to the easternmost room was closed. Or maybe it was an office, I didn't know. The last time I stood here, I'd felt dark magic seeping through the hollow-core door. I also had a party of monsters at my back. Now it was just me, a fledgling necromancer, and no magic for at least a mile or so.

"This is it?" Mory asked. Her voice didn't betray any nerves or trepidation. She was cool for a teenager. Maybe that was the way they came now — or maybe seeing ghosts had prepared her for a lot of things.

"Yes. Do you want to talk about anything before we go in?"

"Like what?"

"Like, if Rusty comes to you ... how will he look? Do you ... should you know ..."

"No. He'll come as himself. His projection of himself. I think."

"You don't see the ... scenes?"

"Like in a movie, except real life?"

"Yeah."

"No. Not yet anyway. Death visions, you mean."

"I wasn't sure it was a thing, except that investigator crew came through."

"Yeah. The one with the YouTube cube thing was a reconstructionist. That's different. Not a necromancer thing." Mory spoke matter-of-factly, but to me, the magic we'd witnessed at the tribunal had been awesome and overwhelming. "And I only saw the one with the werewolf. Mom made me leave."

I didn't know what to say to that, though I was really, really glad the fledgling necromancer hadn't seen the reconstruction of her brother's murder.

"They had a hired necromancer with them as well," Mory continued. "Mom said the necro should have been able to speak to Rusty, to help piece together the moment of his death, but she didn't testify. So maybe he wouldn't talk to her."

"Well," I said, "let's hope this isn't your first death vision." I really didn't want Mory to see the last moments of Rusty's life. I didn't want her to see my sister eating Rusty's soft parts as he lay dying, either. The very idea of that still sickened me.

We stepped into the room. It was completely empty. New blinds hung closed over the windows. New light-gray carpet on the floor. I could still smell the glue. No candles, no pentagram, and no blood.

"Here?" Mory asked as she stepped into the room and turned around.

"Yeah," I answered. It had all been wiped clean. Logically, I knew it would have been, but seeing it was different. It wasn't just a surface wipe. It was a deep, magical clean. "The magic has been totally scoured away. Will you ... does that make a difference?"

"No," Mory answered. She pulled a small mason jar containing a tea light candle out of her bag. "He's not here in that way."

"Not on this plane of existence."

Mory shrugged. "Don't know about that, but you can't clean shades or ghosts like dirt. You can release them. Let them go if they're trapped. But I'm not looking for Rusty's ghost. I want to connect with his spectral energy."

I had a feeling that the fledgling necromancer's ability to connect to this spectral energy, or life force, or soul, was what bothered the vampire so much. But whether that was because vampires didn't actually have souls, I didn't know.

Mory lit her candle and sat cross-legged in the middle of the room. Now was not the time to ask her whether she could see Kett's soul. Actually, now wasn't the time for me to even be here.

"Mory, do you need me?" I asked quietly, just in case she was already in a trance or something.

"No," she answered. "Either he'll come or not. I just have to wait." Her voice betrayed the first hints of worry.

"I'm ... maybe I should —"

Mory's shoulders, slumped over the candle in her hands, stiffened and straightened. She looked directly ahead of her and slightly upward. She held the candle aloft just over her head, as if using it to light some darkness I couldn't see. The candle flickered, though there was no wind.

"Rusty," she said. "It's just me."

I stumbled away from the pain in her voice. I stumbled, tripping over my own feet until I made it to the hallway, spun around, and pressed my back to the wall beside the open door. I slid down into a squat and covered my eyes with my hands.

The ache in my heart — the sharp point that had lodged there when Sienna died — flared but I stuffed it back down. This was about Mory not me. I needed to not make it about me.

"Rusty." Mory's voice was clear — bright even — through the open door. Full of joy. "I've missed you so much."

I squeezed my eyes tighter, but not tight enough to stop the tears. I could taste Mory's magic as it filled the room behind me with the flavor of toasted marshmallows and the same candied-violet base she shared with Rusty. I couldn't sense anything or anyone beyond that, even though I could hear Mory's one-sided murmured conversation.

"Jade brought me," I heard her say, but then she paused as if listening.

Looking for a distraction, I pulled the jade stones out of my pocket and rolled the skinwalker magic around in the palm of my hand. I wasn't sure what I'd created by combining the skinwalker bindings with the natural magic of the jade, but the last time I'd left magical objects lying around, things hadn't turned out so well ... for many people, including Rusty. I felt better with the stones in my hand.

"No!" Mory cried out from the room behind me. "But ... why?"

I brushed the tears from my cheeks. Mory was getting bad news, and she didn't need to see me blubbering like a baby when she came out the other end of it.

"They say you knew before that," Mory said. "They say you helped." The fledgling's tone grew angry and hurt. I thought about getting up from the hall and pulling the necromancer from the room. Maybe this kind of truth was too much. She'd already lost her brother. Did she need to tarnish all her memories as well?

I didn't move. Mory had stopped speaking. I tucked the jade stones back in my pocket and listened, but I couldn't hear anything further.

I stood and went inside. Mory was seated as before, though her head was bowed. The mason-jar candle was still lit, sitting on the floor before her crossed ankles.

I found some Kleenex in my satchel and crossed to dangle it over Mory's shoulder. She took it and blew her nose.

"He wants you to know he's still here," Mory said. She blew her nose a second time. "Because you can't see him."

"Oh," I said. My stomach bottomed out. "I ... should I look somewhere specific?"

Mory gestured over the candle in front of her. "There. Standing."

My stomach lurched as I tried to make eye contact with something that didn't exist. Rusty had been about my height. I remembered him sprawled naked and half-eaten on the floor at my feet.

"He's says he's sorry ... for Hudson," Mory spat angrily, as if she didn't want to relay the message.

I nodded before I could stop myself, then switched to staring at the candle. "He wasn't mine to mourn."

"Rusty says he helped Sienna that night because she was scared of the werewolf. She was scared he was going to hurt you."

A slew of retorts flashed into my mind, but thankfully I managed to not speak them out loud. Things such as *How could you be so blind?* and *Well, that's convenient,* and *I don't even remotely believe that your girlfriend was combining sex and blood magic and you didn't even notice.* I wasn't going to say any of those things. I wasn't going to start any argument with Mory in the middle.

Hudson had been drained of blood and magic while he was alive. Sienna couldn't have done such a thing on her own. Not even with five of my trinkets anchoring her own binding magic. Rusty was culpable through, through, and through. And he'd paid the price.

"Jade," Mory said. She rested her head back against my thigh. "He'll stay with me. If I ask."

"All the time?"

"He can come and go. But yeah."

I touched Mory's hair. The purple dye was fading badly from its shaggy tips, creating a terrible, unintentional ombre effect. It also needed a wash. I pressed the palm of my hand to her head. She wanted my guidance but I had none to give. At least, I didn't know what the right choice was here. Should she keep her brother's spectral energy by her forever? Would he help or hinder? Would he protect her? Could he protect her?

"What would your mom say?" I finally asked.

"She'd say that I've made contact now, and I could make contact again."

"Okay. Would you need to come back here?"

"I don't think so." She twisted the large bracelet — the one I was certain belonged to Rusty — on her wrist. I found myself wondering whether I could take the residual magic in that bracelet and combine it with Mory's magic to make a beacon of sorts. So Rusty could always find her, but not be tied to her. Maybe necromancer magic already worked like that ...

"Is there ... is there anything you would be denying him? Does heaven exist?"

Mory fell silent for a moment, listening. Then she said, "Umm, I don't know. He goes to talk about that, but then he can't talk. Like something blocks him. I don't know."

"If you tie him to you, can you let him go later?"

"Yes."

"So what's the worst case scenario?"

"That I go crazy."

"Well, that's always the worst case."

Mory laughed. "It's a problem for all necromancers."

"I imagine."

"And, well ... constantly talking to your dead brother might ... you know."

"Hasten the process?"

"Yeah."

"Life is never going to be normal anyway. Is it?"

"No."

"You got some answers. Whether they were the truth or not."

"Yes."

"Then maybe you need to think on those before you make a decision."

Mory nodded and pulled away from my hand on her head.

"See you later, Rusty," she said to the air in front of her. Then she quickly leaned over and blew out the candle, as if she didn't want the time to change her mind.

All the toasted marshmallow magic that had filled the room snapped back into Mory.

"You use candles like a witch," I said.

"It's a focal point," Mory said, shrugging as she rolled to her feet and grabbed the candle.

"No circle, though." I scanned Mory's eyes for traces of magic, but I couldn't see anything beyond her normal amount. A witch would never cast magic without the protection of a circle.

"I am the circle," Mory stated.

"Yeah. I see."

"I want bubblegum."

"What?"

"The ice cream?"

"Right. Let's call a cab."

"You should get a car."

"Nah, too expensive. Maybe I should sign up for one of those car co-ops."

Mory made a noncommittal noise and headed for the door as I pulled out my cellphone. The gelato place was close enough that we probably could have walked, except I wasn't sure a teenager could actually walk that far. Plus, Mory's ratty combat boots looked like they were two sizes too big for her.

Three voicemails and ten text messages lit up my screen. I ignored them all.

Ice cream waited for no woman.

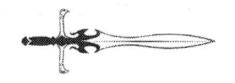

Mory's witch friend Amy — her magic only a glimmer behind her eyes — was waiting for us at Mario's Gelati. I surmised that the quarter-witch had been delivered by text message. I bought them both cones and had a one-liter tub of black forest cake hand-packed for myself. Then I got my third-wheel ass out of there before they made me feel any older or unwanted. I was glad Mory had someone to talk to, because I was certain she couldn't hide behind chocolate and cupcakes like I could. Nor did I have any other wisdom to offer, other than "grin and bear it."

That philosophy wasn't currently working for me, anyway.

I walked home, eating the entire tub of ice cream while I did so, hoping the calorie burning would offset the intake but also not really caring. Too much shit was rattling around in my head, and none of it was constructive or helpful.

My sandals — purple Joni's with green laces; Fluevog's, of course and always — were gorgeous and perfect for ghost hunting, but weren't made for three-hour strolls along the seawall. However, blisters that would probably heal in minutes weren't enough to snap me out of my head shit. And yeah, it freaked the hell out of me that I healed so quickly now. That I kicked a grizzly bear in the gut and he felt it. That I felt every drop of magic all around me all the time, so much so that I had started avoiding the things I'd loved before … dancing, dinner out, etcetera.

And I'd freaking kissed Desmond.

If by 'kiss' I meant 'practically molested.' Though he'd more than obviously been a willing victim.

I ran out of ice cream before I even made it into my own neighborhood.

Trinkets, Treasures & Other Bloody Magic

I avoided West Fourth Avenue and the bakery by using the back entrance and slipping up to my apartment through the kitchen.

Scarlett, thankfully, wasn't home.

I thought about checking the messages on my phone and then didn't. I crossed to the kitchen and pulled out my Mixmaster. The ice cream was begging for a brownie chaser.

Someone knocked at the front door. The stovetop clock read 4:47 P.M., but I was pretty sure I'd never bothered to spring it forward for daylight saving time. The knock didn't sound like Kandy, who probably would have just come up through the bakery kitchen. Not being able to feel magic through the wards, I assumed it was the green-haired werewolf anyway.

Shucking my sandals as I crossed to the door — and yeah, the blisters had already healed — I opened it to reveal a nice-looking man with a perfect dimple and sexy suit.

Joe.

Oh, shit.

Joe's smile faltered as I stared at him. His brow wrinkled slightly as he took in my just-walked-for-three-hours-eating-a-tub-of-ice-cream look.

"Friday." I exhaled the word with the realization.

Joe tried to widen his faltering smile. "Dinner?" he said. "Tickets to Avenue Q?"

My heart sank and I felt like the utter shit I was. Joe, the cute lawyer whose office was just down the street from the bakery, had finally gotten a "Yes" from me two weeks ago for an actual date. It hadn't been difficult putting him off, what with my sister's death and all, but I'd actually felt ready to go out again. But then obviously —

"You forgot," Joe said.

"No. I ... it's been ... I'm sorry." God, I was lame.

"Invite me in?" he asked, so sweetly.

"Yes," I said, stepping back from the door. Then I saw the vampire in my living room. What the freaking hell was Kett doing in my living room? He shouldn't be able to pass through the wards on the apartment.

I held up my hand and Joe walked right into the flat of my palm. All the air whooshed from his lungs and he hunched over slightly. Oh, shit. Mind your freaking strength with the human, Jade. "Oh, Joe. I'm sorry."

Joe gulped for air. I noted Scarlett crossing into the living room from the bakery stairs. Her magic, I felt. The vampire had been doing his dampening thing, which only worked this well when I was distracted. My mother had let the vampire into my home. I was going to freak out. Right after I got Joe to a safe nonsnacking, nonmesmerizing distance. At least that was the excuse for my behavior that I was going to latch onto.

"Jesus," Joe muttered, rubbing his chest.

"Sorry," I said. "That was ... right on your solar plexus. Just the wrong spot. God, Joe. I'm sorry."

"Just say no next time. I understand no."

"Yes, no. No, no. I wanted to say yes. I just ..." I stepped closer to Joe, and dropped my voice. "My mother is here and ..."

Joe's eyes flicked up over my shoulder, his face confused. I'd angled him so he couldn't see much behind me.

"It's not a good time," I sighed. I was a total asshole. I mean, it wasn't a good time, but I knew what Joe would assume since he didn't know vampires existed.

"Oh, I see," he said. He shook his head — compassionate and extremely cute — and stepped back. "I understand. Grief comes in waves like that." He touched my arm lightly and I smiled at him. He was a sweet, kind person, and I was not. At least not right now.

"I'm completely jerking you around. I should have called."

"You forgot. You're human. Family is most important."

"You can find someone to go with you on short notice?"

Joe grinned. Yeah, I was quite certain he had a long list of phone numbers at his fingertips corresponding to many women who would jump at the chance. I sighed ... again.

"Text me later," he said as he turned away from the door.

"I don't want to ruin your evening a second time."

Joe stepped back, placed his fingers on my shoulders and tugged me forward into a light, chaste kiss. "I'll wait, Jade," he whispered against my lips. "I'm not in a rush."

I nodded.

He looked up over my shoulder and winked at Scarlett, who'd crossed to stand a few feet behind me. "Have a good night, Mrs. Godfrey."

I laughed and glanced back at my mother. Her answering smile was pinched around the edges. Mrs. Godfrey. Hilarious.

"Hey," Kandy said as she appeared at Joe's shoulder.

Joe jumped and spun to face the green-haired werewolf.

Kandy, completely ignoring the human, sidestepped around Joe and me into the apartment. "Pow-wow o'clock," she said.

I sighed. All I did was sigh these days. "Sorry," I whispered to Joe. He, not looking so sure of himself now, nodded and crossed to the stairs.

Then, pissed that the normal evening I'd been looking forward to — before I was distracted by skinwalkers and communicating with the dead man my sister murdered — I reached out for the magic of the wards.

I turned to face the living room with this magic at my back and on my fingertips.

Kett, still standing by the couch where I'd first seen him, took a step back.

Kandy was in the kitchen peering into my mixing bowl. Scarlett was putting iced tea and glasses out on a tray.

"You understand I can eject you at any time," I said to Kett.

He nodded. Scarlett frowned, but didn't comment on my rudeness.

"This is a one-time entry," I said, backing up my declaration with the magic of the wards. "Once you leave tonight, you will not be able to reenter without my express permission. Mine, not my mother's."

The magic of the wards moved beneath my hands, almost from within my skin, accepting this intention as gospel ... so I said, so it shall be.

Scarlett opened her mouth to speak, perhaps to chastise. But then, catching my gaze, she didn't follow through.

The vampire nodded and sat down on the couch. The magic settled behind me.

"Now," a steely voice said behind me. "Let me in, dowser. Or I'll huff and I'll puff and I'll tear all your wards down."

I turned to see Desmond standing as close as he could without triggering the wards protecting the doorway between us. Well, I guess I was the idiot who'd been standing with my back to an open door. Serves me right that the wards cut me off from detecting magic the same as they stopped the shapeshifter from entering.

"That would be a show," I said, my murmur coming off more inviting than I'd intended. The fact that I totally checked out his tight T-shirt-clothed abs probably didn't help with the cool demeanor I'd decided to adopt when dealing with him.

Kandy snickered from the kitchen. Damn werewolf hearing. Desmond's eyes flicked over my shoulders to three points. Taller than Joe, he could obviously see Kandy, Scarlett, and Kett behind me. If the vampire's face was carved of ice, then Desmond's was hewn from stone.

I fought the urge to run my fingers along McGrowly's bulging biceps and coyly inviting him to enter. He smirked as if he could follow my train of thought. He was clothed — yes, damn clothing — in jeans that were snug in all the right places.

"Done staring, dowser?" Desmond said. His voice was so low I barely heard him.

I nodded, caught red-handed and without any witty retort coming to my rescue.

Then I stepped back and let him through the wards. Same invitation that Mory and — belatedly — Kett had. One-time entry.

Desmond hesitated as if he didn't exactly trust me, and I smiled at him — challengingly, not invitingly.

He stepped through the wards and brushed by me on the way to the living room. "We have unfinished business, Jade," he said. His breath was hot and promising on my neck.

Great.

I returned to the kitchen as my mother served iced tea to the predators in the living room.

All we needed to make this more delightful was Gran.

So, of course, Pearl Godfrey chose that exact moment to enter the apartment from the bakery stairs. "Good evening," she said to no one in particular. Her greeting was quite crisp.

I started to chafe, to protest this invasion, and then I saw it. I saw the way Gran twined her fingers around the necklace I'd made her. The way Scarlett's magic rimmed her eyes. The way Desmond stood stiffly at the back window with Kandy pacing between him and the rest of the room. Only the vampire looked at all comfortable, and that was because he was in his active-listening mode.

They were all uncomfortable and all in my living room to protect me in some fashion, with or without ulterior motive.

I sighed, shut my mouth, and made brownies while they discussed Blackwell's invitation and a trip to Portland.

Chapter Ten

Oddly, Gran wasn't opposed to me meeting the sorcerer Blackwell, but Scarlett and Desmond were dead set against it. Though it was obvious that Desmond just didn't want me anywhere near Portland. McGrowly practically ate the entire first batch of brownies himself, so I was fairly certain he didn't have a problem with me, as long as I stayed in Vancouver. Gran and Scarlett were the bigger surprises.

Gran, who'd coddled me throughout my childhood and teens — channeling my unknown magic into arts and crafts and making sure I didn't come face to face with any Adept capable of comprehending that I was more than half-witch, half-human — felt the trip was "an acceptable risk."

An acceptable risk? Why did I suddenly feel like I was being abandoned rather than supported? Because Gran had eyes for Blackwell's collection as much as Kett did?

"What if," I asked as I mixed up a third batch of brownie batter, "this is some sort of elaborate ruse to — I don't know — add me to his collection of magical artifacts? Or even force me to treasure hunt for him?"

Everyone turned to look at Gran. Except Kett, who'd remained in his fugue state throughout the serving of my dangerous but delicious double-chocolate brownies. They were instant migraines in a chewy, dense square.

"Blackwell is a renowned sorcerer," Gran answered. "If he's settling into my neighbor's backyard, I want to know what he's bringing with him." Gran and Desmond exchanged a formal nod.

Well, it seemed that Blackwell certainly knew how to manipulate my so-called protectors.

"Pearl," Scarlett said. She'd called Gran that for as long as I could remember. "I've met this sorcerer, and I don't want my Jade anywhere near him."

Yes, my free-spirited mother who lived life as an endless joyride was now cautious and questioning. That said a lot of not-so-fantastic things about this Blackwell, and had a lot more pull than the lure of magical treasures.

"Scarlett," Gran answered, "Jade is not you. It is likely that Blackwell simply wants to enlist a dowser to assess a few items he's thinking of acquiring."

"He's a sorcerer, mother," Scarlett said. Her voice was nowhere near its usual degree of warmth. "If he couldn't already feel the magic in something, it would be worthless to him. You're willfully ignoring the danger. The value of being forewarned is not worth risking Jade's safety." I'd never heard Scarlett snap at anyone before, let alone Gran. My mother never needed to get angry to get what she wanted — she simply asked. Except this was about me, not her.

"You really don't want me to go?" I asked as I wandered into the living room with the second plate of brownies. I had one of those pans that made individual squares. It had been a gift from a friend but this was only the second time I'd used it. I usually only baked downstairs.

"No," Desmond answered before my mother could elaborate. "It's easier to keep you contained here. Portland, though pack territory, is full of the Adept."

"You have hundreds of shapeshifters at your command," Kett said, rising out of his fugue state at the chance to piss off Desmond. "I'm sure one or two of them could be spared."

"We have lives, vampire," Desmond answered. "Those lives are not subject to your whim for a play date."

I made sure that Scarlett and Gran each got a brownie before passing the plate to Kandy. The green-haired werewolf immediately passed the plate to Desmond, who was still staring out the dark window despite his speech. The sun had set an hour ago, but I hadn't bothered with the blinds. The mountainside across English Bay was filled with the lights of the North Shore neighborhoods. Kandy hadn't eaten a single one of the last batch of brownies until Desmond pushed the plate toward her. This time he took two and waved the rest off. Kandy eagerly started in on the remaining eight.

"I took Mory to speak to Rusty's ghost today. Or, rather, his spectral energy." I snagged a brownie from Kandy and attempted to muffle my confession by cramming it into my mouth.

Kandy choked on her brownie. Green flared across Desmond's eyes as he reclenched his jaw at a different angle. Scarlett blinked her perfect blue eyes at me. Kett didn't even twitch.

"I beg your pardon?" Gran said. Actually, she sputtered. Yes, I made my grandmother sputter like a fool in front of powerful Adepts in her own territory.

"She asked and I made a decision. There isn't much more to explain."

"You brought a necromancer to the death site of a blood relative?" Gran's surprise was quickly being overtaken by anger.

I sat down beside Kett and crossed my legs. Granted, it was the only open seat in the living room, but the fact that it would place me next to a vampire would only serve to irritate Gran further. So yeah, I had unresolved feelings about the woman who raised me. Who didn't?

"That's extra bad for some reason?" Kandy asked.

"Necromancers can use the blood connection to tie a soul to them, until death. Perhaps beyond, if you believe in such things," Kett answered. The vampire must be in a good mood to offer actual information to a werewolf so freely.

"Sure," I said. "Mory explained that. She also said the ghost could choose the binding and that it could be undone."

"She said that, did she."

"You know different?" I asked, despite the fact that Kett's comment had obviously not been a real question.

"You understand the moral implications, Jade," Gran said. "Mory is a child."

"She's fifteen."

"Exactly my point."

"She's more than old enough to make her own choices. As was Rusty. As was Sienna."

"We don't always simply get what we want, Jade. No matter how much we work for or wish it."

"How can you think I don't know that already?"

"Because you took a fledgling necromancer to the site of her brother's murder. A death full of violence and the need for retribution. On a whim. You could have allowed corruption and hate to enter the soul of a child. On a whim."

"She had a right —"

"She could have waited a few more years to exercise that right. It wouldn't have made any difference."

"So, what should I have offered her? Cupcakes and half-truths?"

"Yes," Gran said. "If that's what you had to give."

I let the argument drop as Gran's last statement sunk in. Scarlett, sitting on the other side of me, sighed. It was a soft noise full of years of pain. And it all clicked into place for me. The relationship that had been built from mother to daughter to granddaughter. I'd been making up for my mother's supposed mistakes my entire life, but not in the way I'd thought.

"Because that's all I'm good for," I finally said. "The cupcakes and the pretty smiles. That's all I'm capable of."

Gran straightened her spine but didn't contradict me.

"Jade ..." Scarlett whispered.

"Wait, I'm having some sort of epiphany."

"Yes, sugar. But maybe not now?"

I laughed at the idea of controlling the timing of an epiphany, then forged ahead, clicking the pieces together. "I'm not good enough, strong enough to watch over the portal. That's what you mean ultimately, Gran. Send me down to look at Blackwell's pretty trinkets, come back and report on all the pretty magic, and go back to making pretty cupcakes." I paused to see if Gran wanted to deny my charges, but she simply squared her shoulders and gave me a look that informed me I was too much — too dramatic and too worked up — and very, very rude about it all. And to air any of this in front of strangers? Unforgivable.

"What does the rest of my life look like to you, Gran? I meet a nice boy ..." — Gran's eyes flicked to

Desmond — "Oh, no. Not a nice boy. A powerful one, maybe, who likes pretty things in his kitchen. I have pretty babies, who if they're very, very lucky, grow up to be powerful enough for their Great Gran."

"Are you done?" Gran asked.

"Not yet," I answered. I raised my hands to hover palms-up over my crossed knees. The magic of the wards came to my call, dancing over my fingers and along my arms. "You've never asked, Gran. You never asked what I figured out about my magic while you were supposedly off surfing. You just demanded that I close the portal, cleaned up Sienna's so-called mess, and tried to ignore that anything had ever happened."

"I raised Sienna from the time she was thirteen."

"But any love you had for her, you erased from your heart as you eradicated her blood magic in the basement."

"As it should be —"

"What if it had been me?"

"It would never have been you, Jade." Gran softened her tone, but I wasn't ready to back down yet.

"You don't even know what my other half is … what if I'm some sort of demon?"

"You aren't," Gran snapped at my stupidity.

"But I could be."

"Scarlett," Gran said, turning to look at my mother as if she was going to step between us. My mother was anything but stupid, however.

No, Scarlett had never been as naive as I was, even when having sex with a being of unknown power during a fertility rite at age sixteen. I'd always thought of my mother as frivolous and inconsiderate. Now I understood that every step she took was deliberate. A witch bred from a long line of witches who turned out to manifest powers of charisma and charm rather than … than whatever power Gran expected her to have. And then there was good little girl me, who never expected to be anything — because it was never expected of her.

"I'll go to Portland," I said, completely letting the subject of power and magic drop as I watched the wards' magic pool in my palms. Desmond huffed out some sort of laugh behind me. Gee, so glad I amused him.

Gran watched me with hooded eyes as I allowed the magic to snap back into place. I'd been gearing up for some sort of power-display tantrum but stopped myself. The tantrum had been expected, I saw, and now Gran was perhaps a little unsure of what was going on in my head.

"I'll go with you," Scarlett said. Gran flicked her gaze to her daughter. "Since you need to stay here, Pearl."

Gran pursed her lips but didn't speak. Kett leaned back on the couch and crossed his legs — a gesture full of satisfaction that I was surprised to see on the vampire.

I had so much to say, so much to ask, but I really didn't like the answers I was stumbling upon. "I'll need to bake in the morning," I said instead. "Bryn already takes the Sunday shift, and we're closed Monday. So we have two days."

"We might need more," Kett said.

"Blackwell has an agenda," Desmond added. "Why else set Portland as the meeting place? We'll figure it out before Monday." So everyone was on board now. The troops were rallying — but to what end, I had no idea.

Gran rose and I followed. I walked her to the door, down the stairs, and out into the alley. She'd parked her car right next to the dumpster. Towable, if I ever felt like being a real asshole. But then, she held the lease on the bakery and my apartment, which was something I'd never had to worry about before.

Gran had clicked the car locks with her remote key before I found what I wanted to say.

"Nothing will ever be the same now. For you, that's not because of Sienna's death, but because I can open the portal."

Gran looked as if she was going to chastise me for speaking of such things out in the open. But then she simply said, "I gave you everything you ever wanted, Jade. Including Sienna."

"Yes. In bite-sized, chewable pieces. An easily digestible life. Never knowing who I could really be."

"I will not apologize for loving you."

"I scared you. In the basement," I said, finally voicing what I'd seen in Gran's face that night. When Sienna tried to kill us and ended up dying herself.

Gran squared her shoulders. "No, Jade. You surprised me. Enjoy the trip to Portland."

I nodded. Gran climbed in the car and pulled away.

Well, that was what loose ends and unspoken pain felt like. Another new and oh-so-delightful experience. A wedge between me and the child I once was, as if I was both and neither at the same time. Moving forward and stepping back.

I blinked up at the stars overhead and thought about Mory. Had I inadvertently, out of guilt, thrust her forward without giving her time to mature in her grief? Had I blundered ahead, blind but ever the perky go-getter? Thinking I was making my own choices but just doing so out of spite, not deliberation?

"Are you going to stargaze all night, dowser?" Desmond's deliberate drawl confirmed he was behind me. Though, I'd crossed through the thinner wards of the bakery when I stepped into the alley, I had actually felt a trickle of magic move when Desmond leaned in the alley doorway.

I turned to look at him, all muscle and meat. His hair would be naturally shaggy if it wasn't cut so short. He didn't have a charming bone in his body.

"What are you thinking?" he asked. I was surprised he cared.

"I was thinking it would be nice to skip the heart-to-heart."

"Talking only leads to fighting with us anyway."

"Yes."

He waited for me to step back into the kitchen. I waited for the impulse to do so, very glad that his magic was dampened by the wards so I couldn't claim I'd been overwhelmed and intoxicated by it.

"You don't want me in Portland," I said.

He chuckled. "So you choose the talking option even knowing where it leads."

He moved out into the alley. I didn't step away, though I had to lift my chin as he neared.

He looked up at the moon. It was a half sliver, low in the sky. The dim light softened his features, but with the sharp taste of his magic now so near, I wasn't fooled. I wondered if the moon called to him, as I thought it might for Kandy. He was a cat, though, not a wolf.

"I haven't eaten dinner," he said.

"Is that an invitation?"

"Yes." No chocolate and flowers in his directness. But then, I could buy my own chocolate, and I thought cut flowers were a waste of money.

"I'll cook. I'm not dressed to dine out."

"We'll order in." Some sort of caution edged his reply. He didn't want me cooking for him, but accepted the baking? I'd always been more of a baker than a cook, but I could put a meal together.

He looked at me, then. With the moon behind him now, his features were cast into deep shadows. "I liked you better in the forest," he said. He flashed a white-toothed grin.

"The feeling is mutual." I turned back to the bakery.

He laughed and followed me. I was tired of talking, but I also had to restrain myself from having my way with him on the stainless steel workstation as we passed by it on the way to the apartment stairs. That restraint didn't stop me from imagining the sequence of events in great detail, though.

"A pizza," I said. I folded the apartment wards around Desmond as we walked up the stairs without really thinking about it.

"Three," Desmond answered. "Five, if Kandy is joining us."

Right. My mother, the vampire, and my werewolf bodyguard were all upstairs.

I turned around in the middle of the stairs and opened my mouth to say something cute and flirtatious. I couldn't really see Desmond in the dark of the stairwell. I hadn't even thought to turn on the light.

He pulled me to him, his tongue in my mouth before I even invited it. I wrapped my arms and then legs around him, as I had in the forest. I was barely able to twist my fingers in the hair on either side of his head. I'd never kissed anyone I could cling to like that. My weight was nothing to him.

His mouth locked on mine, he swiveled on the stairs and descended so quickly that we created a breeze. Obviously, I wasn't the only one who'd fantasized about the stainless steel tables in the bakery kitchen.

Desmond settled me on the edge of one of the workstations, and I arched my back and neck up for his attention. He obligingly nuzzled my neck, nipping my collarbone at the edge of my T-shirt while I tugged on his shirt and yanked it up and over his head.

I ran my hands across his now-bare shoulders, over his taut skin, and curled my fingers in the pool of hair in the middle of his chest. In the forest, the hair there had been the same color as the fur of his mountain lion form, not that I could see it in the darkness of the kitchen.

"Are you dampening your magic?" I asked, taking the opportunity to nibble on his neck. The dampening was a skill both he and the vampire possessed. Gran would be jealous.

"Hmm," he answered as he tugged my hips closer. My ass was practically hanging off the table, but I wasn't even remotely in danger of falling. I assumed that was a 'yes,' but before I could tell him to stop it — I liked the way his magic felt underneath my skin — our mouths were locked again and I forgot the thought.

He ran the heel of his hand up my spine and I arched back into it. The strength in that one hand should have been frightening, but it wasn't.

I leaned away from him to lie back on the table as he turned his mouth to my neck and shoulder again.

My eyes had adjusted to the low light offered by the digital clocks on the ovens, and I caught a flash of white teeth as he grinned again. I liked this smile. It was completely unsuited to Desmond's usual brusqueness, his all-business and no-play demeanor.

He splayed his hand across my lower ribcage, then shifted his thumb up and over the mound of my breast to tease a nipple through my clothing. I moaned softly and tried to pull him closer with my legs.

He pressed his other hand to my hip to hold me down, inadvertently covering my knife, which was invisible to him. He grunted, slightly surprised, but just shifted his fingers higher to curl around my waist.

He tugged my T-shirt up and leaned down to kiss my belly. I moaned again.

He laughed, his breath hot on my sensitive skin. Self-satisfied prick. He was completely confident that he could have me — that I would probably beg for it — right there and then.

Well, I guess he was right. And the confidence made him more, not less, sexy.

He continued to softly kiss my belly and abs, running the tips of his fingers along the top edge of my jeans.

"I will not beg," I said as I tried to not squirm. Or perhaps writhing was the better description.

He laughed and looked up at me. "Begging doesn't suit you, Jade. You taste good. Do you taste this good everywhere?"

I freaking melted into a pool of hot, sticky desire. I knew he barely contained a monster beneath his skin. I had seen said monster in the flesh just yesterday. And still, here I was, all wet, pliant, and ready to writhe for him. I didn't have a witty comeback, so I simply sat up, pulled my T-shirt off, and locked lips with him again.

"I see the bond is misfiring again."

A cool voice cut right through the literal heat Desmond and I were generating, skin to skin.

His hand stilled at the clasp of my bra as I — just barely — managed to not start shrieking obscenities at the intrusion.

"Fuck off, vampire," Desmond growled, but he didn't turn around. Thankfully, he never gave a shit about being polite.

Kett's voice had come from the stairwell. I figure he had a pretty good view of McGrowly's back and my legs from that vantage point. Not that I was naked, but I didn't go around just flashing my bra — though it was terribly pretty, a light-blue demi-cup with white flowers up the straps.

"Yes, of course. I understand the attempt to settle the bond. If this doesn't work, my offer still stands."

"What?" I mumbled. My lips were actually swollen from kissing, a first for me.

"This is not about the bond," Desmond snarled. "And what fucking offer?"

That last part was directed at me. I admittedly was still fuzzy from desire. Desmond was putting things together quicker than I was.

"I would never have offered, shapeshifter. Had I known you were going to make a claim."

"I'm not a freaking piece of land," I said. Then I started looking around for my T-shirt.

"What did the vampire offer you?" Desmond asked. "To break the bond? Again?" By his growl, it was obvious he didn't like to ask twice. Hell, he didn't like to ask at all. He preferred having everyone jump at the snap of his fingers.

"Is that why you were dampening your magic? You want to have sex to settle the bond?"

"You initiated. Both times."

Yep, I had. I could also uninitiate, even without my T-shirt.

I untangled my legs and pushed Desmond away. He stepped back, though voluntarily. I wasn't sure I could dent him even if I tried. Maybe with the SUV.

I snagged my shirt off the floor but didn't bother wrestling it over my head. I was going for dignified, not mortified.

"Dowser," Desmond said.

So I was back to being dowser, was I?

"Get your own pizza," I said over my shoulder as I reached the stairs to my apartment. "And don't wreck my kitchen."

"We aren't going to fight over you."

"You already are," I answered. "Too bad it's for all the wrong reasons. Otherwise, it would be the sort of thing that could turn a pretty girl's pretty little head."

I climbed the stairs, deliberately laying my feet to each riser and not stomping like I wanted to. My jeans chafed my inner thighs and groin. That pissed me off further. I was going to need a cold shower and maybe some quality time with the showerhead ... except I wouldn't be able to masturbate with Scarlett and Kandy in the apartment.

So, cold shower it was then.

At least I had the upper hand with both the vampire and the shifter. Neither one was getting back through my apartment wards without my invitation again.

When compared to the sizzling make-out session, it was a dull victory.

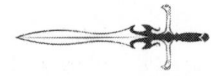

So Scarlett cooked. I packed and grabbed three hours of sleep, which was all I seemed to need these days.

When I got up, it was still dark out, but I padded down to the bakery to make double batches of batter and icing to lighten Bryn's load on Sunday morning. The extra batter would keep for twenty-four hours, no worries. We opened early — at 9:30 A.M. — on Saturdays and always needed extra stock on the weekends.

While I baked the cupcakes needed for the day I thought about Mory insisting that Sienna was still alive.

I wondered how wrong it would be to ask the fledgling necromancer to go down into the basement and try to talk to her. I hadn't been anywhere near the basement in three months. I would have nailed the door shut if it wouldn't have come across as utterly cowardly. Though I wasn't just avoiding the site of Sienna's death — I was hiding from the portal. Yes, hiding. Yes, like a coward. The magic and the promises it contained, though invigorating at the time, freaked me out in hindsight.

It would be terribly wrong to drag Mory anywhere near any of that ... Jesus, get your head out of your self-centered ass, Jade.

I boxed a dozen cupcakes for the trip, remembered Desmond would be with us — I thought — and boxed another dozen.

I fished my passport out of the small safe I kept in the tiny back office of the bakery. I tried to spend as little time as possible there, and I noted it really needed to be dusted.

"I'm totally messing around with Desmond," I muttered out loud, not knowing why — standing there with passport in hand — that thought had just occurred to me.

Magic shifted behind me, announcing Kandy's arrival. I felt the green-haired werewolf as she came in through the alley door, paused to steal something from the kitchen, then turned toward the office. I stuffed the passport in my back pocket and slammed the safe shut.

"I like these," Kandy said. She was leaning in the doorway, nibbling on a dark chocolate cupcake that I was testing chocolate-cherry buttercream icing on. It was supposed to be a *Kiss in a Cup,* but it wasn't gelling for me.

"Too sweet. Not cherry enough."

"You're just too picky."

"Am I?"

Kandy looked up at me with a genuine grin — not her predator smile. "Life is short. You should enjoy it more."

"Yeah, you're really cutting it up. Hanging around here."

Kandy shrugged and licked icing off her fingertips.

"See, it's too moist as well. It dripped all over your fingers."

She laughed. "I like it here with you, Jade. You make treats. Your magic is tasty too. Worth protecting."

"Don't you miss your pack?"

Kandy shrugged again. "Wolves are ... conformist." Ah, Kandy was anything but traditional or conservative.

"And cats?"

"Wolves are the dominant species among shapeshifters. Most of the pack alphas are wolves. Cats are rare. They're dominant, but usually prefer to run alone."

"But ..." I definitely heard a 'but' in Kandy's tone.

"Desmond is alpha."

Alpha, spoken as if with a capital A. The subtleties of that were lost on me. "He makes the rules?" I asked.

"Sure. And enforces them. Cats might be loners by nature when they hunt, but you can't be alpha without the pack. Desmond worked hard to achieve his position."

"I'm not getting where you're going, Kandy."

"He won't marry you."

"What? You think I want to marry McGrowly?"

Kandy grinned at the nickname. "No, but I think you're the marrying kind."

I scoffed at the idea. Kandy shrugged her shoulders a third time, then retreated into the bakery kitchen. Todd, my other full-time employee/coffee aficionado, hadn't arrived for his shift yet, though he wasn't technically late.

"These the rejects, then?" Kandy asked while stuffing another cherry-chocolate-iced *Kiss in a Cup* in her mouth.

I nodded. Kandy happily boxed the extras, adding them to the two boxes I had already set aside.

It was only just after eight o'clock when I started arranging the cupcakes in the bakery display case. A few people tried the door, then glared disappointedly at the posted hours printed on the glass.

Crap. I had totally forgotten to text Joe last night. Damn. I fished my phone out of my pocket.

It was going to be a long day.

Chapter Eleven

Actually, the trip was smooth and practically effortless. It had been a while since I'd traveled with Scarlett, and I'd forgotten how easy everything always was around her. No traffic. No lines at the border. No petty fights in the car.

Too bad I didn't get any of that magic along with the indigo eyes.

We traveled in three cars. Scarlett, Kandy, and I drove in the green-haired werewolf's SUV. Kett inexplicably hopped into some sports car I'd never laid eyes on before, while Desmond thankfully drove in another beast of a vehicle. The idea of a vampire driving a sports car was hilarious for some reason. Then I realized the car belonged to creepy Hoyt, spellcurser extraordinaire.

Given that he'd obviously driven up, why the hell Hoyt had bitched about driving rather than flying was a mystery. Many Adepts preferred to not fly — magic often didn't get along with technology — but that had never stopped Scarlett from globe-trotting.

Later, I discovered that Desmond's pickup truck belonged to the young werewolf attending UBC who Sienna and Rusty had killed. It was this murder that had brought Desmond and the pack to Vancouver. Kett as well. Desmond had left the vehicle for Kandy, but the green-haired werewolf didn't want to drive it. He was returning it to the pack now.

I'd never thought about him settling the estates of his murdered pack members. I'd known that Hudson's body had eventually been shipped back to the Midwest, but now I realized that I'd mourned him for three months and didn't even know his last name. Now was not the time to ask. There never was a right time to talk about any of it, actually.

As we'd loaded into the cars in front of the bakery, I thought I tasted Mory's magic. Hoyt had been sullenly waiting, all blurry-eyed and sallow-skinned. He had only flinched — but not protested — when Kett took his keys. Desmond hadn't bothered getting out of the idling truck as Scarlett and I settled in with Kandy. I was sure the young necromancer was fast asleep somewhere, and I'd just been imagining things. Surrounded by Kandy, Scarlett, and Kett, I wouldn't be able to pick up any other magic, anyway. Hoyt didn't even register on my senses.

I demanded we stop at the first See's Candies store we passed after entering the United States. We pulled off the I-5 at the outlet mall in Burlington, just before Mount Vernon, and spent far too much money. Kandy and Desmond included. Desmond had used his NEXUS pass to breeze through the border even faster than the rest of us, and was bitchy about having to wait the extra five minutes in the mall parking lot.

The clerk calmed him down instantly by offering him a second sample of their scrumptious *Dark Cocoanut*, a creamy soft center with angel-flake coconut covered in dark chocolate ... yum. She was smart enough to guess his wallet matched the size of his appetite. With my custom box packed and paid for, I contentedly commenced consuming and snoozing as we continued through Washington State toward Seattle.

Kandy's music taste was eclectic but road-trip worthy — Maroon 5 to Marianas Trench, Flo Rida to Paul Simon, Fleetwood Mac to AC/DC. Scarlett was poring over some spellbook in the front passenger seat. I'd never seen her study before. Her magic kept flaring, as if she was triggering spells but not following through with them.

I sprawled out in the back seat and attempted to slip into a chocolate coma. I would have been more successful if I hadn't been forced to eat lunch in Seattle. We stopped just off the highway at a diner I didn't recognize, but the fries were tasty so I was appeased. Desmond and Kandy each ordered two meals, then cleaned off Scarlett's plate, then cleaned off mine.

Kett and Hoyt didn't join us for lunch. Unfortunately, I ran into the spellcurser and his day-old magic outside the ladies washroom. He'd more than obviously been waiting for me.

"They keep you pretty covered at all times, don't they?" Hoyt's tone was oily around the edges.

"You might want to wonder whether that's for my protection or yours, Hoyt." Yeah, rude of me, but the spellcurser bothered me. I didn't like the nothing taste of his magic.

Hoyt smirked. "I know a lot about you, Jade Godfrey, and none of it has anything to do with you being dangerous. Though I hear your cupcakes are to die for." His eyes flicked down to my chest on the word 'cupcakes.' Moron. My necklace was far more interesting than my breasts. And it wasn't nearly as interesting as the knife I wore at my hip, though the spellcurser was nowhere powerful enough to see through Gran's invisibility spell.

I ran my fingers along the hilt of the afore-mentioned invisible knife and turned to the parking lot exit. I knew I should probably interrogate Hoyt — under the guise of flirting — to find out what exactly he knew about me, and what to expect when I met Blackwell. But instinctively, I knew he was a bluffer. He knew nothing of value, but was probably great at reflecting people's reactions back at them — thus appearing more knowledgeable than he was. Plus, I couldn't even pretend to like him. His dull magic soured my stomach that much.

"You're not scared of me, are you, Jade?" Hoyt jogged a couple of feet behind me, out the glass front door and into the restaurant parking lot. "Is that why I'm riding with the vamp? Because I wouldn't hurt a hair on your pretty head."

I stopped and turned back to him. He stumbled. Yeah, I could move faster than a human. "Call him vamp to his face," I said, then offered him one of my total-bullshit-but-still-blinding smiles.

This confused him — like I said, he was a moron — and I turned away to continue cutting through the first row of parked cars toward Kandy's SUV. The green-haired werewolf was lounging against the front side of the vehicle — she'd reversed into the spot, total show-off — and enjoying the Jade-disses-Hoyt show. Scarlett was two cars over chatting to Kett, who'd found the only tree-shadowed spot in the lot.

Desmond had already left. He was in a super chatty mood today. He hadn't looked at me once during lunch, not even when stealing fries off my plate. But he wasn't pouting like a jilted teenager. He was just his stoic self.

"Trouble?" Kandy asked as I approached.

I laughed, but her gaze stayed locked on Hoyt as I climbed into the back seat and she crossed around to the driver's side.

Kett flashed me a grin over Scarlett's head as she turned to join Kandy and me. Underneath his baseball hat and sunglasses, even with his white blond hair, he looked All-American. It probably helped that he'd obviously — by his skin tone — recently fed. I didn't like the implication of the grin, or how the vampire watched Hoyt as the spellcurser crossed to the sports car. Hoyt kept his eyes on me. The moron really had to sort out the predator ranking and his priorities more quickly.

Though I'd never spent any time in Portland, Scarlett took Sienna and me on a road trip down the Oregon Coast when we were eleven, and we'd driven through on the way back. I didn't remember much, though. As we approached, I immediately saw what Mory had meant about the bridges. I could see at least four spanning the broad river that cut directly through the city.

Almost trapped in the seriously congested four-lane I-5 traffic, we drove by each bridge until Kandy turned us onto the very last one. We looped off, around, and along an underpass to pull up to a boutique hotel on the south bank of the river. A large patch of struggling-to-be-green grass stretched along the riverbank walk to the west, while a marina occupied the eastern section.

The grassy area — which turned out to be a narrow but long park — was currently filled with large white tents. The park, and therefore the river, ran through the city along the edge of the downtown core. It wasn't nearly as pretty as Vancouver, but it was close.

"What are the tents for?" I asked Kandy as we climbed out of the SUV. She'd stopped in the guest unloading zone by the main doors of the hotel.

"Jazz festival," Kandy replied as she hustled Scarlett and me inside.

"Wait," I said. "My bag."

"Let the valet get it."

"But ..." Then I noticed the 'valet' looked suspiciously like Jeremy, a tall blond teenaged werewolf I'd met three months ago in Vancouver. He flashed me a grin and caught the keys that Kandy threw at him. I turned to question my green-haired werewolf friend/bodyguard only to find her smiling as well. There were suddenly too many smiling predators around ... though I guess I should have been used to it by now. Speaking of which, Desmond and Kett obviously had other destinations, because neither of them had followed us into the hotel.

We entered the lobby. As the SUV pulled away behind me, I noted that Jeremy wasn't even wearing a regular valet uniform. We turned toward the reception desk only to be intercepted by Lara of the bee-stung lips — another werewolf I'd met in Vancouver, who pulled off purple like it was her natural skin tone. Yeah, I was jealous.

"I've checked you in. A suite on the fourth floor. River view," Lara said, addressing Scarlett and me.

"Great," Kandy said. "Let's get on with it."

Lara pouted prettily, which further agitated Kandy. I imagined that was the point. Werewolves weren't naturally prone to pouting.

She led us toward the elevators but then cut off to one side and opened the door to the stairs. Um, okay. I guess I looked like I needed the cardio.

The stairs led down.

"Err," I said. Maybe I'd eaten too much chocolate, though that usually sharpened my thoughts rather than dulled them.

"We're leaving," Kandy said. "Clandestinely."

Yeah, okay. I wasn't a complete idiot. I could add two and two. I just needed the complete equation. I had dropped algebra as quickly as high school had allowed. Same for geometry, actually.

"Where are you taking us?" I asked, attempting to keep up to Kandy and not trip on the stairs. I had chosen my aqua Assured sandals from Fluevog — of course and always — for the trip. The color was perfect for me, and the two-and-a-quarter-inch leather-wrapped heel was cute yet completely walkable. Scarlett practically floated down each step beside me. Her slight smile was permanently in place, and there was never even a hint of whining in her voice. I needed to adopt her as my new role model.

"You'll like it," Lara answered from behind us. "The kitchen is gorgeous."

Obviously, today was everyone-knows-Jade-inside-and-out day.

"I practically cleared Cacao out of their dark chocolate and cocoa," Lara continued.

"Oh! I've heard they have a fantastic selection of small craft chocolate makers." Yeah, I was gushing, but not drooling ... yet.

"Desmond said the darker the better."

Desmond said? And I was going to have time to bake, was I? Why did this feel a lot like being kidnapped? Well, the fake check-in, the side stairs, and the big black SUV waiting in the underground parking lot — with a werewolf at the wheel and two others on either side — might have something to do with it.

House arrest was more accurate. An absolutely beautiful, modern, sprawling house on a hill with a breathtaking view of downtown Portland and the river. But still, it was rather obvious that I was a detainee and that Lara and Kandy were my jailers. Scarlett too.

Moments after we arrived, things got even more tense when Desmond showed up with a spitting mad Mory in tow. McGrowly wasn't so pleased either.

The fledgling necromancer had stowed away in the covered bed of his pickup truck. That had to have been a nasty seven-or-so-hours, including lunch. But smart girl. The pickup placed her far enough away from me that I wouldn't notice her magic, other than the hint of it I'd tasted this morning and brushed off. And Desmond, having never met her, wouldn't have caught on to his stowaway until he actually got a whiff of her when he opened up the truck bed to retrieve his bag.

I had two immediate concerns. One was the pained look on Mory's face, which had nothing to do with the fact that she was practically dangling by the back of her hoodie, currently clenched in Desmond's meaty fist. She was so tiny I thought that McGrowly might not actually be aware he was holding her off the ground, the tips of her too-large army boots just scraping the granite tile of the entranceway.

"Desmond," I snapped. Jeremy behind McGrowly and Lara beside me both winced. "She has to pee. She's been trapped in the truck for seven hours."

Desmond released Mory. "Third door on the left," he said. The fledgling necromancer took off down the hall that Desmond indicated. "Do you know the shit I could get into, smuggling a child across the border?"

"She's a smart girl," I retorted. It was easy to cover my concern and confusion with bravado when Desmond was near. "I'm sure she had her passport."

McGrowly sneered in my direction, but I was now focusing on the second of my concerns.

Namely, the bag in Desmond's other hand. His overnight bag, to be exact.

I did a second scan of the house. I was currently standing in the living room area, which was directly off the entranceway. Dark green — almost black — granite tile turned into some sort of deep brown hardwood — walnut, maybe — through what I could see of the remainder of the house. The granite tile reappeared in the chef's kitchen, which was beyond the dining room far off to my right. The house was huge. A modern open-plan home perched among trees over the river below. Leather furniture, glass, and steel made up the Spartan finishings. I was trying to not salivate over the kitchen or the massive river-rock fireplace on the left. Nothing blocked the view.

A man's home. A wealthy, no-nonsense man. Sigh.

"Your place?" I asked. "We're supposed to stay here?"

"Thank you for your protection and hospitality, alpha," Scarlett interjected.

Desmond's frown smoothed and he nodded his head curtly in my mother's direction. "You're welcome to my home and my city. It is an honor to host the scion of the Godfrey coven."

What the hell? And Jesus. I was a blundering, freaking fool.

"I will see you at dinner," Desmond said. He dropped his bag in the entranceway and turned to a hall that branched off in the opposite direction from where Mory had run. The house extended in two wings. The front section was all open windows and entertaining area. I assumed the wings led to bedrooms, bathrooms, and whatnot.

"No one has taught me anything," I said, hissing unbecomingly at Scarlett.

"This will be a fun crash-course then, my Jade." Scarlett brushed her fingers on my forearm, forever soothing the riled baby ... Unfortunately, it worked. My mother's charm was formidable. "First lesson," she continued. "Interlopers on pack territory are usually executed unless they can prove allegiance to a stronger alpha."

"We're not shapeshifters or interlopers."

"No, but a stowaway is, and the law applies to all of the Adept. Ignorant or not. I assume the fledgling claimed allegiance to you when found, but let's just make that clear."

Oh, freaking great. I leave Vancouver to get away from Gran's lack of expectations and find myself subject to martial law.

"I would love to freshen up before dinner," Scarlett said, turning to Lara.

"Please allow me to show you to your room, scion." Lara picked up our suitcases, which Jeremy had retrieved from the SUV, and headed off in the direction of the bathroom. Jeremy had already picked up Desmond's bag and hustled off after his alpha.

I mouthed 'scion' over Lara's shoulder to Kandy, who grinned but then shrugged. I was beginning to see why the green-haired werewolf might have been assigned to guard me in Vancouver. Formalities weren't her strong suit, though she ranked rules and loyalty very highly.

"I'll go talk to Mory," I said.

"Better you than me," Kandy replied. "Plus, I'm worried about the rest of the cupcakes in the car. Jeremy might try to claim desertion and eat them."

She spun to trot back out through the entrance doors. I wandered down the hall after Lara and Scarlett. No art or crown moldings decorated the walls — just perfectly flat, white-painted drywall. The others were about twenty feet ahead — it was a huge house — when I found the bathroom door. Third on the left. It was closed. And locked.

I knocked.

"Oh, Jade," Scarlett called from down the hall. "Dress for dinner."

Dress for dinner? Hell. "I didn't pack any dress," I hissed back loudly.

Scarlett glanced at Lara, who nodded solemnly. I took this to mean that a dress would be acquired. It would probably be purple. I'd look hideous. Who the hell cared? It wasn't as if I was trying to impress anyone. At least not anyone who hadn't already seen me covered in dirty bruises and bloody hair.

"Mory," I said as I knocked on the door again. "Let me in."

"Who was that?" Mory cried from the other side of the door.

"What are you doing here is the more pertinent question, Mory."

Silence was all that followed. I sighed. Man, I was turning into a dour old biddy. "That was McGrowly. He's the alpha around here. And you probably shouldn't call him that to his face."

"I don't want to say anything to his face." Mory's whisper was almost lost behind the door.

"Scary, huh?"

"Yeah."

"He gets that a lot, I imagine." I remembered my first impression of those scary eyes. The fact that making out with him — twice — hadn't altered that first impression said a lot about my state of mind. Good thing I wasn't interested in analyzing myself outside the door of a bathroom while cajoling the teenager within.

"At least come out, Mory. You're here now. There isn't much we can do about it right away."

Mory thought about that for a moment, then unlocked the door. I had no idea why a shapeshifter would bother with locks he could snap with a fingernail. They'd probably come with the house.

Mory's eyes were red rimmed, the tip of her nose unbecomingly pink. McGrowly had really scared her. She also needed a shower. The small black-and-white checked wallpapered powder room boasted a pedestal sink and toilet but no shower.

"Where's your bag?" I asked. "I'm guessing you knew where we were going?"

"He took it," Mory pouted.

"Desmond took your bag?" This sounded completely beneath the Alpha of the West Coast North American Pack.

"No," Mory whined. "The other one, who thinks he's way older than he is. The blond."

Ah, Jeremy. "Cute, isn't he?" I asked, turning down the hall toward Scarlett's room.

"No. He totally stole my phone."

"He's going to be drop-dead gorgeous in a couple of years."

"So?" Mory said, sneering convincingly.

I laughed. Desmond must have embarrassed the hell out of Mory in front of Jeremy, and that was the biggest reason for the fledgling's tears. Oddly, that relieved some of my tension, which had amped up at her appearance.

I fished my phone out of my satchel and texted Kandy about Mory's missing backpack. Then I started opening hallway doors at random. "Let's pick a room."

"Okay." Mory wasn't as begrudging about this task as she'd like to be. Like I said, the house was gorgeous. Completely under-furnished, but still modern and classic. Just the way I liked it.

"You need a shower before dinner."

"I'm not showering."

"Jeremy will probably be there."

"What do I care?"

"Maybe you can get him to take you to the nearest graveyard or something tomorrow."

"Really?"

"Sure. Right after we call your mom."

"Ah, Jade."

Yeah, that's me. Responsible, no-fun, Jade. I was like the school-teacher-aunt rather than the cool older sister.

My stomach bottomed out at the thought of being a sister. Mory continued to chat about the famous Portland ghosts she'd heard about. I tried to ignore the taste of bile in my mouth. Bile that tasted a lot like Sienna's blood magic ... the aftertaste, at least.

Chapter Twelve

The dress was purple, of course. Deep purple silk that twirled around my knees and hung from my shoulders and waist like it was made for me. I didn't look half bad at all. And, happily, I'd packed my black and beige Elif Minis. The diagonal strap made them sexy enough to pull off with this dress.

I wore my knife and necklace as well, of course, but stashed the jade stones underneath the bowl of cotton balls in the en suite bathroom. I figured that was pretty damn random and that no one who could feel magic like I could was going to get anywhere near my bedroom without one of Desmond's wolves noticing.

The dinner — of course and despite the beautiful dress — was boring as hell. But then, keeping myself shielded as much as possible from all the magic in the room might have dulled things for me.

When I wandered out into the living room with Mory in tow, I found Scarlett holding court among five shapeshifters. The only familiar face in the room was Kandy, who stood off to one side of the unlit fireplace gazing out the picture window. She was wearing a satin, collared shirt and black dress pants that fit her like a second skin. Scarlett turned as I entered, pulling every other gaze to me as well.

A flare of green rolled over the eyes of the well-dressed shifters as they accessed some part of their magic — most likely scent. No one else stumbled back at this display because no one else in the room could see and taste magic as I could. The reminder was crystal clear and adrenalized. The living room was full of potentially deadly beasts like McGrowly. Though I understood the half-form that Desmond could manifest wasn't a common shifter ability, these five felt almost as powerful as their alpha.

"Ah, my Jade. Do come meet everyone." Scarlett beckoned me forward. "This is my daughter, Jade Godfrey. Jade, these lovely people are a few of the West Coast pack's Assembly members."

Was the entire Adept community just a series of councils, conclaves, and assemblies? All politics and governing bodies all the time? No wonder Desmond was so perpetually serious and Kandy was perfectly content to be in Vancouver. If the room got any stuffier I was going to need to climb out a window.

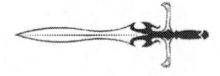

So, yeah. Dinner was boring and politics were in play all over the place in Portland. Though Desmond looked damn sexy in a suit that downplayed his broad shoulders by emphasizing the taper of his waist and hips. I didn't stare. Much. He didn't spare me a second glance. I got the impression that Scarlett's presence made it impossible for McGrowly to sneak us into the city. My mother was referred to as scion or Convocation member all evening. If the food hadn't been so tasty, I would have fallen asleep in it.

I was bombarded with magic — utterly surrounded — from Desmond and Scarlett in addition to the five other highly ranked pack members. I assumed that the pack ranked their members based on good looks and magical wattage. Then there were the shapeshifters guarding and serving us — not one pure human in the bunch. Despite the grounding presence of my necklace and knife, I was itchy and antsy with all this magic.

It also didn't help that a breathtaking brunette — the only uncoupled shapeshifter — sitting next to Desmond didn't take her eyes off him all evening. She didn't have Scarlett's charm or laugh, but her killer body made up for it. Her ratio of breasts to waist made me want to slap her. And no, I wasn't even remotely jealous. I didn't even remember her name ... Ashley, Alison, Alicia?

So I spilled my wine on Mory. The fledgling necromancer was perched on a low stool beside me. Desmond was at the head of the table with Scarlett and what's-her-name on either side. I was at the opposite diagonal from Scarlett, with Mory tucked on the corner between me and some old dude, who was the alpha Desmond had succeeded without having to kill him. Not something, by the way, to just blurt out when meeting an ex-alpha. Fortunately, that had been Mory's mistake, not mine.

Anyway, it was only a small spill. Mory shrieked like it was molten lava or something.

I hustled her off to the washroom, throwing out mumbled apologies, with Kandy following closely behind us.

I shoved Mory into the powder room where we'd had our first chat of the day, shutting the door behind us before Kandy could enter. I almost wilted from the relief of being a few steps away from all that magic.

"The skirt is ruined," Mory moaned.

"Shush," I said. "It's my skirt, and it's only a drop of wine on the hem. Rinse it off with cold water." I'd had the blue miniskirt crumpled in the corner of my suitcase.

Thankfully, it had a drawstring waist so Mory could borrow it. It looked crazy cute with the fledgling's old combat boots, which was good because her feet were way too small to borrow any of my shoes.

I climbed on the toilet and tried the window. The lock was stiff, as if it had never been opened, but eventually I got it to slide upward. I noted the alarm sensor on the window frame, but assumed it would be deactivated with so many people coming and going from the house.

"What are you doing?" Mory asked. She was dabbing the rinsed wine spot with a black hand towel. The thread count of the towel looked thick enough to use as a pillow. Nice.

"All I've been able to hear all night is the music playing down by the river," I answered without actually answering.

"You can hear music?"

"You can't?"

"Nope."

Whoops. Do I admit I was more than a witch or just let the fledgling think I was slowly going crazy? "Do you want to go dancing?"

Mory's face lit up. "With you?"

"Yeah, who else?"

"But ..."

"It's a totally stupid idea. And has nothing to do with why either of us are here." Mory, I had established, was still seeking vengeance on Sienna — confirmed death obviously wasn't enough for the fledgling — and she'd stowed away just in case we happened upon a clue in Portland. This logic sounded a little weak to me — and to Mory's mom. Scarlett had called the necromancer, who was calmer than I would have been once my mother put Mory on the phone. But then, Scarlett had that effect on people, even if her magic didn't pass through satellites and carrier networks.

"You game anyway?" I prompted Mory. "I can go on my own and you'd be in way less trouble."

"Less trouble? I'm already grounded for life."

"I've been grounded for life. It wears off."

"Did you ever stow away to Portland with witches, werewolves, and a vampire?"

Err, no. She had me there. "Okay. I'll get Kandy to take you back to my room. Like you aren't feeling well —"

"Forget that, I'm coming with you."

I laughed and yanked open the bathroom door. Kandy was standing on the other side with her arms crossed. Her make-up was generous around the eyes and practically nonexistent on her lips.

"I can hear you through the door," she said.

"I know. I'm not a total idiot." I had totally forgotten to factor super-hearing into my getaway plans.

Then Kandy handed me an evening purse. I rarely carried anything other than my Matt & Nat satchel. I opened the bag. It contained my lip gloss, credit card, and phone.

"You rock."

"I know," Kandy answered. "So we're going out the window?"

"I'm coming with you," Mory insisted in a whispered hiss from behind me.

"I got that part, fledgling," Kandy said. Then the green-haired werewolf shouldered by me to survey the open window.

I closed the door. It was rather cramped with three of us in the powder room. Granted, with how tiny Mory was and how slim Kandy was, I was the one taking up all the space.

"Don't lock it," Kandy whispered. "Desmond hates breaking locks in his own house."

"Yeah, who wouldn't?"

Kandy slipped through the window into the rhododendron bush outside. Then she reached back for Mory.

I had a slightly more difficult time getting through without ruining my dress. So I didn't have the hips of a teenager. I'd never heard a single complaint from anyone who had his hands wrapped around them.

"We can't take a car," Kandy said. She led us away from the front drive and entrance through the manicured yard. We slipped through a side gate — I was thankful I didn't need to scale a stone wall or anything — and stepped onto the road. The neighborhood was upscale in that expensive-property-close-to-downtown-but-not-actually-full-of-downtown-buildings-and-people way.

"OMG. OMG," Mory kept repeating under her breath. Really, for a teenager who'd just stowed away to Portland in the back of a shapeshifter's pickup, I would have thought she'd be harder to thrill. But then maybe it was the conspiratorial thing. I knew that nothing had felt this fun for me since Sienna left me to my boring life. And I'm not counting wrestling with skinwalker grizzly bears or alpha shapeshifters, as neither of those made me want to grin uncontrollably, twine my arms through the arms of my friends, and laugh out loud.

The sound of muted music pulled me forward, and I didn't marvel at my ability to hear that while filtering all the traffic and other noise out. I'd always been able to obsess over things that way, so why should this be any different?

Then a taxi rather conveniently pulled around the corner. I eyed Kandy, who smirked at me with her predator grin. I climbed into the cab despite whatever was hinted at in that smile. I didn't care what the green-haired werewolf was up to — not when I was going dancing for the first time in three months. I rolled down the back window to listen to the jazz music filtering through the houses and trees. It grew louder and louder as we wound down the hill toward the park on the edge of the river. The breeze struggled to free my pinned curls, but I didn't care. I felt a glimmer of freedom, and I would ride it to the probably short and bitter end.

The taxi pulled to the side of the road, blocking traffic on what the signs said was Natio Parkway, but none of the vehicles behind us seemed to care. They, like me, were happy to gawk at the dense crowd spreading among and spilling from the multiple white tents covering the narrow strip of green grass along the river's edge.

We tumbled out of the cab and into the crowd, Kandy at my shoulder and Mory's fingers twined through mine. Beer and wine were flowing within the boundaries of several fenced-in areas. Portland's liquor laws were obviously less stringent than Vancouver's. We cut through the diverse crowd to the river walk, then headed west away from the hotel Lara had supposedly checked us into.

"We're never going to pass Mory off as twenty-one," I said, eyeing the entrance and ticket booth of the nearest tent. "Are there free venues?"

"Further down," Kandy answered.

"Oh! Do you think Voodoo Doughnut is still open?" I asked. I had to get my hands on some of their famous donuts.

"Sure, till midnight, I think. But the line is a killer. Your choice."

"What time is the meeting with Blackwell in the morning?" I asked. Mory was wide-eyed and staring at the crowd as we walked along the path at the river's edge. I almost reached over to tuck her chin closed, but she caught me smiling at her and snapped her mouth shut herself. "Nine o'clock, right?"

"Ten thirty, actually. Desmond changed it." Kandy smirked. Wolves loved to play games. Green rolled over her eyes as she scanned the crowd that pressed all around us.

"Speaking of which, Desmond is so going to freak that you came out with us," I said.

Kandy shrugged.

"My point is you might as well have fun. I'll know if any unknown Adepts get near before they even lay eyes on us."

"You're easily distracted."

"Please — Oh, dancing!" I pointed to a large group gathered around a four-piece band on a raised platform. People near the band were dancing together. Other audience members sat on folding chairs or blankets in smaller gatherings on the outskirts of this central group. The band was playing some kind of jazz fusion, that wasn't familiar, but it was conducive to movement.

"Come on, Mory!" I cried, tugging the teen off the walk and onto the grass.

"Jade, no. I can't. I can't —"

"Don't be silly. You're with me."

"When Jade dances, everyone dances." Kandy pitched her voice over the music, though it wasn't as loud out of doors as it would have been inside.

I pushed through the edge of the crowd. They politely let us pass. My smile and bouncy curls — and other things — were usually a ticket through a crowd. I wanted to be in the very middle.

The audience was more colorful here than it would be in Vancouver. At least a third of the dancers were

African American, with a smattering of Hispanics mixed in. I'd picked up a few faint magical signatures as we walked through the pockets of people along the edge of the river and near the other venues, but there were none nearby now.

And that was okay. I'd come for the freedom and the dancing. I was actually happy to get away from the press of magic at Desmond's.

The band finished the song they'd been playing as we reached the middle of the dance crowd. The dancers paused to clap. I kept Mory tucked in front of me as we faced the stage. My foot was already tapping in anticipation of the next song.

"We're Dizzy Coltrane and the Brubecks. Thanks Portland, for letting us play. This is our song, 'Take Nine.' " The lead singer was a scrawny white guy, as most musicians tended to be, but he had a good voice and a great smile.

The sax opened the song. I'd never danced to jazz or fusion or whatever this music was before, but my body didn't care. I picked up the beat and started to move.

Mory laughed and jumped up and down. Younger than her fifteen years in her joy. I knew I'd made the right decision to climb out the bathroom window with the fledgling. How dark must her life be every day — not just since Rusty's death, but seeing dead people all the time?

Kandy flashed her predator grin at me — she liked it when I danced — and moved her lithe body next to mine. The crowd eased back from us and those nearest turned to face our way. It wasn't only the Adept that found Kandy and me dancing together something worth looking at.

I lifted my hands in the air and a weight shifted off my shoulders. A weight I hadn't acknowledged before in such a substantial way. I closed my eyes, threw my head back, and opened myself to Kandy and Mory's magic. Dark, dark chocolate and toasted marshmallows flooded my senses, pushing everything else out of my mind.

"Perfect," I murmured as I let the music move me.

One song stopped and another began. It was a warm night. The lead singer stripped off his T-shirt in between songs and mopped himself with it. I wagged my eyebrows at Mory, who blushed. My hair was sticking to my neck and face, but I just let it be, knowing it would soon be out of control in the humidity anyway.

Kandy fielded a text message, and glanced around, but I just kept dancing. The silk dress made me feel wild, as if I was barely wearing anything even though I was fully covered. I reveled in the feel of it shifting across my skin, as I tried not to think of the last time I danced like this and the beautiful — possibly perfect — man who'd approached me from the crowd.

Kandy peeled away, drawn toward a group at the fringes of the dance crowd. They were laughing and falling over each other, perhaps a little tipsy. Easy prey. Kandy definitely knew her type as she honed in on a tall girl with brightly dyed red hair. They would look like Christmas together.

Mory was dancing with her eyes closed. A couple of younger-looking guys near her smiled at me when I caught their gaze. Ah, there was fresh meat in Portland tonight. The attention would be good for the fledgling.

And then I felt the tingling — like a warning, maybe — at the base of my neck. I scanned the crowd ... still dancing, obviously. I was here to dance.

A man stepped toward me. The crowd parted before him, even though no one seemed to notice as he passed. His magic was potent. He tasted of red wine ... an earthy cabernet. The kind that dried your mouth but was perfect when paired with rare prime rib. Not a hint of berry. But there was something else on him. I narrowed my eyes, honing my focus, as he strode toward me. His hair was black as if it was dyed that way, because there was nothing Asian, or Native, or Persian about his features or skin. He wore a light gray pinstriped suit that looked expensive, with a crisp white shirt underneath. No tie. The heat didn't seem to affect him in the least.

There ... as he moved, a gap between the buttons of his dress shirt shifted. He was wearing some sort of amulet with a red stone. The magic of it was completely dissimilar to his own. It was fresh, like the undertones of the magic of the portal in the bakery basement. Layered with something earthy like witch magic, and something rich like whipped cream ... or maybe not so sweet ... sour cream and butter on a baked potato.

I laughed at my silly analogy and the dark-haired Adept smiled at me. He didn't bare his teeth.

"Good evening," he said as he stepped into the space before me. He had an accent I couldn't place. England, maybe.

"It is," I answered, slowing my movements to the consideration of the conversation. "You look out of place."

He glanced around. His gaze lingered on Mory to one side and then on Kandy, who had moved a few feet closer with her group of giggling girls. "I suppose I do. But you, Jade Godfrey, look like you would fit in anywhere lucky enough to have you."

"You're awfully charming, sorcerer," I said. His magic, though more formidable than anything I'd felt from a sorcerer before, identified him as such.

He grinned. The tips of his teeth were showing now, so maybe he wasn't a complete stick-in-the-mud. "Mot Blackwell. At your service."

"That's not a made-up name at all," I teased. He wasn't even bothering to move to the music but I kept dancing.

"Perhaps," he answered. "Though the lineage is long enough to come with a castle."

It wasn't every day that a guy could drop the fact he had a castle into a first conversation. But then, maybe it was and I just didn't run in the right castle-owning circles.

"And where would this castle be?"

"Scotland."

Ah, that explained the accent.

"Perhaps you will honor me with a visit some time?"

"I've never been to Scotland," I answered. His grin widened. "But the trinket around your neck is far more interesting to me."

Blackwell's face blanked. His dark eyes searched my face. I guess he hadn't taken a close enough look the first time.

"Your reputation has not been understated," he said, his face not even close to smiling now.

"It's powerful," I said with a shrug. "Though I wouldn't mind knowing who you've been discussing me with."

Blackwell didn't answer. Instead, his eyes dropped to the necklace I wore openly over the purple silk desk. It was nowhere near as impressive as his, but I imagined it felt like magic to him. All sorcerers had to be able to feel magic to some degree. It's how they exercised their powers.

Blackwell touched his amulet lightly through the fabric of his shirt, then let his hand drop to his side. "It is one of my most precious possessions."

"I imagine the maker thought so as well."

He smiled, though the gesture was tight on his face. I'd upset his plans somehow. "You cannot feel the age of an object? The maker must be long passed. No one lives this many centuries."

"Except vampires, of course."

Blackwell scanned the crowd again. "Where is your ... mentor? Protector? His reputation also precedes him."

I knew Kett was also called 'the executioner." I imagined it was this that Blackwell referred to.

"I don't like Hoyt at all," I said. No point in beating around the bush about it — we both knew where Blackwell had gotten his most recent information. How he'd heard about my dowsing abilities in the first place was another matter. A board member from the witches Convocation was the most likely source. After the tribunal, perhaps. "His magic tastes ... dull."

"Is that the worst thing you can say about him? You didn't get to know him at all, I see."

I shrugged and picked up the pace of my dancing. Conversation was boring when there was music underneath the stars.

Blackwell leaned closer. "Your magic is delightfully intriguing."

I laughed. "Get in line, sorcerer. I think you'll find it a bit long, though."

Blackwell didn't smile. I had a feeling I was nothing like he'd expected.

"I would speak to you alone."

"Not tonight," I answered, easy and kind about it. He wasn't my type, though I'm sure many would swoon for the accent. Plus, I had Mory with me, who had just folded her fingers into mine behind my back.

I could feel that the fledgling had stopped dancing, and by the way Blackwell was now looking over my shoulder, that she was staring at the sorcerer.

He frowned. I wondered if sorcerers could identify Adepts but not their brand of magic? He tipped his head to bid me goodnight and turned away into the crowd.

Mory pressed to me, practically clinging as she stared at Blackwell's retreating back.

"What is it?" I whispered to her.

"Shades," she said. "He's ... surrounded by shades."

"Did they notice you?"

Mory shook her head, but I could feel how scared she was by the way she gripped me.

I sought for Kandy in the crowd and noticed her trailing after Blackwell already. Smart wolf.

I tucked Mory to my side and pulled her in the opposite direction, toward the edge of the crowd and then out onto the grass of the park.

"How many shades?" I asked the scared teenager. She was cranking her head back in the direction Blackwell had walked. I couldn't see him or Kandy's green hair.

Mory shook her head, stumbling over her own feet, and finally answered, "Too many to count."

Jesus. Why would shades follow a person — a sorcerer — around? Because he'd killed them? If so, why or how could they remain solid enough to follow him?

"Shades, not ghosts? Not spectral energy like ... like Rusty?"

Mory shook her head again. I pulled her across the grass to the river walk. I was moving as quickly as I could toward Desmond's, hoping I could find a cab, but then realized I didn't know the exact address. Kandy would find us. She could track my magic ... though probably not if we drove around in a cab randomly looking for McGrowly's house.

"Do Kett or Desmond have shades around them?" I asked, knowing they both must have killed people, intentionally or otherwise. Kett to feed, or for his job. Desmond in his rise to alpha, or exercising the duties of his position.

"No. The vampire is different ... he has a darkness. A shadow within him. But the werewolf, no."

I didn't correct her on calling Desmond a werewolf.

"And me? Mory, do you see a shade around me?" I asked, not sure if I was hoping she did or not. Knowing that the only thing that could be haunting me would be Sienna.

Mory shook her head, and I dropped the interrogation.

Chapter Thirteen

"Is this the way we came?" Mory asked. It was the first thing she'd said in ten minutes. Blackwell's shades had really scared her.

I'd just been wondering the same thing. We'd reached the end of the park, and crossed by the hotel that Lara had checked us into. I'd thought about grabbing a cab there and texting my mother or Kett for Desmond's address. Except — if he caught wind of it — I was pretty sure McGrowly would over-react and disrupt the jazz festival with a dozen werewolves in full hunting mode. So then, giving Kandy a few more minutes to catch up to us, I'd cut up a road that I thought would eventually lead to Desmond's residential area on the hill. Except I might have cut up too soon, because we still seemed to be in the city. An oddly unpopulated city. Everyone was at the festival.

"Sure," I answered. "A short cut, maybe." I tried turning left again. I knew Desmond lived vaguely left, but I couldn't get a clear view of the hillside through the tall, night-shrouded buildings. Even the stars seemed farther away here. The streets were angled, one-way only, and the grid of the city was confusing.

"Maybe a short cut?" Mory mocked. I stifled my smile. I liked the mouthy teenager better than the scared fledgling necromancer, but I didn't want her to think I was laughing at her.

"You can't be lost if you know where you want to go, right?"

"Not being able to get there is the actual definition of lost, Jade."

I laughed and fished my phone out of my evening purse. No texts or missed calls appeared on the screen. I was going to have to break down and call someone to pick us up if Kandy didn't catch up to us soon.

But seriously, I'd never seen a city so quiet before. Even the homeless had left their cardboard huts and shopping carts.

I didn't like the feeling of the magic we were moving toward — a dark, oily patch that had manifested ahead. I left the sidewalk, and cut right up the next alley to avoid it. It was past time to loop back to the park. We could grab a taxi at the hotel. If we picked up the pace, we were maybe only five minutes away. I pulled out my phone and texted Kandy to tell her we were heading back to the hotel.

Here, farther away from the riverside jazz festival, a few street people slumbered tucked against the building walls and behind dumpsters. None of them did more than stir as we passed. I seriously thought about pulling out my knife, which I'd rigged up on my right thigh beneath my skirt so it didn't invisibly crush the silk. However, wandering around downtown Portland with an eight-inch blade seemed like a super stupid idea. Plus, I didn't want to freak Mory out any further than she already was.

"Jade," Mory moaned. Too late. The fledgling necromancer's eyes were darting all around the alley.

"More shades?"

Mory nodded and bit her lip.

"Do they see you?"

"Not yet, I'm ... I don't shine as brightly as my mom yet. And they are pretty entrenched. But they look ..." Mory shuddered instead of finishing her sentence. I got the gist.

Off to my left, beyond the building that backed onto the alley, the oily patch of magic was shifting or growing. I wasn't sure it had anything to do with us yet, but I was starting to wonder if I could run as fast as I had in the forest with Mory piggyback. She was awfully tiny, probably not topping ninety pounds. Still, I hadn't ever tried to pick up anything remotely that heavy before.

I reached up, unwound my necklace, and pulled it off over my head. The feeling of the oily magic and Mory's fledgling magic intensified. I compensated and it dulled, though not to the low level it had been simmering at before.

"Here. Wear this," I said as I stopped to loop the necklace over Mory's head. It looked way too big and chunky on her, even after I looped it a third time.

"This ... isn't this ... yours? I mean, it feels like it belongs to you."

That was an interesting observation coming out of a necromancer's mouth. I didn't question her, though, because I could feel something rapidly approaching.

Something magic — a curse, by the taste of it — glimmered behind me and I stepped to the side, pulling Mory with me. The curse hit the dumpster behind us and actually rattled it.

"Nice dodge, witch." Hoyt attempted to affect a drawl but his voice was too reedy and weak to pull it off.

I ignored him and asked Mory, "Do you have your cell phone?"

Mory nodded.

"Check to see if Kandy programed her number in it."

I didn't take my eyes off Hoyt as he stepped around the corner of the building at the mouth of the alley. I couldn't tell if he'd been following us or coming from the direction of the oily magic. Hoyt was rolling something silver in his hand. I didn't like the fact that silver made it seem like he was armed for werewolf.

"She did," Mory said.

"Dial the number and run by Hoyt. Back the way we came. Stay on the same streets we walked. Do you understand?"

"Jade, I don't think my phone works here. In Portland."

"That's a pretty valuable trinket you're wearing, little one." Hoyt stopped about ten feet away, which was probably the exact distance he needed to accurately throw his curses wrapped in silver. Yeah, I could feel the magic within those silver ball bearings now. He had no idea what species of Adept Mory was. He might think she was a werewolf, and that would be bad, because silver-coated or not, Mory couldn't take the same level of curse that a werewolf could.

My phone started to ring.

Hoyt threw a curse.

I flipped my skirt up, drew my knife, and slashed the curse out of the air. Hoyt's eyes widened. To him, the knife would have appeared out of thin air and cut through his magic like it was softened butter.

Mory spun, circled around behind me, and ran for the mouth of the alley. Hoyt threw two curses at once — a silver ball at me and a self-generated one at Mory. Great, he could cast two handed.

I slashed the curse meant for me and charged toward Hoyt. The second curse hit Mory. She grunted but kept running, slightly ahead of me. The necklace did its job brilliantly. Hoyt reached for Mory as she dodged around him. His fingers brushed through her hair, but I was faster than he anticipated. He took my kick straight to his gut without warning. I wanted to stab him, but something held me back. Respect for life, maybe. I was after all the 'Cupcake Witch' according to Mory and her friends.

Hoyt flew back into a pile of cardboard boxes. Thankfully, the resident of the boxes wasn't at home.

Mory faltered at the mouth of the alley.

"Go," I yelled at her. "Keep calling Kandy if she doesn't pick up. Keep to the same streets we've already walked. I'm right behind you."

Mory nodded and ran. I pushed the image of her scared face out of my mind and stalked toward Hoyt.

The spellcurser was struggling to his knees, clutching his lower ribs. "Fuck," he gasped. "I think you might have smashed my liver."

"Likely," I said. I grabbed him by the foot and dragged him out of the nest of boxes and into the middle of the alley, hopefully moving him away from any weapons of convenience that I couldn't see. I could feel how the silver ball-bearing curses had fallen out of his hand, but I couldn't see them in the dark.

"What kind of fucking witch are you?" he groaned.

"Not the kind you were thinking I was. You know, the open-hearted, earth-loving kind."

Hoyt wheezed out a laugh but didn't bother trying to get up again. That worried me. I doubted he'd attack without a plan.

I could still clearly feel Mory running away, so I brushed my worry for her from my mind. But I could also feel the oily patch of magic expanding behind me.

"Your magic stinks, Hoyt. In more ways than one," I said. "Did you really think you could just lift the necklace off me with a couple of curses?"

"Nah. The point was to keep you on track and then just get the necklace off you. I did the first and you took care of the second. Thanks for that."

Then, inexplicably, he covered his head and rolled away from me.

The spell hit me from behind.

Now, I thought I'd felt pain before. Getting stabbed — twice — in the gut was no picnic, but it was sunshine and lollipops compared to this.

Fire burned through my veins to the very end of every capillary of every limb and digit. I couldn't even fall to my knees. I just arched forward, screaming internally, suspended in pain.

Through the haze of my vision, I saw Hoyt scramble to his feet and flee the alley. That was not a good sign.

The fire was burning every cell of my brain, but it finally eased enough that I could collapse to my knees.

Someone was approaching. I couldn't lift my head.

Someone whose magic tasted like something I'd once known. Someone who had cloaked herself from my senses in the oily magic, but hadn't factored in how strong my dowsing abilities had become.

I looked up. It was an effort unlike any effort I'd ever made before. A cloaked figure stood twenty feet

Trinkets, Treasures & Other Bloody Magic

from me. She'd circled around and in front of me while I suffered. While I fought off the hold of the spell.

"Nice cloak," I said, my voice coming out in a thin croak. "Very urban chic."

"Fuck off, Jade," she snarled. Her voice was nothing and everything like I remembered. "I'm the one with the upper hand here."

"Nah," I said. I attempted a laugh. "You left me with the knife. You should've tried to grab it when I was down." Except she wasn't stupid. Stupid enough to make a mistake, of course. Just not stupid enough to make it twice. Her learning curve had always been way higher than mine.

"I've missed you sister," she said, her anger gone. She'd always been capricious with her emotions but this was a quick change. "I have something I need you to do for me. And I promise, no more fireblood spells."

I made an effort to straighten. I wasn't terribly successful. I couldn't see her face within the cloak. I desperately wanted — and didn't want — to see her. If I didn't see her, she could be an apparition or someone crazy good at impressions.

Except it would be impossible to fake her magic, wouldn't it? The taste of candied violets and earth soaked in dirty old blood.

That taste was uniquely Sienna.

I might have lost a little time, because I realized that I'd managed to stand upright, though I was still shaking with pain. The spell was still in my bloodstream. At least that's what it felt like.

Extremely disjointedly, I thought about trying to channel the spell into something magical. Except I had only my knife on me, and I didn't know what adding such a spell would do to it. Serves me right for wearing a pretty dress without pockets. Serves me right for thinking I was worthy of such a dress in the first place. That my life was one where such dresses were wearable and —

"Standing already," Sienna said. "Impressive. One of my test subjects was out for two days. And the other — a human — died."

Jesus, I couldn't believe what I was hearing. My ears had to be lying, right along with my dowser senses. Was this just a crazy, creepy extrapolation of Sienna's tendency to exaggerate? Or was my sister actually as blood-frenzied as she sounded?

"How did you get to Portland?" I asked. I was attempting to control my convulsing limbs. I wasn't sure I was capable of doing anything more than standing.

"It seems a strange choice, doesn't it?" Sienna took a few steps closer to me. I still couldn't see inside the hood, though. "Cute dress."

"I wore it just for you."

Sienna laughed and clapped her hands together. She'd let her nails — painted black, obviously — grow too long. They were beginning to curl. Totally icky. Her laugh hit me like chewing glass, running all along my spine. Not that I'd ever chewed glass before. Ironically, it cleared more pain away from my overloaded nerves.

"Sienna —"

"No," she snapped. "Not Sienna. Not some dull witch name. I'm Valencia now."

I laughed. It came out through my pain a lot like gurgling. "Like the orange? Disney called. They're alleging copyright infringement —"

"It means power in Spanish, moron."

Sienna hit me with the spell a second time.

I brought the knife I still clutched in my right hand up in time to cut through it, but half of it still hit my left side, shoulder to hip. My left knee buckled and I fell sideways to the ground. I tasted blood in my mouth. I must have bitten my tongue. That typical sort of pain was easily and utterly overwritten by the fireblood spell.

Except ... it wasn't quite as bad as the first time. This time I was capable of screaming.

Sienna crouched down beside me and brushed her fingers through the riot of curls covering my face. I couldn't even lift my head, let alone my knife.

"Amazing now, aren't I?" she said. "I figured it out. Well, one in three times, anyway. How to bind the magic to me."

"More stolen magic," I croaked. I was starting to worry about whether the pain was more than just a spell perceived by my brain as painful. I was starting to worry it was doing permanent damage to my veins and arteries.

"What do you think you do with your little trinkets? That magic doesn't belong to you, either."

The spell was wearing off quicker than it had before, but I didn't move as Sienna ran her fingers over my forearm, then down to my hand clutching my knife.

"I don't kill for power," I said, desperate to keep Sienna focused on me and not Mory, who had obviously backtracked contrary to my explicit instructions. Damn willful teenagers. I could feel the fledgling necromancer's magic just around the corner. That magic was expanding even though she wasn't moving closer, as if she was triggering something. Stupid, stupid, brave, brave girl.

"You will, Jade," Sienna said, crooning at me as if I was a pretty kitten. "You will kill for me, but now it's time to go."

I abruptly straightened from my fetal position. Sienna stumbled back, her hood falling over her shoulder.

I'd rolled, still crouched, to my feet with my knife ready, but I didn't press my attack further because ... because ... Sienna's face.

Sienna snarled and yanked the hood back up over her head. Magic danced around her fingertips. She was readying another spell but it was a slow build, as if she couldn't cast such heavy magic multiple times in a row.

"Your face ..." I said. I wanted to cry, to lie down and weep. Yes, I'm aware I can be a softhearted idiot. But my sister —

"Stop gaping at me like a moron, Jade. You think I care what I look like when I have this power?"

Sienna threw the fireblood spell at me. I knocked it away with a slash of my knife without really trying. It was barely half the strength of before, disintegrating underneath my blade just as Sienna had in the portal.

"The portal," I said. Clicking things together in my mind. "You survived the portal."

"Obviously," Sienna answered. "Fuck, Jade. I should kill you just to save you from your ignorant, dull existence."

"But you have something you want me to do."

"As I mentioned previously. Think much?"

I took a step toward her. Just one deliberate step forward. I hoped it looked threatening, because I was really sure it was all I could currently manage.

Sienna took a step back and began readying her spell again.

"You need more in your arsenal, Sienna. That spell isn't going to take me down again."

"I told you not to call me that."

The tone of Sienna's voice reminded me so much of fighting with her in our youth. My heart pinched right in the place that constantly — no matter how much chocolate I consumed or how many shapeshifters I kissed — ached for my sister.

"I never knew ..." I stumbled on my words. "I never knew I loved you best."

Sienna stilled. Her hands were in front of her, the spell on her fingertips. "I know," she whispered. "I know, sister. Just come with me, then."

"No, Sienna. I meant I never knew I loved you more than you loved me."

Mory stepped around the corner of the building at the mouth of the alley. Her eyes were wide and way too big for her pixie face. A too-pale child in dress-up clothing.

"I invoke my blood right to retribution for the death of my brother, witch," Mory said. Her hands were spread wide at her sides. I could feel the power rolling off her ... almost as if she was feeding something with it.

Sienna twisted to look behind her, but she couldn't keep both Mory and me in her field of vision with her hood up. So she knocked it back. Mory winced at the sight of her face.

"Sienna, you've met Mory, right?" I asked.

"Rusty's sister," Mory added. "You remember Rusty, don't you? Because he sure remembers you."

The dumpster to Sienna's left shifted. I stared at it in shock. Though I couldn't feel any magic moving it, it spun sideways as if pushed, clipping Sienna as she tried to jump out of its way. Sienna hit the far wall and stumbled, but managed to stay mostly on her feet.

Mory sagged and swayed as if exhausted. Jesus. Was she somehow transferring her energy to the shades she'd seen in the alley before Hoyt showed up?

Sienna raised her hands, but not at me. At Mory. Fuck. That spell would kill the fledgling.

I lunged for Sienna, knowing it was too far, knowing I wasn't going to be able to protect Mory. But at the last second, with a black-lipped smile stretched across her face, Sienna pivoted and hit me with the spell right over my heart.

I fell.

The night got even darker around the edges. The spell burned through my heart and into every vein and artery that came and went from it. I was vaguely aware I was arched back on the filthy, garbage-strewn concrete, with only my head and heels touching the ground.

Sienna's face came into my field of vision. All the veins and capillaries that connected to her eyes were black. They stood out on her pale skin as if drawn in permanent marker. Same for her lips. That wasn't lipstick.

I collapsed on the ground, the pain easing much quicker than the first two times.

I licked my lips and tried to speak. Sienna's smile widened. Jesus, her gums were black flesh as well. She leaned over me.

I stabbed her in the gut.

"That's one," I croaked. "For payback."

Sienna shrieked and tried to pull away from the blade.

"Get her, Rusty," Mory said. She was only a few feet behind me.

Sienna twisted away. She clutched one hand to her belly while the other batted at something that appeared to be attacking her. I couldn't feel any magic but Sienna hissed and scrambled backward. Small scratches appeared on her face.

Mory touched my hand and then felt her way up my arm. I wasn't sure until I caught her in my peripheral vision, but she was crawling along to sit beside me. Her eyes locked to Sienna fighting with her invisible demon. I couldn't move yet.

"You bound him," I croaked.

"He came when I called," she answered. "She was going to kill you." She swayed, struggling to keep her eyes open.

"That's not why you did it, Mory."

Mory smiled at me. Death was gnawing on her bones. "You're not the only one who gets to take care …"

"You have to let him go, Mory. He's draining you." Rusty. She'd called Rusty and he'd come to fight Sienna for her. Except ghosts have no form, so he was using Mory's magic — and maybe even her life force — to attack his murderer.

"I can't let him go now. I gave it all to him." Mory collapsed forward over my chest and belly. Her eyes, when they managed to stay open, were still locked to Sienna, who was shrieking and clawing at her own face.

I looked away from my sister's struggle and focused what little strength and energy I had on Mory. I wrapped my fingers through my necklace where it was still around the fledgling's neck. I gathered all the magic I found there, then I pushed it out and around Mory like a shield, like a ward of sorts.

The edges of the alley blurred. Pain lanced through my brain and down my spine. I thought I might be passing out but I only pushed harder, adding my magic through the necklace and then up and over Mory.

Sienna stopped shrieking and clawing at the air. She straightened, shaken and bleeding but intact.

"No," Mory moaned. Then she slumped into a full faint.

"You're such a bitch, Jade." Sienna was holding her stomach again, looming over me.

"Come closer, Sienna," I whispered. "I owe you another." I raised my knife but it was just a show of bravado. Sienna hesitated. I wondered if she had another of those spells in her.

As if she had come to some decision, Sienna reached for Mory as if to pull her from me. But before I could slash her with my knife, she screamed and snatched her hands away from Mory as if burned.

I laughed again, like a gurgling monkey. "You never learn, sister. Don't take my stuff."

Sienna snarled and raised her hands to cast another spell. But then I felt more magic speeding in from behind her.

"You better run, sister. The good guys are coming."

Sienna looked around distrustfully, but then I felt a ping of magic from a medallion she wore around her neck. Perhaps she'd set up perimeter warning spells.

The good-guy magic was closer. Sienna stood. Stumbling, I was pleased to note. And she walked away. Just like that.

I guess we'd already said our goodbyes for this lifetime.

I released the magic of the shield I'd woven around Mory. As I felt that power settle back into the necklace, it glowed with a gold-blue hue. Well, that was a new trick.

I sat up and gathered the tiny teenager into me as best I could. I wasn't capable of standing and carrying her.

Sienna's magic and the oily patch she somehow traveled with to cloak her presence moved away. Behind me, Scarlett, Kett, Kandy, and Desmond approached from two different directions.

It was from this half-propped-up vantage point that I watched McGrowly burst into the alley. He tossed the dumpster that Mory — or rather, Rusty — had moved, hard enough to dent the concrete building. Then he leaped to land on two massively clawed feet one step in front of me.

He reached down with clawed hands, tearing the back of my silk gown to shreds as he scooped Mory and me up in his arms.

A gray wolf with blazing green eyes shot by us, fixed on Sienna's trail as McGrowly turned back the way he'd come. He began to close the gap between us and Scarlett, who — even with a vampire at her side — still traveled at human speed.

"I was hoping for the transformation," I said, whispering into McGrowly's furry shoulder. "You have the best ass ever."

He growled something that might have been a chuckle.

"I'm going to sleep for a bit now," I said. Then I blacked out.

Chapter Fourteen

I became aware of a set of cold hands touching my arms. Kett.

"Leave her," Desmond said. His voice sounded human again. By the feel of the magic burning into my skin everywhere I was touching him, I was still in his arms. I couldn't open my eyes.

"At least let him take the fledgling, alpha," Scarlett's voice was melodic and filled with magic.

Desmond grunted as the weight on my chest shifted. Mory.

Is she all right? I tried to speak but then I was pulled under by sleep again.

The second time I woke, I was indoors — the lighting was low and the sounds muted — but still, to my pleasure, in Desmond's arms. He was seated with me draped over his lap. His very naked lap.

I snuggled my ass further into his groin, pleased at the immediate quickening response I got. I curled my fingers through the pelt of hair on his chest.

"We're not alone." His low voice rumbled in his chest.

I opened my eyes to confirm that I was nestled in Desmond's lap in an armchair. The green flecks in his eyes were doing their crazy kaleidoscope thing. He smirked, oddly painfully, at me. He nodded over my head, which I turned only to be rewarded with shooting pain up my neck. "Oh, God," I said as I blinked past the tears that had rushed to my eyes.

"You and me both," Desmond said, resting his head on the high-backed, plush chair. The light bronze fabric looked familiar. We were in one of the guest rooms at Desmond's place.

I tried turning my head again and was rewarded with a smile from Scarlett, who was perched on the edge of the bed and dressed head to toe in black.

"You hate black," I said.

Scarlett's smile widened. "When you want to blend into the night, black is necessary."

I was getting quicker at putting two and two together. "You were out hunting Blackwell." Hell, Mory and I hadn't escaped that stuffy dinner. We'd been set up and let go.

"You could have waited until after dessert," Desmond said. His tone was almost teasing, but in a tired way. "My guests were displeased."

"Kandy totally played me," I said. "Mory?" My chagrin whiplashed into concern.

Scarlett shifted to the side, and I saw Mory curled on her side sleeping on the bed.

"Okay, so it looks like there is more room on the bed ... and, though I've made it fairly clear I don't have an issue being in your arms, my mother is, like, right there." I mock-whispered the last part to make it clear I was neither whining nor complaining.

"I, too, have no issue with holding you," Desmond said. His murmur was pitched low for my ears only.

"But ..."

"There was some issue with putting you down, Jade," Scarlett said. "Have you been intimate with the alpha, sugar?"

"Mom?!?"

"Exchanged bodily fluids?"

"I know what being intimate means!"

Scarlett sighed. I shifted my legs to the floor, not that they wanted to move, and attempted to sit up in Desmond's lap. He helpfully wrapped his hands around my waist to steady me. His thumbs almost touched at the small of my back. God, I could really get used to a set of male hands that could make me feel slim like that.

"What was the issue?" I asked, pausing to absorb the pain twisting through my joints and bones.

"Same issue when we tried to remove the fledgling," a cool voice said from the deep shadows by the door.

I flinched. Kett stepped into the moonlight filtering in through the open window. He was dampening his magic so much that I hadn't tasted it underneath Scarlett's and Desmond's.

"Stop doing that!"

"His presence was agitating the alpha further." Scarlett was using a tone that one might normally reserve for a rabid dog. "But I felt it necessary for him to be nearby, just in case."

"What the hell is going on?" I asked. "Give me all the information at once and quickly."

"You bound the fledgling's magic," Kett said.

"No. Yes," I answered. "For her own protection."

"We cannot remove her from the room without her going into convulsions."

"What?" I shot to my feet without another thought of my pain.

"I believe you need to remove the necklace," Kett continued.

I raced around the bed to Mory, aware of Desmond rising from the chair and stretching behind me. My dress was hanging off me in shreds of purple silk. Thankfully, I was wearing a good bra and matching underwear.

"I used the necklace as a shield. A personal ward for Mory," I said.

"Yes, ingenious," Kett responded.

"Her brother Rusty, or his spectral energy or whatever, came to her call. But the connection was hurting her, draining her."

"She is young."

I reached for the necklace, which was still glowing with juiced-up magic. Kett cradled Mory's head in his hands, and together we got the necklace untwined. As I pulled it from Mory, the taste of the fledgling's magic filled the room.

"Toasted marshmallows," I said.

"Yes?" Kett asked. "I have never tasted such."

I brushed the hair from Mory's forehead. She was still too thin, but she looked healthier than she had in the alley.

I looked up at Desmond, who'd — unfortunately — pulled on some track pants. His chest was still a welcome sight. He was watching me. I looped the necklace around my head and he inhaled a long breath, then exhaled in relief.

"The bond?" I asked. He nodded, then he ran his hand through his hair and over his face as if trying to wake himself up.

"Where's Kandy? I saw her in the alley, and —"

"Fine," Desmond answered. "Healing, but fine."

Scarlett spoke up. "We were tracking Blackwell from the festival with Kandy on point. And suddenly Desmond was ... hurt."

"Practically incapacitated," Kett added.

"I was never off my feet, vampire," Desmond growled.

"Sienna's spell."

"What was it?" Scarlett asked.

"Fire in my veins. I couldn't move."

"A fireblood spell," Scarlett murmured, pulling her spellbook to her lap. She flicked on the side-table lamp, not noticing the three of us reel back from the sudden light. Some warning would have been appreciated. She was making notes. That wasn't weird at all.

It was also interesting that no one seemed shocked that Sienna was alive. While I was relieved to not be bombarded with questions before I'd had a chance to sort through my own feelings, I was also a little put out imagining that they'd had discussions and — obviously, by their outward calm — made decisions that they were once again keeping from me.

"Were you wearing the necklace then?" Kett asked. I shook my head.

Yep. They were putting something together. A puzzle that I didn't even see the pieces of yet.

"Kandy, Kett, and I continued after Blackwell, but Desmond turned back to track you." Scarlett didn't look up from her spellbook. "The alpha assured me you weren't dying."

Yeah? Thanks, Mom.

"I had to transform to shake off the second hit," Desmond said. "It helped that you dealt with it more easily."

I nodded.

"We lost Blackwell," Scarlett added. "He turned the corner and disappeared."

"Disappeared?"

"Magic and all," Kett said. If the user was powerful enough, the vampire could feel magic like I could. Not the glimmers and residual energy I could pick up, but anything strongly imbued.

"He wore an amulet. Called it his most precious possession. He seemed put off that I noticed it on him. It tasted, just a little, like the portal."

"A transportation device," Kett said, practically gushing — in his icy, offish way — over the idea. "Did it bear a ruby?"

"A red stone, yes. So let me get this. Desmond feels what happens to me through the life debt bond?"

"We already established that via the skinwalkers." McGrowly was back in pissy mode.

"Excuse me?" Scarlett interrupted. "Skinwalkers?" Her voice was as steely as I'd ever heard it. Her eyes were on Kett, who oddly and actually appeared to avoid her gaze. "You said you were seeking some sort of treasure."

"And we found it," Kett answered smoothly.

"Off topic," Desmond said.

Scarlett actually pointed a finger at Kett. Then, as if nothing had interrupted, she continued her conversation with me. "The bond has intensified. Which is why I questioned you about …"

Yeah, yeah. Intimate relations.

"The necklace seems to dampen it."

Okay, good to know. "But I don't feel anything. I mean … do you think I'm … pushing the spell, or fear, or whatever into Desmond through the bond?"

"Perhaps," Kett answered.

"But I don't feel ... I mean, I can feel the magic of the actual bond, but I don't feel Desmond specifically."

"It must be connected to how your magic works," Scarlett said.

"Yes," Kett added. "You've said you visualize it as solder or mortar when you're making the trinkets?"

Yeah, and while draining the skinwalker spells into the jade rocks, and making my knife, and so on. That would mean that the bond, though active until I fulfilled its parameters — namely to bring Hudson's killer, Sienna, to justice — only went one way. And I couldn't blame the bond for my practically attacking Desmond twice.

But I could blame him for returning the advances so enthusiastically on the life debt. Damn, that was a sour twist.

"So each time I ... we ..." I couldn't finish the thought. Couldn't look at Desmond. My cheeks flushed with mortification. Had I inadvertently been compelling Desmond to kiss me? Jesus, that kind of coercion was damn close to assault.

"It could have been the necklace, Jade," Scarlett said as she crossed the room and gestured Kett toward Mory. "The necklace might block the intensity of the bond. You're usually never without it."

Kett picked up Mory and exited the room with Scarlett trailing after him. Her head was bowed to her open spellbook, her look thoughtful. She seemed to remember something, turning back at the door to blow me a kiss. Then she shut the door behind her leaving Desmond and me alone in the room.

I looked at my feet. My pretty shoes were scuffed. I felt like crying but I wasn't going to cry over my shoes. "Just what every girl wants to hear about the boy she's been kissing," I finally said.

Desmond sighed. "Don't be dramatic, dowser. I'm the alpha of a large pack, all of who are tied to me with fealty bonds. Their magic is my magic, otherwise the bond between you and I could never have existed in the first place. I'm not easily compelled."

He crossed to me. I tilted my head to look him in the eyes, but he was looking at the necklace. "Just keep the necklace on, yes?"

I nodded.

He crossed by me to the door, opened it, and stepped out.

My stomach churned, but I wasn't sure if I was disappointed or anxious.

"You haven't forced anything on me, Jade," he said over his shoulder. "I extracted the life debt from you. I was angry, and frustrated, and you seemed uncooperative. Any man would give his left arm to kiss you, dowser. Don't go thinking otherwise."

I nodded again. He left, shutting the door behind him with a soft click.

He didn't — I noticed — kiss me goodnight.

I couldn't sleep. Not even after I texted Kandy and received an obscene emoticon in response. I was relieved the green-haired werewolf was well enough to be cracking jokes, but it didn't settle me. The room was too hot even with the window open, and was too chilly with the air conditioning on. Though that might have just been my thing, not being a fan of air conditioning in general. This heat wasn't an issue in Vancouver, which is exactly where I should be ... making cupcakes ... or trinkets.

Trinkets.

I had to keep my necklace on to mute the life debt bond between Desmond and me, but now I'd also inadvertently dragged Mory into a shitload of trouble. She had needed all the protection she could get from Sienna, and — if I wasn't mistaken, because hell if I had any idea about how necromancy worked — from her dead brother, Rusty.

Maybe Rusty's ghost, or shade, or spectral energy hadn't known he was killing Mory in order to go after Sienna. But maybe he was beyond caring. Maybe he'd never cared about killing in the first place. The tribunal had found him equally as guilty as Sienna for the werewolf murders.

I could make Mory a necklace of her own if I could find the glimmers and bits I needed. A lot of the Adept came and went from this house. I should be able to cobble together something temporary at least.

I pulled on a crumpled *Keep Calm and Eat a Cupcake* T-shirt and short shorts — that rolling/packing trick never actually worked for me — and didn't bother with shoes. The clock informed me it was just after 5:00 A.M. That seemed like a sane time to be up to me, but when I padded out into the hall, the house was very quiet.

I chose to explore further into the house rather than immediately backtrack to the rooms I'd already seen. Though I skipped Scarlett's room, which was right next to mine. I gathered — after I came across three more empty bedrooms — that I was in the guest wing. The fact that Desmond needed a guest wing was mind-boggling. He didn't come across as a big-Thanksgiving-or-Christmas-gathering sort of guy.

A glimmer in one of the bedrooms led me to three thin gold bangles that must have dropped behind and underneath a dresser.

In the next room, I found a Montblanc pen. I had no idea what I could do with a pen, but I took it anyway.

I hadn't made a magical object without motivation yet. Kett had been coaxing me to do so, but it seemed that unless I was in danger, I stuck to making cupcakes, not trinkets. It helped that Scarlett was currently occupying my crafting space, because I was still sickened by how Sienna and Rusty had used my trinkets to fuel and aid their killing spree. I'd left all the trinkets hanging in the bakery, though I'd wanted to destroy them initially. I also kept a daily count — yeah, maybe that was overkill — but I hadn't made anything new.

I backtracked through the hall until I arrived at Scarlett's room. A knock gained me a sleepy permission to enter, and I found my mother curled up in bed looking perfectly mussed.

"Oh, good," I said. "I was worried there'd be a vampire in your bed."

"Why would there be a vampire in my bed?" my exhausted mother asked. "Vampires don't sleep."

"What? At all?"

"They do that fugue state thing that bothers you," Scarlett said. "I believe that's like sleep for them."

"Wow, life must be insanely boring for them. How do you fill all those hours? Months? Years?"

"I think you will discover that most vampires prize their immortality above all else. They do not have the comfort of reproducing without great cost, so very few choose to attempt it."

"Kett was turned, not born."

"Yes," Scarlett said. "Again, as far as I have gleaned, that is a painful process that is rarely successful. Are you waking me for a lesson in vampire reproduction?"

"God, no. I was wondering if you had any jewelry. I want to make Mory a necklace."

Scarlett regarded me. Her normally sunny demeanor was dim and her expression more neutral than I usually saw it. Then she swung her legs off the bed and padded over to the bureau.

Speaking of vampires, Kett had taught me — inadvertently — to milk the silence in a conversation a little more. To pause when someone was obviously thinking and let them broach their own concerns instead of constantly drilling for conflict.

Scarlett lifted a padded, embroidered-silk roll out of the top drawer of the high bureau. Yeah, she'd unpacked. No, I hadn't. My mother untied, then unfurled, the roll to reveal an impressive collection of necklaces, bracelets, and earrings.

"You travel with this? I've never seen you wear half of it."

Scarlett shrugged and crossed to climb back into bed. "When you travel as much as I do you learn how to pack."

I hadn't thought about my mother's nomadic ways like that before. She didn't actually have a home of her own. How odd was that?

I ran my hands over her neatly stored necklaces. The padded fabric roll had compartments and clips and pockets to keep the jewelry separate and the necklaces untangled. Scarlett's magic was potent where it imbued many of the items.

I selected a heavy-linked silver chain that would drape just over my collarbone if I wore it. On Mory, it would practically hang to her waist. I also took a thinner flat-linked gold chain of a similar length. I'd never seen Scarlett wear either item.

I wandered back to the bed and held the necklaces out to Scarlett. She hadn't fallen asleep.

"Can I take these? Permanently?"

"Yes. I'm not sure I've worn the silver in years."

"It glistens with your magic."

"Does it? The Adept world must look interesting for you, my Jade."

"It's normal for me, I guess."

"Are you making the necklace right now? We could talk about Sienna, if you wish."

I nodded, but I didn't actually want to talk about the sudden reappearance of my sister. Back from the never-dead and all.

"I called Pearl," Scarlett added.

"Will they … will the tribunal be reformed?"

"I imagine."

"And Sienna hunted."

"If that is the verdict."

"Everyone is always one step ahead of me," I said, changing the subject — though not completely.

"Everyone — of the Adept near you, at least — plays their cards close to the chest. The witches don't want to share information with the shapeshifters. No one wants to collaborate with the vampires. And you are a new unknown. It took all of Gran's influence and my vote to quash an investigation into you and your new abilities. We still kept as much hidden from the Convocation as we could without blocking their investigation into the death of the werewolves."

"I meant with you all using me as bait. First with the skinwalkers, and now with Blackwell. I mean … I saw Sienna dissolve. How is she whole again?"

I sat down on the spot my mother had left beside her on the bed. Scarlett rubbed my back. Her magic soothed me, though maybe I gave too much weight to it. Maybe being babied by my mother was what soothed me.

"Kett ..." Scarlett spit the name, but then regulated her tone. "The vampire will not be using you as a dowsing rod anymore. I weighed the value of having his protection at your side too lightly. It is in his nature to be secretive. I thought treasure hunting was simply an exercise, not a means to accumulate power."

"He won't hurt the skinwalkers."

"No. But he views such knowledge as power in and of itself. As he views you. I've never met an Adept who can create magical objects. And as far as I can tell, neither has Kett."

That was surprising. Scarlett and Kett could cover a lot of time and distance between them.

"We're lucky, in one way, that vampires are so secretive. Kett was easily persuaded to leave you off any official reports."

"But?"

"But it is always best to know where you stand, ally or not. Right now, you're caught between us all. At least two of us love you, Pearl and me. But the other two powerful players are ... well, they're tied to much larger things than a bakery in Vancouver."

"They answer to someone."

"Eventually."

"I can't control any of that."

"No, you can't."

"But I can make this necklace."

"Yes."

"Maybe we'll talk about Sienna after that."

"All right."

I stood and walked to the door.

"It's okay as well, Jade," Scarlett whispered behind me. "To love her. Your sister."

"I don't even know her anymore."

"That never stops love." Scarlett smiled.

"She wants something from me."

"She always did. And you her."

I nodded, and let the painful subject drop. Scarlett snuggled back into bed.

I stepped into the hall and nearly ran into a sleepy-looking Jeremy. The tall blond werewolf blinked at me a few times, then grinned.

"I need wire cutters and a soldering gun," I said.

The grin slipped off Jeremy's face and was replaced by a frown of confusion. "I don't even know what that is," he said.

"Desmond will have them in the garage. Any man who sees himself as being as self-sufficient as Desmond does will have a large, probably mostly unused, tool collection neatly displayed in his garage. Check there. Please and thank you."

"I was just doing rounds. I'll look on my way back."

"Perfect," I said and continued up the hall. "Oh!" I called back over my shoulder. "And stay away from Mory. She's too young for you."

Jeremy squared his shoulders and jutted out his chin. "Wolves don't run with necromancers," he said.

I grinned back at him sunnily. "Good. Keep it that way." By the end of the day, Mory was going to be thanking me. Forbidden fruit was always the most appealing, especially to teenagers.

I searched the other wing of the house. I found a completely nonmagical tray in the kitchen to carry my bounty, then I snooped through the library, gym, and Desmond's suite. I added an antique watch from the library and a ring that had rolled underneath an elliptical machine in the gym. But I hesitated to trespass in Desmond's rooms, even though I could tell he wasn't there.

Where I spied them from the doorway, those rooms were sparsely decorated like the rest of the house in wood and glass. His bed was gigantic — custom sized and custom made was my guess — and swathed in brown fabrics. The stone-tiled fireplace had a thick rug in front of it that looked like the perfect place for a large cat to nap. Not that Desmond seemed like the napping type. A large family tree — built from photographs and sketches — dominated an entire wall. The Llewelyn family was serious about their lineage.

I backed out of the bedroom and carried my tray to the final room at this end of the hall. The door stood slightly ajar, and I could feel Desmond's magic from within. I hesitated and thought about turning back ... but I needed permission to use some of these items in Mory's necklace.

"Come in, dowser," Desmond drawled. I sighed and pushed open the door.

Desmond was sprawled in a swing-back leather chair, his feet on a massive walnut desk. He was holding a phone to his ear but not speaking. He raised an eyebrow in my direction. "Not like you to hang around outside doors, dowser." Then he spoke into the phone. "Yes? Wake him, then."

The wall to my right boasted full-height windows with a seating area just in front. An abstract painting, its strokes thick and multicolored, hung behind Desmond's desk. Like the rest of the house outside of his rooms, there were no personal pictures or items strewn around.

Rather, like my own apartment before my mother moved in, I got the sense that Desmond had either recently moved in or didn't really consider this house his home.

"What have you got?" Desmond asked with the tone of a man hoping for food.

I placed the tray before McGrowly and he swung his legs off the desk to peer at the items arrayed there.

"I'm sorry to wake you, father," Desmond said, speaking into the phone as he sorted through my collection. "Blackwell showed himself last night. No, no casualties. We believe he has a black witch" — I stiffened at this mention of Sienna — "working with him." Desmond paused, listening. He took the pen from the tray and tried writing with it on a pad of blank paper. It didn't work. Still listening, he swapped out the ink cartridge from a box in his desk drawer.

"I wasn't seeking advice," Desmond finally said. "Nor am I asking permission. I just wanted to inform an Assembly member that I will be hunting today, as I have no second —" Desmond paused again, cut off in midsentence. He toyed with the antique watch I'd found in the library.

I began to pace, restless but trying not to be rude. Jeremy poked his head around the open doorway and held a set of wire-cutters tools and a brand new soldering gun out to me. Brand new, as in still in its original packaging.

"Thank you," I said.

"I appreciate your concern and your opinion, as always, father," Desmond said into the phone. "I'm sorry to have disturbed your vacation. Love to mother." Desmond hung up the phone, then studied it as if expecting it to ring. It didn't.

"Are you making something?" he asked.

It took me a moment to register that he was talking to me. I approached the desk again and added the wire cutters and soldering gun to the tray. "Hopefully," I answered.

"All these items are magically imbued?" He ran his fingers over the objects on the tray again.

"Glimmers. From being in contact with an Adept. Either a powerful one, or over a long period of time."

"The pen is mine. Thank you for finding it. The watch is my grandfather's."

"I'll put it back. And the bangles?" I really needed the bangles.

"I don't know. Where did you find them?"

"Fifth guestroom."

"Audrey's, perhaps. Just use them if you need them, dowser. Same with everything else here."

"Audrey won't mind?" I asked, having no idea who this person was.

"Losers weepers," Desmond said, then he showed me his teeth in that nonsmile that I thought Kandy had patented. It was a shapeshifter thing, maybe. Obviously, this wasn't just about gold bangles.

"We're still going to meet with Blackwell?"

"No. I'm going to meet with Blackwell. You, the necromancer, and your mother will stay here. Under guard, if necessary."

"Don't act like you didn't set me up last night."

"Not me, dowser," Desmond said. His growl clearly outlined his feelings about last night. "I protect my assets. The vampire engineered that."

"But Kandy —"

"Should verify the vampire's directions through me much sooner. She's been gone from the pack too long."

"She is loyal —"

"I don't need to be told so from an outsider perspective, dowser. I know my wolf."

"I really didn't want to get Kandy in trouble."

"If it had just being you sneaking out, dowser, that would've been different."

"Expected."

"Yes. Can you deny it?"

No, I bloody well couldn't. I picked up the tray.

"I stocked the kitchen," Desmond said. "In case you wanted to bake."

Something intimate was hidden in this request-formed-as-a-statement, but I didn't want to delve into it. Desmond's mention of not having a second on the phone had reminded me of Hudson. And where Hudson haunted my thoughts, my sister was sure to follow.

"Thank you," I finally said, then I moved toward the door. There were so many questions in my head, so many demands for information, I didn't know where to start. I just wanted to channel it all, put it all in one place to be examined at a later date. Except thoughts didn't work like that.

"Will you hunt her?" I finally asked. Forget Blackwell and his stupid magical artifacts. This was now all about Sienna. If Desmond was right and Sienna and Blackwell had somehow teamed up, then this entire trip had been orchestrated by my sister. To what end, I had no idea.

"It's my right," Desmond answered.

"So I'll just go make you cupcakes while you hunt and kill my sister."

Desmond's jaw shifted like he was grinding his teeth, but when he spoke he was calm. "The tribunal found her guilty."

"Without a defense."

"No defense, even if Sienna had been alive to voice one, would have cleared her name, Jade."

I shut my mouth, then my eyes. Everything he was saying was true. It just wasn't true in my heart.

"People change," Desmond said. His tone was almost tender. "The magic is too much sometimes. I've seen shapeshifters go berserk. We lose about a third of our teens to berserker rages."

I nodded and tried to look him in the eye. I knew he was trying to share something, trying to speak to me. I tried to listen. He looked like he hadn't slept. This diminished him somehow, which was okay. He could handle some diminishment.

"I keep getting pain, spasms, in my joints," I said.

"The necklace dampens the connection. I feel no pain."

"There goes sleeping together," I said, trying to bring some levity into the conversation, into my beleaguered brain.

"That's crazy talk, dowser," Desmond answered. "I plan on bedding you, well and often. Just as soon as you invite me."

"Oh, yeah? The ball is in my court?" I asked, seriously thinking of closing the door, tossing the tray, and testing out the strength of the desk. It looked sturdy.

Desmond grinned. "From the moment I laid eyes on you."

"You thought I was childish, irresponsible, and naive."

"I still do."

Right, just what every girl wanted to hear from her next lover. "You need to work on your pillow talk."

"I don't generally talk while anywhere near a pillow."

"Here's a hint. Try flattery. It'll get you nearer the bed."

"I haven't needed it yet."

"Well, then, have it your way." I turned to exit the room. He was insufferable. Why the hell did I get so hot and bothered at the mere thought of spreading my legs for him? Damn it.

He called after me, laughing. "You'll still bake, right?"

Desmond hardly ever laughed, and now he was compelled to laugh at me. I didn't answer. I would have liked to swear to never bake another cupcake for him ever again, no matter how childish it sounded. Except there was no way I could uphold a self-imposed injunction of that sort for more than an hour or two. If there was good chocolate in the house, at some point, I would bake.

I might be able to walk away from sexy, dangerous shifters, but chocolate had me at its beck and call. Of course, having not slept with Desmond yet made walking away easier. I had a feeling that if I knew what I was missing, I wouldn't have any more willpower than I did with baked goods.

Chapter Fifteen

I was never more sure of who I was, than when making a trinket. Or, in this case, a necklace. My hands moved of their own volition. My fingers surfed the glimmers of magic in the found items, bringing them together to create a new whole.

With my thoughts filled with the urgent need to protect Mory — to protect Rusty's sister as I hadn't protected Sienna — from her own magic and the harmful magic of others, I wove the fine gold chain through the thicker links of the silver necklace. I clipped off the clasps and soldered the ends together with the extra metal. Then I snipped the large man's wedding ring off my own necklace and linked it to Mory's necklace with a soldered piece from one of the gold bangles. I'd used this ring, combined with some of Sienna's hair, for a seek spell in the very first magical object I'd knowingly created. I hoped that the ring still held enough of Sienna's magic that it would help inoculate the necklace, and therefore Mory, against my sister.

What if I'd done this for Sienna six months ago? Would she still have dabbled in black magic? If yes, then would it have rooted in her so deeply that it created ... whatever she now was? A black witch who cared for nothing beyond the accumulation of power?

I remembered Mory lying across me in the alley, the life slowly being pulled from her by a force I couldn't see or feel. Thinking about shielding her from that magic, I began to bend and shape one of the thin gold bangles into a small cage of sorts with the wire cutters.

"Excuse me," a snobby female voice said. "What are you doing to the alpha's coffee table? And are those my gold bangles?"

I looked up, peeved that my focus had been pulled away. I'd dragged the coffee table to the front living room window so I had a view of the river, and the bridges, and Portland beyond. I'd spread my cobbled-together jewelry-making bits and tools on what appeared to be the oldest towel to be found in the linen closet. The towel wasn't actually particularly old, just dark colored. There'd been a bunch of them, so if I ruined this one, I hoped it would go unnoticed.

The striking brunette who'd been fawning all over Desmond at dinner last night was looming over me. She looked just as good dressed in some sort of business chic as she had in eveningwear. I felt instantly grubby in my shorts, T-shirt, and pinned-up curls.

"What are you doing?" she repeated, as if I might be a terribly dense two-year-old about to eat cat poo.

"How is it your business, Audrey?" Kandy asked. She was stretched out on the couch, eyes closed as if sleeping. I hadn't even noticed her there. The house was so full of werewolf magic that I didn't bother to distinguish.

Oh, shit. This was Audrey? These were probably her now-ruined bangles.

"I'm sorry," I said. "I'd be happy to replace these —"

"I don't care about some cheap baubles," she said. "Just what do you think you're doing here, witch? A spell of some sort? You will not practice magic in this home."

"She's not only a witch. And she has permission." Kandy, her attitude still deceptively relaxed, shifted half upright on the couch. She had one foot on the floor, one arm propped on the back of the sofa.

Green — the glow of the shapeshifter magic — rolled over Audrey's eyes as she finally acknowledged Kandy's presence in the living room with a turn of her head. "The alpha is not currently in residence —"

"And you're not Desmond's second," Kandy interrupted, emphasizing her use of McGrowly's given name.

"Not yet," Audrey said. "I'm here at Lord Llewelyn's request —"

"Lord Llewelyn, esteemed member of the Assembly, is not alpha here."

Audrey squared her shoulders. Her high heels were so spiky they sank into the rug. They looked difficult to fight in. But I assumed that if she was vying to replace Hudson as Desmond's second, Audrey was an accomplished scrapper, high heels or not.

I bowed my head back to the half-finished necklace before me. I slipped one of the jade stones imbued with skinwalker magic into the gold cage, then cinched the spokes closed.

I'd been rolling the jade stone in my hand, thinking of the skinwalker magic ... how it rolled up and over the walkers like a cloak. I thought about how that magic would combine with Scarlett's glimmer in the chains, Sienna's glimmer in the ring, and Audrey's glimmer in the bangle to create a cloak of protection for Mory.

"You will not talk back to me, wolf," Audrey said, once again interrupting my focus. She and Kandy had continued their argument over my bowed and occupied head.

Kandy had risen beside the couch. She had some half-healed burns on her arm that I hadn't noticed before.

"What are those burns, Kandy?" I asked, completely undercutting the tension and the magic building between the green-haired werewolf and Audrey.

Kandy glanced at her arms and shrugged. "Stupid spellcurser riding point for the black witch last night." She curled her lip in Audrey's direction.

"Hoyt hit you with one of his silver ball-bearing curses? I thought he ran off."

"I run faster," Kandy said.

I laughed.

"If you're done with the girl talk?" Audrey said.

"We aren't," I said. "And you're interrupting my work." I stood. Slowly. A grin spread over Kandy's face — her predator smile.

Audrey didn't step back, but her head pivoted between Kandy and me, now unsure which of us was the bigger threat.

"Perhaps you could continue this discussion at another time?" I asked, my tone civil.

"The discussion is about you, witch," Audrey answered. She had two tones, snooty and snappish. I wouldn't make her my second. I thought about mentioning this to her — reminding her of Hudson's charm — but the thought of the handsome werewolf made me sad.

"The dowser," Kandy said, correcting Audrey from calling me a witch for the second time. "Is not your concern. She's an invited guest. The items on the table and in the kitchen have been provided for her." That wasn't technically true, but I didn't want to argue the semantics.

"I asked," Audrey repeated, "what she was doing. I expect an answer."

Now this was a sticky subject. I wasn't going to blurt out that I was making a magic necklace, because very few people knew I was capable of such. Audrey obviously wasn't one of those in the know, and I wasn't interested in enlightening her.

"I'm simply tinkering. I'm not going to unleash some spell in your alpha's home."

Audrey turned her green-eyed gaze on me. She scented the air, looking ridiculous enough that I had to fight a smirk. Then she curled her lip toward me. "I don't like the way your magic smells. Like spicy spring rolls."

"I do not smell like —"

"It's a good thing you aren't staying," Kandy said before I could start an all-out brawl.

"You have no right to question me." Audrey had settled on snarling instead of snapping now.

"I stand as the dowser's protection. You're disturbing her —"

"I'll question who I want, when I —"

"Perhaps this dominance display could be postponed or moved to another location? I'm very certain that Desmond would be pissed if you trashed his living room."

Audrey and Kandy immediately backed off their aggressive posturing. The mention of a dominance fight was some sort of a deterrent, which made sense. Kandy was tough but didn't want to be involved in pack politics. Audrey did want to be involved, but if Kandy kicked her ass, she'd lose her chance. I had a feeling Audrey thought out her power plays more thoroughly than that.

Kandy turned her grin on me. "You could at least have pulled out the knife and threatened her a bit."

Audrey looked startled. Her eyes darted over me in a futile search for the afore-mentioned invisible knife.

"Play nice, Kandy," I said, "and I'll make you some cupcakes."

"I bought blueberries. You said you wanted to test a new frosting."

I smiled. I had wanted to test a blueberry buttercream. "Deal."

Audrey looked as if she wanted to spit nails. I turned back to my work.

"No cupcakes for you," Kandy hissed over my bowed head. Audrey spun on a high heel and stomped from the room.

Using another piece of Audrey's bangle, I soldered the gold cage around the jade stone to the man's wedding ring. When I was done, it hung off the necklace like a pendant.

The necklace still felt unfinished, but I wasn't sure what to add.

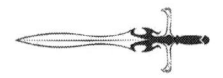

I wandered back through the bedrooms looking for Mory. It was after eleven.

I found the fledgling necromancer leaning against the wall in the hallway, next to the guest room I was occupying. What was interesting was who was currently looming over her, his height even more awkward and gangly next to Mory's super-petite form. Yep, Jeremy, the teen werewolf himself. The werewolf I'd expressly warned off the necromancer only six hours ago.

I suppressed a smirk at my amazing ability to manipulate a teenager as I cleared my throat.

Jeremy flinched, then looked chagrined when I tapped my nose. Yeah, he should have smelled me coming, or heard my footsteps, bare feet and all.

"What are you doing?" I asked, singsong and ever so sweetly.

"Talking," Mory answered, with her regular chin-jut firmly in place.

I grinned, then dangled the necklace out in front of her. "I made this —"

"For me?" Mory cried, all her sulky teenaged angst dropped without hesitation.

"Yes. It's not going to be as reliable as mine yet. I've added to mine for two years."

Mory's fingers fluttered over the necklace but she didn't touch it. "You'll add more?" she asked quietly, not looking me in the eye.

"As I come across them."

"Because you just know which are the right ones?"

"Something like that. It's not finished. I …"

Mory cupped her hands around the gold cage pendant and I saw what was missing. The necromancer's magic. I had to show the necklace who I wanted it to protect.

"Here, let me put it on you." I lifted the necklace over Mory's head. It could loop only once, not three times like my chain, but it still rested about an inch beneath Mory's collarbone. "I have to seal it with your magic. You okay with that?"

Mory nodded solemnly. Jeremy took a step back. Smart wolf.

Having never done such a thing deliberately before, I wasn't sure of the right way to go about it. I spread my fingers across Mory's chest, some resting on the necklace and some resting on her upper ribcage. I could feel her fledgling magic. It was dim compared to the powerful beings I was now accustomed to being around. I remembered it being drained from her in the alley, along with her life force. My heartbeat picked up, unsure and anxious.

"Mory," I whispered as I called her magic toward, up, and over the necklace. "You know this is just for fun. You don't go looking for trouble just because you have it."

"That guy hit me with a spell in the alley, and —"

"But this is a different necklace, yes?" I looked for some understanding in Mory's face.

The necromancer nodded.

"It's a trinket."

"A trinket," Mory repeated.

"Is Rusty here?"

Mory glanced over my shoulder at Jeremy and bit her lip. Then she nodded once, quickly. I could feel Jeremy shift behind me, looking warily around. Wolves, even more than most people, didn't like things they couldn't see, smell, or hear.

"Can Rusty understand me?" I asked.

Mory nodded again.

I lifted my head so that I was speaking over top of Mory and slightly to the side. "Rusty. You will never harm Mory again —"

"He won't," Mory interrupted. Her words were anxious and rushed. "He didn't mean it. He —"

"Never again," I said. Then I soldered Mory's magic to the combined magic of the necklace with my own, thus creating a completely new magic — one that would protect Mory from any other magic. Well, any other weaker magic. But, factoring in Scarlett, the skinwalkers, Audrey, and me, it would have to be a high-powered spell and not cast by Sienna ... hopefully and in theory. Unless my sister had found a way to fundamentally alter her base magic.

"No one but you can remove this from around your neck," I said, running my fingers along the chain.

"Can I use it to protect someone else, like you did with me?" Mory asked. Her eyes were once again on Jeremy.

"I wouldn't," I answered. "It needs to ... get to know you. To accept you. You understand? Like new shoes."

"I have to wear it to break it in, to make it mine. Then, maybe?"

"Maybe," I said. "But let me work on it a couple of more times before that. I'm ... I'm not sure how it would react to someone else. I've added so much of your magic to it."

"Okay." Mory threw her arms around me — catching me unaware — and gave me a fierce hug. Startled, I felt her magic twirl around me, filling my senses with the taste and smell of toasted marshmallows. My chest constricted. I was going to cry when it was the last thing I wanted to do. I patted Mory's back and cranked my head to meet Jeremy's gaze. "We should make lunch, eh?" I asked, my tone overly bright.

"Sure," Jeremy answered. His hands were stuffed in his pockets.

Mory disengaged from me and immediately started showing off the necklace to Jeremy. I headed toward the kitchen, barely keeping my tears at bay.

"Jeremy's going to take me to the shifter graveyard later," Mory called after me.

"All right," I said back over my shoulder, but I didn't stop. "Just ask permission first. Ask Audrey."

Jeremy moaned. "Audrey is never going to let us go," he muttered to Mory. She giggled in response.

I brushed a tear from my cheek and hoped neither of them noticed. Damn you, Sienna. Damn you. I could feel that intense ache in the flesh of my heart, that knife tip that had been lodged there since I thought Sienna had died.

Except this was worse. She was still alive and still very willing to hurt whoever stood in her way. Her way toward what, I had no idea, and I'm not sure Sienna really knew either.

Damn you.

I was all ready to test the blueberry buttercream, then frost the dark chocolate cupcakes I'd made, when Desmond and Kett lumbered into the house. Well, Desmond lumbered, while Kett glided over to the window and took up his still-life position.

Kandy swiped a finger worth of icing while I was distracted. Audrey jumped to her feet. She'd been hunched over some sort of paperwork in the dining area, but she had no idea where to place herself when Desmond slumped onto a stool in front of the kitchen island and stole a bare cupcake from me.

"Don't eat the paper," I said.

Too late. Desmond inhaled the entire cupcake. He reached for a second one. I slapped his hand with my icing-smeared spatula. "I'll ice one."

Audrey lunged for me — her eyes blazing green — and smacked into Kandy like she was a brick wall.

Desmond licked the icing that had splattered on the back of his hand. "Mmm, good."

"Not too sweet?" I asked, ignoring the growling woman attempting to dart around Kandy, who kept sidestepping to block her.

"You always think it's too sweet," the green-haired werewolf said.

"It has to balance out the cake. More cocoa, maybe?"

"Just put some on a damn cupcake," Desmond said. "And calm the fuck down, Audrey."

"She … she … smacked you —"

"She has touched me many times, and I have suffered no damage … other than the need for a cold shower on occasion."

All the fight went out of Audrey. She alternated from staring wide-mouthed at Desmond to gawking at me, disbelief etched across her face. Jesus, it wasn't like I was some hideous monster … wait, maybe that was the problem.

I frosted a cupcake. Desmond watched my hands intently as I did so.

"You usually put on more than that," he said.

"I'm not done, and I thought you were in a rush."

"I can be patient."

I laughed. He grinned.

I got that we were deliberately not talking about something and didn't push it. The neck and armholes of his T-shirt were stretched out, and he was wearing track pants again. The kind shapeshifters stored in places like the trunks of their cars.

I passed Desmond the iced cupcake, and frosted a second for Kandy. Then, with only a moment of hesitation, I made a third for Audrey.

I licked the frosting off the spatula. It was on the edge of being too sweet.

Desmond watched me with hooded eyes. I grinned, wishing briefly that we were alone with the bowl of icing.

"What will you call these ones?" he asked. His gaze was on my mouth.

"They aren't ready for a name yet," I answered, sauntering over to the sink to wash the spatula. "So you had to go all McGrowly?"

"What?" Desmond asked. He grabbed the cupcake I'd iced for Audrey. Kandy hadn't eaten hers either.

"Your shirt is stretched out," I said. "You went all man-beast for some reason while meeting with Blackwell?"

"He wasn't there," Kett answered from the living room. His gaze was still out the window.

Ah. I added a quarter cup of cocoa powder to the icing. Lara had picked me up some Valhrona cocoa powder that was only 21 percent cocoa butter. This pleased me. It would also cut the sweetness.

"Blackwell left a gift," Kett continued. "I gathered you were the one who was supposed to open it. The shifter disagreed."

Desmond grunted. Kett's implication was that Blackwell's gift had hurt McGrowly and he'd transformed to speed his healing. I'd seen him heal easily without needing the magic of the transformation, so it must have been a hell of a gift.

"What about Scarlett?" I asked as I offered a taste of the amped-up chocolate icing to Kandy.

"She didn't go with us," Desmond answered. "Some witch thing."

The green-haired werewolf carefully directed my extended hand and the icing-filled spoon toward Desmond. He didn't bother taking the spoon from me. He simply ate the icing off with one lick.

"A witch thing?" I asked.

"The local coven is missing a couple of members," Kett answered.

"Sienna." I had managed to turn my sister's name into a swear word.

"It seems likely," Kett replied.

"Where's the gift?"

"We'll have to take you to it." Kett pulled out a cell phone and began texting. It always wigged me out when I saw the vampire using technology. I guessed he was texting Scarlett.

Desmond smacked his lips. "Yes. On the cupcake part now."

His language skills were degrading rapidly. But then, great chocolate had that effect on me as well, so I couldn't judge.

I began to systematically frost the remaining cupcakes. I was surprised that Desmond didn't snatch the first one I put down.

No one spoke while I finished frosting. Desmond just watched me with that stoic, granite look of his while the other three busied themselves. Or slipped into a fugue state in Kett's case.

I wiped my hands on a tea towel and plated the cupcakes on a pretty, seventies-inspired, earthenware serving platter I'd found. It came with a matching set of side plates that looked like they'd never been used.

I set these down in front of Desmond. He looked over the cupcakes and nodded his approval. Then he looked up at me.

Kandy shifted anxiously. I was missing something.

Desmond waited, his face giving me no hint. Kandy toyed with the spoon she'd guided me to offer to Desmond.

He wanted me to serve him the cupcakes? I opened my mouth to say something snarky, then paused.

Desmond lifted his eyebrows questioningly. I remembered how he'd countered my offer to cook dinner. Food was significant to shapeshifters. Kandy displayed that every time she was with Desmond. He always ate first or got first pick.

Kett's phone pinged. "Your mother is on her way."

I picked up a side plate and put a cupcake on it. Then I topped the cupcake with a few fresh blueberries and scattered more around the plate.

I placed this plate in front of Desmond. His eyes crinkled around the edges. His approval was obvious. I was playing some hierarchy game I didn't understand, but I made up five more plates anyway. I started to place one of the five in front of Kandy but she shook her head sharply and looked briefly toward Audrey.

I crossed around the kitchen island into the dining room and placed the plate on the table beside Audrey. She bobbed her head in thanks, but I could tell by her tensed jaw and averted eyes that it took every ounce of discipline to do so.

Then I served Kandy. Desmond bit into his cupcake. Kandy and Audrey followed suit. They made appreciative noises while they ate. I took a bite of my cupcake as I noted the two extra plates.

"Where are Jeremy and Mory?" I asked Kandy once I cleared my mouth.

Kandy shrugged and kept eating.

I glanced at the clock on the oven. I couldn't recall seeing them since lunch. I reached out with my dowser senses to find Mory's magic. She wasn't near.

"Did they go to the graveyard?" I asked.

"What?" Desmond replied.

"Jeremy and Mory," I said around the last two bites of my cupcake. "They were talking about some shapeshifter cemetery."

"What have you done now?" Desmond's tone said so much more than his words. It implied I'd been nothing but a headache for him for many, many years ... and really, it had only been three months.

I stared him down. He never liked it when I did that. Then I licked a dab of frosting off my fingertip as if I had no care in the world. I was learning the rules of this dominance game pretty quickly.

Green rolled over Desmond's eyes. It was a really bad idea to play games with an alpha in his own home. If McGrowly made an appearance, he would totally ruin the kitchen trying to get to me. I liked the kitchen. I just loathed Desmond's all-knowing, all-suffering tone.

"Don't think you know me, shifter," I whispered. I didn't lay my hand on the hilt of my knife, but I really, really wanted to. God. Where was all this aggression coming from? The constant feeling of having no control of my own life? Desmond's dominance games pulled me right out of the contentment I'd felt from making Mory's necklace.

"I know you, dowser," Desmond growled. He spread his large hands on the granite counter before him. His fingers were each thicker than my thumb.

"I gave them permission." Audrey whispered so quietly that I barely heard her.

Desmond rolled his shoulders, then slowly turned to look at her. She stumbled to her feet, knocking her chair back, and knelt on one knee with her head bowed.

"Explain," Desmond said, "why you have allowed two pups to leave this house unaccompanied."

"I sent your enforcer, Lara, with them." Lara was one of Desmond's personal enforcers. He'd brought her, along with Kandy and Jeremy, to Vancouver when they were investigating the werewolf murders.

"So you chose to lighten the guard when we had a guest in residence that has been offered our protection?"

"No. I ..." Audrey faltered.

"Actually, I changed my mind. I will take responsibility." I swore a vein in Desmond's forehead twitched when I spoke. "They told me their plans. I foisted them off on Audrey, assuming she could rein Jeremy in better than I."

"A fair assumption," Desmond said. He didn't look at me.

"I should have said no. I practically threw them together."

"Werewolves do not mix with necromancers," Desmond said, completely rebuffing my attempt to take the blame. He wasn't big on the shades-of-gray concept.

"Werewolves don't mix with anyone but other werewolves," Kandy muttered under her breath.

"Except in the wild," I said, smiling at the little bit of information I'd somehow accumulated. "They can mate with coyotes and dogs, right?"

Kandy looked at me, her mouth was wide open. Then she started to laugh.

Desmond growled. But then he seemed to give in and start laughing along with Kandy.

Audrey glared at me from her position kneeling on the floor when Desmond wasn't looking. She didn't find the subject of interspecies mating at all amusing. Did shapeshifters mate across species of animal? Desmond was a mountain lion, which I understood was a form practically exclusive to his blood relatives. They had to marry wolves and what-not, didn't they?

Now wasn't the time to ask.

"To the graveyard we go," Desmond declared. He swiped another cupcake off the platter.

I'd once found him stoic and unreadable, but now the Alpha of the West Coast North American Pack's mood changes seemed abrupt and confusing. Perhaps I'd been spending too much time with Kett.

Speaking of whom, the vampire was watching me. He then deliberately looked down at the coffee table. I'd tidied up after making Mory's necklace but hadn't put everything away yet. Kett raised his gaze and rewarded me with a very rare, very human smile.

"Yeah, yeah," I said, embarrassed that I was pleased with pleasing him.

His grin widened. "Alchemist," he said.

I shrugged. Desmond frowned as he glanced between Kett and me.

"To the graveyard, and then I get to unwrap my gift from Blackwell?" I asked brightly. I crossed out of the kitchen toward my room.

"You will at least look at it, dowser," Desmond answered.

I ignored him, thinking only of what sort of shoes to wear to a shifter graveyard, then to open a gift from a sorcerer whose intentions were unknown and perhaps deadly.

Something with laces and a bit of a heel, perhaps.

Chapter Sixteen

The shapeshifter cemetery was about a five minute drive from Desmond's house. The private plot, which was situated on the edge of the hill overlooking the river, was the size of three or so residential lots. It was well-maintained, though the trimmed grass was brown from lack of rain. The graveyard itself spread out from a crypt that sat about ten feet beyond the low wrought-iron fence that ran along the edge of the road. It was as old as anything I'd seen in Portland. This had obviously been shapeshifter territory for hundreds of years.

Lara's bashed-in SUV was parked at the roadside edge of the spiky, wrought-iron front gate. Through and to the side of the gate, the door to the crypt was canted to one side, half-ripped from its heavy-duty hinges. As I raced by the door, pulled frantically forward by the low pulse of magic I could taste from the other side, I saw that the interior of the crypt was empty ... excepting the shifter remains, of course. Shapeshifters seemed to favor cremation. No bodies to exhume was a good policy in general for the Adept community in the twenty-first century.

Lara was lying crumpled to one side of the white stone mausoleum. By the marks and the blood trail, she'd fought even after she'd fallen, perhaps taking cover behind the crypt. Or perhaps she'd simply been left there to die. Even though my senses told me that the teenagers were nowhere near, I couldn't stop myself from frantically looking for them.

I wasn't sure the vivacious werewolf was alive until she moaned when Desmond brushed by me. He held me back even as he moved forward. Lara's magic rolled toward him, as if she sensed him on another level. She was covered in burns and what looked like pockmarks. Her wounds were bloody, sore, and similar in pattern to the partially healed burns I'd seen on Kandy's arms this morning.

She reached out for Desmond as he knelt beside her, but she couldn't hold on after he'd gathered her in his arms.

"Change," he ordered. The green of his magic blazed from his eyes. I'd never seen them so bright without being followed by a transformation.

Lara shook her head, the movement forcing a painful moan. "The kids ..."

"Change," Desmond demanded.

"We need to know what happened here." Audrey spoke up from behind me. Kandy's grip was rubbing the bones of my wrist together, but I didn't mind the pain. The green-haired werewolf had stepped up to hold me back after Desmond passed by.

"We have the dowser for that," Desmond answered. His magic rolled off him in a way I hadn't tasted or felt before. It crashed over Kandy, Audrey, and me. The two werewolves involuntarily fell to their knees.

"The dowser," Lara moaned. She was still fighting whatever Desmond was attempting to do with his magic. I could see her own magic answering and twining through his, though. Her green was dim — so much dimmer than Desmond's or Kandy's. My heart began to ache as my mind urged me to look away. But I didn't.

I shook Kandy off my wrist. The green-haired werewolf couldn't hold me and withstand whatever Desmond's magic was doing. I stepped into Lara's eyeline.

"There's a ... gift ... for her ..."

"We know," Desmond said. "Now change."

Lara arched up in pain. Her magic gave way to Desmond's, which spread out over her body. Desmond grunted. I had a feeling he was trying to siphon off the werewolf's pain somehow, while also triggering her to transform.

"You can do it, little wolf," Desmond whispered.

Audrey and Kandy shuddered as if paying a price for resisting the call of Desmond's magic. Kandy's fingers, wolf-clawed, dug into the dirt on either side of her feet.

Lara screamed as if her soul was being ripped from her body. Green finally flooded her eyes and rippled across her body. Then she transformed into a gray wolf.

The wolf, draped in Lara's shorts and tank top, lay panting over Desmond's knees. Her fur was matted and bloody in places, but I understood that the change was supposed to help her heal.

Desmond pulled the shorts off the wolf, who whimpered. Then leaving the tank top on, he resettled her in his arms and stood. He turned to stand before Audrey, still kneeling with her head bowed. He gazed down at the stylish werewolf, then glanced up at me.

"I gather the fledglings, my wolf and your necromancer, are not nearby?" he asked. It was an oddly formal question. His magic still whirled around him, shimmering from his eyes as if he was barely holding onto it.

I shook my head. I couldn't taste Jeremy or Mory's magic anywhere near ... except ...

"There's a glimmer of Jeremy by the SUV," I said.

"Blood," Desmond said. So he'd smelled it already. "Kandy. I'd have you on your feet please."

Kandy straightened but kept her eyes averted from Desmond.

"They hid behind the SUV," Desmond said. "Then fell back here behind the crypt. Probably after Jeremy was wounded and Lara had to stand alone."

"Against the spellcurser," Kandy spat in agreement.

Hoyt. Hoyt had attacked the teenagers and Lara.

"Why not just drive away?" I asked, really, really trying to focus on each moment and not completely freak out that Mory was missing.

"Kandy?" Desmond asked.

Kandy crossed to the SUV and walked around it, looking at the ground. At the driver's side door, she reached through the open window and popped the hood.

"He disabled the SUV, then mounted his attack when they returned." Desmond murmured. "Then they ran?"

As Kandy nodded, I found myself wondering whether he was psychically connected to all the shapeshifters in his pack somehow.

"Jeremy was hit here." The green-haired werewolf pointed at the ground where I could see a glimmer of Jeremy's magic. "There's blood here, here, and here." She gestured to three places that all led toward the crypt.

"Lara's," I said. It was easy for me to tell whose blood was whose.

I crossed to and hunched over the spot nearest the trashed SUV. "This is Hoyt's." His magical signature wasn't so dull in his blood, though the sour fennel taste that flooded my mouth made me want to spit.

"Also silver," Kandy said as she circled the SUV a second time.

"He encases his spells in silver somehow," I said.

"He can make magical items like you?" Desmond asked. I glanced toward Audrey but she hadn't moved from her crouched position at Desmond's feet. He waved his hand to indicate I wasn't to worry about the bowed werewolf.

"No. It's not the same thing. It's like someone making bullets. I doubt they have much shelf life, but he might be able to load them up more than he can throw when he typically curses. Like extra ammunition."

"They have a silversmith," Desmond said, his gaze on Audrey's bowed head. I really, really didn't get what was going on here with the shapeshifters. My fingers itched to grab my phone and text Kett and Scarlett, who'd gone ahead to wherever Blackwell had left the gift —

"Gift," I said. "Hoyt snatched the kids and told Lara about the gift. Why?"

Desmond didn't answer me. Instead, he addressed Audrey. "Rise, wolf."

Audrey rose but kept her head bowed.

"The pack is splintered, disorganized because there is no second."

Audrey looked up to meet Desmond's gaze. "I overstepped, my lord."

"You thought two wolves would be enough protection for the fledgling necromancer, but you had no knowledge of the enemy we were facing."

"No, my lord," Audrey whispered.

"A second must be levelheaded, focused, determined, strong."

"Loyal, diplomatic —"

"Hudson is not easily replaced."

"I don't presume —"

"You presume. You sit by my side. You give orders to my wolves. You're antagonistic with my enforcer and my honored guests. All because you presume your favor with my father will transfer to me."

Audrey said nothing, but she stood her ground before Desmond. In the face of his barely contained anger, that was impressive.

Desmond stared at her long enough that I began to get anxious to get moving again.

McGrowly then held the gray wolf in his arms out to Audrey. "I place this wolf in your care."

Audrey nodded and reached out to gather Lara into her arms. She accepted the weight of the hundred-and-twenty-pound werewolf without effort.

"Kandy, the dowser, and I will join the scion and the vampire. Then we will hunt the sorcerer and the black witch."

Audrey opened her mouth but Desmond cut her off. "You will provisionally step in as my beta, pending the trials. You will see this wolf healed and you will gather the shapeshifters of Portland. If we have not returned by nightfall, the pack will rise."

Audrey shuddered but nodded. "Sunset. Yes, my lord."

I had no freaking idea what all that meant. Except that if their alpha didn't return, Blackwell was going to have a butt-load of pissed off shapeshifters up his ass.

"Kandy, can you get Lara's vehicle moving?" Desmond asked.

Kandy shook her head. "Looks like he poured acid all over the engine."

Desmond growled and started back toward our SUV.

"Wait," I cried. "Can't you track them?"

"No," Desmond answered. He held the back door open for Audrey, who climbed in with the gray wolf still in her arms.

"The trail ends right here," Kandy murmured in my ear as she stepped by me.

"But all that alpha magic," I said. I had a hard time believing that Desmond could exert so much control over the shifters and not track them magically.

"Jeremy hasn't been with us long. He's pack by birth, but he isn't bound to Desmond like some of us are. That comes later, by choice. Jeremy's going away for school in the fall."

Oh, shit.

"Desmond or I, or any of the werewolves with good tracking abilities, could eventually find them. But the quicker the better, right?"

"The gift," I muttered.

"Yeah. Let's go see what the sorcerer left you."

That didn't sound like so much fun anymore. The only thing I could cling to, so that I didn't drown in my fear for Mory, was that I couldn't taste any of her magic in the area. Dead or alive I should be able to feel her magic if it was near. So whatever hurt Jeremy and Lara hadn't hurt the fledgling necromancer ... yet.

A small gold-plated, hinged box sat on an antique mahogany plant stand in the middle of what appeared to be a very dusty, neglected barbershop.

We had dropped Audrey and Lara back at Desmond's house. The gray wolf was still conscious but panting in pain. Desmond was actually twisting the steering wheel in his hands. I wasn't sure how much the steering column could take and still function. But it had at least lasted until we pulled up to an abandoned strip mall somewhere outside of West Portland. Even the 'For Lease' sign had fallen, neglected, half off its posts.

Kandy stood outside waiting by the SUV. She'd done a patrol around the entire complex before I'd been allowed to step out of the vehicle. Even though I could clearly feel only Scarlett and Kett inside.

My mother, her face as serious as I'd ever seen it, was holding some sort of spell over the box when we entered the barbershop.

Footsteps leading to and from the door stood out in the thick dust on the linoleum floor. A few massively sized ones with claws tracked around the inner perimeter of the walls as well. McGrowly investigating, I guessed.

"It's spelled," Scarlett said. "But not necessarily maliciously. Did you try to remove it from the stand or simply open it?"

"Remove it," Kett answered. The disdain in his cool smooth voice was completely obvious to me. His expressions and moods were as subtle as Desmond's were wild. I'd really been spending too much time with the vampire.

"Blackwell's magic," I said. I could taste that much even without touching the box.

"Yes?" Scarlett asked as she dropped her spell.

I instantly missed the comforting taste of her magic. It still lingered, of course, wherever my mother was, but was so much more intense when she was casting. I could remember her using a similar spell occasionally on me the few times I'd been sick as a child.

"Not Sienna?" my mother prodded.

I shook my head. No. My sister's magic was so distinctive now that I would have tasted it from the car even with the doors and windows closed.

"Is Lara all right?" Scarlett asked Desmond over my shoulder as I crossed the room to look at the box.

"She will be, scion. Thank you for your concern," Desmond answered as he followed on my heels.

Scarlett inclined her head and returned to her examination of the box. Though Desmond had answered her with a formal tone, her question was not that of a diplomat. She actually cared about Lara. The realization startled me. Scarlett had always seemed frivolous and fun. Free with her friends and relationships. Maybe she cared so deeply that maintaining close ties to many people was difficult for her? Was that why she'd come and gone from my childhood? There for all the good times and the bad, but absent in between?

I shook off my self-absorbed thoughts and focused on the box. I hovered my fingers over it but nothing leaped out to bite me, which was always a good first sign. I could see the tinge of Blackwell's magic coating the box. It didn't feel like it was trying to repel me. But then, I couldn't see or taste my own magic in the way I saw others', so I couldn't be completely sure.

I touched the lid.

Desmond snarled behind me.

Nothing else happened. "Spelled to me, I think."

"Blackwell shouldn't be able to be so specific," Scarlett said. "Without something of yours ... blood, hair. I sensed none of those foundations here."

I shrugged, losing patience with the not-immediately-tracking-Mory aspect of the afternoon. I didn't want to sit around analyzing everything to death. Kett on his own could spend weeks just looking at the box. This was totally why I made cupcakes and not wedding cakes. An aspect of my personality I accepted years and years ago. If a customer ever wanted a fancy custom order, Bryn did the decorating.

I flipped open the lid. A gold ball the diameter of a quarter sat nestled in a purple velvet cushion within the box.

"Expensive," I muttered. Even not knowing the weight of it, I could tell this wasn't just some pretty gold-plated ball bearing.

"Spelled?" Kett asked.

"Yeah," I answered. "See the solder join? It holds some sort of spell like those silver balls Hoyt uses for his curses."

This spell ball was twice the size of Hoyt's ball bearings and made out of gold, so a hasty guess placed it way higher on the power scale as well.

Scarlett raised her hands — probably to cast her diagnosis spell — but I simply plucked the gold ball out of its nest.

My mother gasped. Yeah, I was tired of talking.

The ball rolled in my open palm, then settled in the center. The spell contained within it tried to attach itself to me. I pushed it back into the sphere. It resisted, but then settled back.

"It's a compulsion spell. Like Blackwell placed on his invitation letter to force Hoyt to deliver it only to me. It's supposed to force me to ... I don't know. Follow it?"

"You have it under control, Jade?" Scarlett asked. I saw worry lines on her forehead that I'd never noticed before. They looked permanent. I seriously hoped I wasn't putting them there, but who was I kidding?

I rolled the gold sphere in my fingers, tasting Blackwell's magic like the fine wine it reminded me of. "Do you think Mory's at the other end?" I asked no one in particular.

"He clearly wants something from you," Kett answered.

"Yeah. Sienna mentioned something she wanted me to do for her."

Scarlett sighed. "I thought you were speaking metaphorically."

"I wasn't."

Scarlett sighed again.

Geez. It's not like I'd had hours to dissect my torturous conversation with my sister with her.

"Can you follow the spell or not, dowser?" Desmond asked.

I lifted my hand and pointed a finger.

"Due west," Kett said.

Desmond dug his phone out of his pocket as he crossed out of the barbershop. At least someone else wanted to be moving as badly as I did.

"Blackwell would make a good vampire," Kett said.

"Find him clever, do you?" Scarlett was clearly not impressed.

Kett reached over and flipped the lid shut on the small box. The spell on it had disappeared once I'd retrieved the gold sphere. "No," he said. "Overly convoluted, heavy handed, and obvious."

"That makes him good vamp material?" I asked as I crossed out of the shop. Kett slipped the gold-plated box into his pocket and didn't answer me.

Scarlett hung back, texting.

"Mom, let's go. Who could you possibly be texting?"

"Pearl," Scarlett answered. She slipped her phone into the outside pocket of her purse and followed me out of the shop.

"Gran is texting?" The world was indeed coming to an end. Gran was a traditional witch. Technology wasn't her friend. I had always thought her magic fundamentally rejected cell phones and whatnot. If she spent too much time near electronics, her magic eventually fried it.

"I bought her the phone before we left. I found a spell to protect it from her magic, though I'm not sure how long it will last. I had to be careful how I phrased things yesterday, as she was getting Todd to answer for her, but then she figured it out."

My phone pinged as I climbed into the SUV. I pulled it out. It was a text message from my grandmother.

Jade.
Be careful.
Take care of Scarlett.
I love you.

Gran texting. Yep, it was the end of days.

The gold sphere led us seriously west. As in, all the way to the Oregon Coast.

"Where are we?" I asked, after peering out the window at the waning sun over the Pacific Ocean failed to illuminate me.

"Near Florence," Kandy answered. That really didn't offer any clarification.

We were driving up a steep hill that offered a craggy cliff drop to our left and what looked to be a series of hiking trails to our right. If I glanced back, south, I could see the famous Oregon dunes, but the sphere had tugged me north when we'd reached the end of west.

A building, perched on the edge of the cliff, came into view as we rounded an S-curve. A building with a rather touristy billboard.

"Turn in here," I said.

"What?" Kandy answered, as the SUV sped past the entrance.

"Turn here!"

Desmond reached over from the passenger seat and cranked the wheel left. Kandy hit the brakes and we skidded into the half-empty parking lot through the exit.

We all sat quietly. I, somehow forced to sit between Scarlett and Kett in the back seat, eased myself off the vampire where I'd been thrown against him. My mother and Kett had left their car at the strip mall, deeming that smarter than taking a chance on us getting separated.

Desmond let go of the wheel. Kandy half-heartedly straightened the SUV into an actual parking spot and then turned off the vehicle.

We all cranked our necks to stare up at the billboard. It read *Sea Lion Caves,* with the subhead *World's Largest Sea Cave* beside a life-sized picture of a sea lion. Though I'd never seen a golden sea lion before.

"Okay. What the hell are we doing here?" Kandy asked.

"I wasn't going to be the first to ask," I muttered.

"The sphere is directing you to the building, Jade?" Scarlett asked. The building in question was a rectangle of beige siding with a red clay-tile roof. It was surrounded by — of all things — a white picket fence.

"I don't think so. Farther away. Down? Maybe the beach? Can we get to the beach here?"

"No. Fuck," Desmond said. Then he all but threw himself out of the SUV and stomped into the building.

"I'm missing something."

"The caves, Jade," Scarlett said. Then she also exited.

I climbed out as well. Kandy and Scarlett followed Desmond into the gift shop, but I wandered over to the edge of the property. I stood on a cliff that looked like it was the end of the world, which was exceedingly appropriate based on how I was currently feeling ... or, rather, trying not to feel.

It wasn't the end of the world. Just the end of North America, which for some was the same difference. I hadn't ever been off the continent myself. There was too much old magic, I now knew, in Europe. An Adept of power would take one look at me and know what I was ... or rather what I wasn't, which was not purely a witch. I still couldn't wrap my head around how Gran had persuaded me not to travel after high school. She was that good.

Waves crashed into rocks hundreds of feet below me, with nothing but ocean from me all the way to China ... or maybe Japan. I always got that mixed up.

The gold sphere urged me to continue, but there was no more road or path.

I turned as I felt Kandy approaching from the gift shop. "Closes in thirty minutes," she said. "We'll hop a ride on the elevator and take a look around after." She handed me a brochure.

"America's biggest sea grotto," I read from it.

"You think the chocolate is any good here?" Kandy asked.

"Since when does chocolate need to be a certain quality for you?"

Kandy laughed. "You're a bad influence."

Scarlett and Kett, who was hiding out behind his baseball hat and sunglasses again, approached.

"Caves," I said to them. "You think Blackwell is hanging out in some sea lion cave with a captive werewolf and necromancer?"

"What do your senses tell you, dowser?" Kett asked.

"Nothing." I snapped. I wasn't interested in being schooled right now.

"He won't be in the main cave," Scarlett murmured. She looked over the pictures in the brochure she'd lifted off me while I was gearing up for my hissy fit.

"Then there must be others, perhaps hidden," Kett answered.

I walked away. The sphere wanted me to move, so I did. I crossed the strip of grass toward the walkway that led to the side of the building. I leaned against the fence. From here, I could see the carefully manicured paved paths on the property about twenty feet below. One led south across this wide shelf, jutting out a hundred feet or so over the ocean, to a lookout point complete with coin-operated binoculars. The second led north to — according to the helpful sign — the elevator and another lookout point. Farther north, I could see a picture-perfect, red-topped white lighthouse. Too bad it wasn't a picture-perfect sort of day.

I knew there was a reason I was always last to figure things out. It wasn't because I was self-absorbed, though I definitely was and that probably didn't help matters. It was because I had less experience than everyone else. Desmond looked only a few years older than me, but he ran an entire community of shapeshifters. Kett was hundreds of years old. Scarlett had traveled the world many times over. Also, both Scarlett and Kett already apparently knew a lot about Blackwell.

No one knew Sienna like I did, though. And that was scarier than being ignorant and slow. Because once again, this was somehow all tied to my magic. Jeremy and Mory wouldn't even have met, let alone been kidnapped together, if my magic hadn't brought me to Blackwell's attention.

So, yeah. I got that we were walking into a trap so obviously engineered by my sister that I'm sure everyone else got it too. Of course, that didn't mean I wasn't going to walk into it. What else could I do?

I thought about leaping the fence and dropping down to the path below, then taking those last hundred steps to the elevator and leaving everyone else behind.

Then what? Threaten Blackwell with my knife? I'm sure he had plenty of magical knives of his own. Plus that nifty amulet that might also be a transportation device. And Sienna had bested me in the alley. It might have looked like I'd won the battle, but I wasn't going to win the war. You had to kill to win wars. Could I kill my sister?

"You're dwelling," Scarlett said as she settled beside me with her back to the fence. "It's unlike you."

"I feel like I don't know anything. Like I barely know myself. I had everything sorted before."

Scarlett laughed, softly. "Shall I tell you that this is just life? Because it is. Or shall I reinforce your feelings and remind you that three months ago, you thought you were half-human, and that we still haven't figured out that riddle yet."

"Or should you just kick me out of the nest and see if I fly?"

"Oh, you fly, my Jade. You soar."

My chest constricted at the pride in my mother's voice. Pride I felt utterly unworthy of.

Scarlett laid her hand across mine. I continued to clutch the top of the fence with both hands. Her magic danced across my skin and settled my thoughts.

"Did you always know you could do that?" I asked. "Or did you learn?"

"Pearl Godfrey's child doesn't learn," Scarlett answered. "She is born fully actualized."

"And when you had to learn?" I was full of questions today.

"I was a disappointment."

"So Gran was more careful with me, then."

"Was she? She made it clear I wasn't to interfere. And honestly, I thought it was better ... I thought you'd have a better childhood with Pearl as your caregiver, rather than me. And I was so very scared to lose you. That someone would take you away. Pearl protected you. Pearl loved you so fiercely. I only got in her way. I should have ... I should have stepped up quicker."

Silence settled between us. My mother had said so much in so few words that I wasn't too sure how to start sorting through it.

"Who were you worried would take me? My father?"

"No, I ... How would he know? I looked for him. I asked, but I couldn't stay. I couldn't have a baby in Queensland. I had to go home to Pearl."

"Would he ... do you think he would have wanted me?"

"I have no idea. He was magnificent. Strong, fierce, and he laughed. When he laughed it felt like the world laughed with him. But we didn't talk, you understand. Not more than passing whispers with the magic of the moon and the Kalkadoon ... the Aboriginals, all around us. We were called together and we answered."

Scarlett had told me all of this, in slightly different ways, the night Sienna had tried to force me to open the portal in the bakery basement. Then, as now, I could hear so many nuances within her words. My father thrilled and scared her. It was the scared part that freaked me out. What could scare my mother, whose magic soothed all those touched by it?

"Kett says he can tell me what magic is in my blood."

Scarlett laughed. "Just like a man to tell you anything you want to hear to get in your pants and then forget his promises the next morning. A vampire will say anything for permission to bite you."

"You think he's lying?"

"I think there's no way he's laid fangs on anyone remotely like your father."

"You talk like he's some mythical being. Some demigod manifested through an Australian Aboriginal fertility ceremony."

"Yes."

The simplicity of Scarlett's answer to my outlandish suggestion threw me. A demigod? What the hell?

Scarlett tapped my chin lightly and I snapped my mouth shut with an audible click. "You look exactly like him," she said. "Every inch of you, a perfectly feminine version of him."

Of a demigod. There was no way. Freaking gods didn't exist. Did they?

"Except my eyes," I said by rote, following the script we'd written together when I was very young ... when she was young ...

"You have my eyes," my mother said. She rewarded me with a full-blown heartfelt smile. "Now, let's go see what the nasty sorcerer wants. I have some new spells to try."

Oh, Jesus. Even my petite, sexy, charismatic mother was turning bloodthirsty around the edges. Must. Not. Hang. With. Vampires ... Or werewolves. They will warp anyone's sense of justice and morality to the core.

Then I thought of Mory ... and Sienna. And my anger didn't feel so unjustifiably bloodthirsty anymore.

Chapter Seventeen

I grabbed an extra-large hoodie from the back of Desmond's SUV — it was chilly so close to the open ocean — then we waited until the tourists had cleared out, and the owner/operators were distracted with ... well, an actual distraction orchestrated by Scarlett, who swore the fire wouldn't spread beyond the garbage can in the parking lot.

Not a subtle ploy, but I figured it was way more subtle than what the werewolf or vampire would come up with.

Speaking of vampires, Kett's cheeks were almost flesh-colored again, which meant that in the forty-five minutes we'd waited, he'd managed to snack on a few tourists. How he did it without anyone noticing, I didn't know. But I wasn't interested in getting a close-up demonstration. I just hoped the tourists were happily sleeping off the buzz that I gathered they got from the feeding. A couple of motorhomes were still in the parking lot.

The elevator took us two hundred feet down through the cliff. I worried that the five of us surpassed the maximum weight, but was assured by Desmond that I was just being silly. It was rather obvious, despite the flirting that we'd been indulging in — if that's what it even was — that he blamed me for everything going on and, specifically, Sienna. Just because he had every one of his pack members at his beck and freaking call, didn't mean I could control my sister's actions.

We stepped off the elevator into an educational center. Hardboard posters detailed the history of the caves and the lives of the sea creatures that called them home. A few more steps — past the preserved and displayed skeleton of a female sea lion that I didn't want to look at too closely — brought us to the observation deck overlooking a vaulted dome easily a hundred feet high. This massive cave looked as if it had been carved into the side of the cliff by the ever-pounding surf. Normally, according to the pamphlet, hundreds of Steller sea lions lounged around the rocks jutting up out of the surf, but this was off-season. A bunch of different birds — the seagulls were all I recognized — nested in the craggy walls and swooped in and out of the cave. The cavern walls were stained green, purple, and rust.

"Take a picture," Desmond said.

"Take a freaking pill, shifter," I snapped back.

Desmond stepped toward me, green rolling over his eyes, only to barrel straight into Scarlett as she sidestepped between us. Looking rather startled, he managed to catch her before completely knocking her down.

"Respectfully, alpha," Scarlett said, as she found her footing on the damp stone floor. "We asked, and Jade agreed to come to your city, because seeing Blackwell's collection was to the benefit of the Adept community as a whole."

Desmond grunted and stepped back from Scarlett. My mother, ever the diplomat. Seriously, the world was all out of whack.

I pulled the gold sphere out of my pocket and held it in my open palm. The magic within it glowed more intensely than before. I pivoted until I felt which way the sphere was urging me forward. I was now facing a set of sturdy wooden stairs that led further west and away from the main cavern. "There's another entrance?" I asked.

"That leads to a lookout point now, but in the sixties, they had stairs instead of an elevator," Kandy said. "There's a southwest entrance as well that fills at high tide, but you can only get to it by boat."

I raised an eyebrow at the green-haired werewolf.

"What?" she asked. "I read the brochure."

I took a step toward the stairs, only to have Desmond hold me back.

"You tell us where to go, dowser. We'll lead," he said.

"Fine. Upward."

Desmond and Kandy stepped in front of me. Kett brought up the rear behind Scarlett and me. I didn't know how my mother felt about being in a monster sandwich, but I was especially not a fan of having a vampire at my back.

We'd climbed about halfway up the stairs — which, despite a series of landings, did appear to dead-end at another lookout point — when the gold sphere tried to yank me over the railing and through the rock wall to my right.

"Wait!" I shouted. My voice reverberated back to me off the cave walls. Everyone froze around me. Kandy in mid-step.

The owner/operators of the Sea Lion Caves had strategically placed red mood lighting in various hollowed-out spots all along the passage that had been carved out for the stairwell. I stared at one of these concave hollows and attempted to see beyond the human-generated light. "Magic," I breathed. "More magic. Right there."

I stepped by Desmond, who was directly in front of me, to stand beside Kandy. The magic emanating off a witch, a vampire, and two shapeshifters had overwhelmed my senses. I hadn't felt this other magic until Kandy was almost past it.

If I angled my head just right, I could see a narrow path veering off ninety degrees from the stairwell, straight back into and through the cave wall. At the mouth of this passage, another small box sat on a rock that jutted out like a shelf. If she'd seen the passage before I did, Kandy could have easily brushed it with her shoulder.

"You can't see that?" I asked Kandy, pointing at the box.

"See what?" she growled.

A ripple like a heat mirage fluttered in the air around the box. "Spelled invisible," I said. I climbed over the stair railing onto the bare rock beyond. Kett was instantly at my side.

"Here?" the vampire asked.

"Can you see it?"

"Not quite."

"Do you see the tunnel beyond?"

"Yes, now. Standing here. Is that where the sphere prompts —"

"Can we pass or not?" Desmond interrupted Kett's interrogation, which was fine with me. The vampire could probably spend weeks analyzing the placement of the box alone, never setting one foot into the hidden passageway. Desmond's growl, a mixture of impatience and stress, completely reflected my own feelings. I'd just been taught to be more polite about it.

"Give me a second," I said. I looked around for a loose rock. There weren't any. "How is there not a single rock in a cave?"

"It's a tourist attraction," Kandy answered. "If the humans could take one of the sea lions home, they would. Did you hear about the guy getting killed by a beaver —"

"Kandy." Desmond's growl was now even more pronounced. "We don't need the dowser more distracted than she already is."

I narrowed my eyes at him, knowing that even in the low light, he'd see my glare. I mean, it wasn't like he was wrong or anything. It was just plain rude to point it out.

"Jade," Scarlett said. Her soft tone was instantly soothing. "How wide does the magical field extend around the object? That should give you a sense of its range without hitting it with a rock."

The rock idea was obviously too simple for the powerful quartet sulking through the cave by my side. Silly me.

I swallowed my pride and answered. "About two inches."

"Meant to be accidentally brushed against," Kett said.

"Or as a warning," Desmond said. "Placed obviously like that. He's met the dowser. So no one brush up against that rock shelf." He stepped by the box and through into the passageway. I wondered how many humans had accidentally wandered in here and were never heard from again ... since the passageway didn't appear in the brochure.

Kett was still staring at the box intently, but nothing happened as Desmond passed it by. Kandy helped Scarlett climb over the handrail, then stepped by Desmond to take up point again.

I followed, with Scarlett right behind me. She snapped her fingers and a blue glow the size of a tennis ball floated up from her hand to settle above her shoulder. The light was bright enough for us to see a couple of feet, but not so bright as to ruin the shapeshifters' night vision up ahead. The comforting taste of Scarlett's magic washed over me before ebbing to its normal levels. I'd always loved that light spell as a child, and coveted it as an adult. I couldn't cast without a power circle, and even then, my spells were more miss than hit.

Kett stayed behind long enough that I began to wonder if he'd tried to touch the box. Then I felt his magic as he closed in behind us. The noise of the crashing waves dimmed as we pushed further through the cliff side.

"Stop," I called two more times for two more magical boxes placed in our path. "He likes to contain spells in things. Boxes. This sphere. Is that a sorcerer thing?"

"Blackwell is a particularly powerful sorcerer," Scarlett answered.

The compulsion spell in the gold sphere ramped up in intensity. It really wanted me to walk through the rock wall to my left.

"Wait," I whispered, as I slowly pivoted in the cramped tunnel.

We were walking single file. Thankfully, none of us was over six feet, or headspace would have been a problem. I couldn't see him well in the low blue light, but shoulder space might already be a problem for McGrowly.

"It … it wants me to go through this wall." I stretched my arm out toward the wall to my left. The magic in the sphere pulsed in response. Scarlett flicked her fingers, and her light ball darted forward as if searching for an entrance up and down the craggy rock wall.

"Magic?" Kett asked.

I shook my head. No magic emanated from the wall. The gold sphere in the palm of my outstretched arm tugged me forward ... and ... to the side? My arm slid around the wall.

"A blind entrance," Desmond murmured from my other side.

Indeed, the cave wall cleverly disguised a perpendicular passage.

"No breeze," Kandy said as she squeezed by Desmond and me to take point once more. "But we must be traveling parallel to the coast again."

We continued forward. I followed Kandy, with Desmond right on my heels. The passage was too narrow for him to push past without manhandling me. Scarlett's light returned to float above her shoulder. Now that Kandy had mentioned the no-breeze thing, I tried to not think about the hundreds of feet of solid rock over my head, and the limited air supply.

The fourth trap sprung before I could even react to the glimmer of magic. Maybe Kandy had gotten too far ahead, or maybe Blackwell had gotten better at masking his spells. As she passed it, something shot out and grabbed the green-haired werewolf by the ankle, apparently yanking her through the wall.

"Kandy!" I shrieked, only to be face-planted against the opposite wall by a rough shove between my shoulder blades as Desmond pushed by me.

"Kandy!" he roared at the wall that had just absorbed the green-haired werewolf.

"I'm here." Kandy's voice was muffled but coming through the rock wall somehow. "Fuck, fuck. Sorry."

"Back away, Desmond," I said.

McGrowly begrudgingly stepped to the side. I peered at the wall. It was difficult to distinguish different magical signatures when surrounded by this many powerful Adepts. "Some sort of residual spell on the wall," I said. I could clearly see the outline of an opening, but not Kandy.

"Yeah," Kandy said. "It's another passage. I can smell sea air now though."

"Are you hurt?"

"No." Kandy sounded pretty pissed, as if she should be hurt in order to justify being grabbed by Blackwell's trap.

"I could maybe cut through the ... ward or whatever is blocking us from Kandy's passage."

"Does the sphere urge you in that direction, Jade?" Scarlett asked.

"No."

"Blackwell knows the dowser wouldn't come alone," Kett said.

"And that we wouldn't put her on point," Desmond added.

"Perhaps a miscalculation on our part."

"Kandy," Desmond called through the wall. "Back track if you can, and come through the tunnels again. Follow our scents and avoid the traps behind us."

"Yes, alpha."

"What?" I cried. "We aren't going to leave her!"

"She's leaving us, dowser," Desmond said. "Step ahead."

"You didn't even let me try to cut —"

"Kandy is a warrior. One who would gladly sacrifice herself to save a packmate who was less able. We find the fledglings, first and foremost."

"Yes," Scarlett agreed behind me. "If we had been more careful leaving Vancouver, the necromancer wouldn't be in danger."

Kett — of course and always — remained silent when others were expressing the opinion he would have expressed himself.

"Kandy?" I called, but there was no answer from behind the wall.

"She's already moving, dowser. She knows how to execute orders."

I shoved by Desmond, making sure to hit him in the gut with my elbow — twice — but he probably didn't even feel it. The magic of the gold sphere had begun to buzz underneath the skin of my palm, as if it was attempting to burrow into me. Its intensity lessened as I moved. I wondered whether if I held on long enough, the magic would manage to grab hold of me completely.

"Blackwell would have assumed the compulsion spell would work on me," I said.

"And you'd have no choice but to leave us behind at the mercy of the traps," Scarlett added.

The glow of Scarlett's light ball was almost completely blocked by Desmond's stupid shoulders, and our voices were startlingly loud in the dark. My mother and I were the only ones making any noise as we moved. Last time I'd been in the dark surrounded by monsters, that silence had freaked me out. Now I expected it. That said something profound about my life that I didn't want to investigate too deeply right now. Not without Mory safe and about ten ounces of single-origin Madagascar chocolate at hand.

"Three traps, and then the one that got Kandy. Five of us," I said, focusing on the immediate issue before me. Trying, for once in my life, to work out the puzzle before it jumped up and smacked me in the face.

"There will be more," Kett said. His voice sounded farther away than he actually was physically.

I stopped. Then slowly and methodically, I stretched my dowser senses forward and to the sides as far as I could. I had become accustomed to dampening my senses as much as possible when surrounded by this much magic, afraid it would overwhelm me. Now I tried to filter out Desmond, Kett, and Scarlett.

"Something up ahead ..." I said as I caught the glimmer of Blackwell's magic. The earthy red-wine notes of his magical signature were obvious, but the sorcerer always worked with some sort of magical object to set or store his spells. This intermingled and disguised his taste enough that it was taking me longer to separate it from the tastes of the witch, shifter, and vampire behind me.

The cave itself smelled of old salt water and dried seaweed. I assumed that it flooded occasionally but hadn't for some time. My shoes were going to be ruined, but I wasn't shallow enough to care ... or okay, I cared enough to notice. I wasn't anywhere near freaking perfect. I made cupcakes for a living, not pacemakers or brain surgery tools.

I was a baker, not a savior. A baker who was blatantly trying to distract herself from her present circumstances via meaningless internal banter ... yet again.

Some seconds/minutes/hours/days, it was difficult being me. But I wasn't sure I could do anything about that.

What I could do was keep moving forward.

So I did.

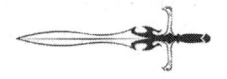

McGrowly smashed his fist through the fifth trap we found. It had been directly and completely blocking our path, and Desmond eventually got frustrated by Scarlett, Kett, and me poking at it.

The spell — similar to the one that grabbed Kandy — blew open and wrapped around Desmond's arm, yanking him to one side. I slashed at it with my knife, severing its connection to Desmond but not nullifying the spell completely. The residual on McGrowly — thwarted from its purpose — seared into his skin. He roared with pain while I tried to get my hands on him, trying to see if I could help by siphoning the magic back into the box or something.

Unfortunately, the second half of the spell — the part that was still functioning — grabbed Scarlett by the shoulder as it snapped back, yanking her off her feet. Kett grabbed her by the other arm, and for a moment, she hung suspended — half in and half out of the cave wall.

McGrowly boiled out of his human skin, changing to counteract the spell, but also managing to knock me farther away from being of any help to my mother.

Then Scarlett's arm — the one in Kett's grasp — snapped. She screamed, a howl of pain I would never want to hear from anyone, let alone my mother.

"Let the scion go, vampire!" McGrowly yelled. His words were mangled by his double cat fangs, but still understandable. Five-inch cat fangs.

I scrambled to my feet as Kett released Scarlett and she was completely pulled through the wall. "Mom! Mom!"

I pushed by the two monsters blocking my path, even though I shouldn't have been able to move them an inch.

"It's all right, my Jade." Even muffled by the spelled rock wall between us, Scarlett's voice was pained.

I started slashing at the magical barrier between Scarlett and me. She'd taken her ball of light with her, so I couldn't see much except for the glimmer of the ward blocking my way. That was enough.

"Sugar, it's all right," Scarlett said again.

I realized I'd been repeating, "Mom, Mom, Mom," over and over again.

"Same as Kandy on this side," Scarlett reported, her voice stronger than before. "I can feel a breeze. I must be near some sort of an exit."

"We have no idea how far we're above the ocean here," I cried. "Climbing the side of a cliff for Kandy is nothing —"

"Jade Godfrey," Scarlett snapped. "You will not underestimate your mother. I have stabilized my arm and numbed the pain. A few more healing spells, well-spaced, will heal the break."

I turned on Kett. His magic illuminated his pale skin, making him easy to identify in the dark. "You!" I hissed. "What were you thinking?"

"That the spell couldn't be that strong."

"Well, it was!"

"Yes."

Yes? What sort of answer was that? "You broke her arm!"

"You slashed an unknown spell with your knife."

"Desmond was caught in it. And it wasn't unknown."

"That's enough children," Desmond said, his voice warped through stretched vocal cords and fanged teeth. The magic in the tunnel shifted, flooding my taste buds with much-needed deep, dark chocolate as Desmond once again adopted his human skin. His human skin, which would be clothed only in tattered jeans and a stretched-out T-shirt now — but I couldn't see anything but magic in the dark. There were no silver linings to be had today.

"Scion," Desmond called through the barrier. "We will continue onward."

"Yes. Blackwell is obviously avoiding hurting us —"

"Too bad the vampire didn't get the memo," I muttered under my breath. Both Kett and Desmond with their super-hearing could still hear me, of course, but they ignored me.

"I'll backtrack if I can," Scarlett continued. "Perhaps find Kandy. Be careful, my Jade." My mother's voice receded as if she was walking away.

The compulsion spell in the gold sphere pulsed up my arm more painfully than before as I continued to ignore it. I turned on the white blob that was Kett. "You broke my mother's arm, vampire. I won't forget it." Yes, I was being completely irrational, but somehow — to me — this was utterly justifiable. He should know his own strength. He should have been able to judge the power of the spell before it snapped Scarlett's arm.

Kett nodded almost imperceptibly in the dark, but I felt his magic shift subtly.

"Keep moving," Desmond said. "The tunnel widens up ahead."

I moved. I didn't want to, but I did.

Chapter Eighteen

The tunnel literally spat us out onto a ten-foot-wide ledge that led nowhere except down. As in, a fifty-foot drop into another cavern. No seagulls in this one. Just two identical fifteen-foot-wide pentagrams side by side, and a portal.

A dozen or so impressive light spells hovered twenty feet above our heads. Blackwell and Sienna, as well as the gagged and bound Mory and Jeremy, stood in one of the pentagrams with what looked sickeningly like a rune-carved stone altar. The second pentagram was empty, but the magic along its edges was active.

The portal, on the cave wall behind the altar group, wasn't dormant like the one in the bakery basement. Not that it was open, or even obvious to anyone who couldn't feel magic. But it was wide awake and waiting to be of service.

The gold sphere went inert in my hand. I shoved it into the pocket of my hoodie, glad I'd thought to grab one. Extra pockets seemed to come in very handy these days. The hoodie was massive on me, of course, but comforting.

"Hello, sister," Sienna called. I couldn't feel a drop of magic from any of the four in the pentagram. That wasn't good.

"So pleased you could join us," Blackwell said. "Though I was hoping you'd have fewer companions. I gather I misjudged your magical sensitivity. Again. No matter."

Jeremy's eyes were glowing bright green, but he hadn't transformed. So I could see magic through the barrier that encased the pentagram, but not feel or taste it. I wasn't sure the young werewolf was even capable of a partial transformation like Desmond was. His clothing was rumpled and dirty, but from this vantage point, he looked unharmed. Mory clutched at her necklace, obviously utterly frightened but also unharmed. Their bindings looked like plain rope, but were probably spelled by the way they glistened.

"Geez, could you be more crazy-dramatic, Sienna?" I asked, finally finding my voice. An awful lot of déjà vu was pinging through my head. No silver chains or half-dead werewolf though ... yet. "You could have just called."

"I told you, my name is Valencia." Sienna snarled. And with no more warning than that, she hit Mory and Jeremy with her pain spell.

I couldn't feel or taste it, but I saw the spell hit. Mory shuddered but seemed to shake it off. Score one for Jade — the fledgling's necklace held against Sienna's magic. However, the fireblood spell hit Jeremy full force. Just like I had been, he was completely unable to scream or move, other than arching up on the balls of his feet with his fingers rigidly splayed.

Desmond lost it. He flung himself off the ledge as if it was a four-foot drop, not fifty. By the time he hit the floor, he was McGrowly once again. Though this incarnation of his beast-man seemed to lope on all fours rather than walk on two. He gouged claw marks in the stone of the cavern floor as if it was crusty frosting.

"No, Desmond," I screamed.

He didn't listen. He covered forty feet in two more bounding leaps. And hit the pentagram full force. Head, claws, and teeth first.

The pentagram wasn't sealed from without — not with Blackwell and Sienna standing in it, not with me unable to taste any magic. It was sealed within, like a witches' protection circle — probably in blood.

It was a testament to Desmond's strength and magical prowess that when he hit the edge of the pentagram, he actually cracked it. Probably with his stupid, meaty head.

Blackwell's eyes rolled up and he collapsed.

Sienna screamed and stumbled. She'd been reaching for Mory but the fledgling necromancer twisted away and kicked Sienna in the knee. She fell.

Mory scrambled for Jeremy. With Sienna distracted, the pain spell had broken. The necromancer tried unsuccessfully to cushion the young werewolf's crash to the ground.

The pentagram held.

Desmond bounced off the protection ward. Sparks of magic lit the fur on his chest and arms on fire.

I screamed again, desperately trying to find a foothold to climb down into the cavern.

Blackwell was groaning, slurring something like, "That was unnecessary." He attempted to pick himself off the ground where the spell backlash had dropped him.

Desmond hit the ground without even attempting to break his fall. His fur was singed and smoking, but he wasn't aflame.

Cool hands wrapped around my waist and knees, and Kett jumped off the ledge with me in his arms. Though he landed impossibly lightly, it was jarring for me. I bit my tongue where I'd been trying to speak. Or, more likely, scream. I also severely dented my back and knees on his steel arms. Gravity — or maybe that was momentum — was a bitch.

I scrambled out of Kett's arms and half-limped, half-ran to Desmond. Black-charred skin was already peeling off him in places, but he hadn't transformed. Nor was he conscious.

I looked up to meet Blackwell's gaze. He was standing but hunched over, with his hands on his knees. His skin was ashen from the effort of maintaining the magic of the pentagram. Sienna was also gaining her feet behind him. Her face was a web of black veins, her eyes just blown-out black pupils.

"Not a great idea," I said. "To piss off powerful people."

Sienna cackled a laugh. "Oh, yeah? Who's that, Jadey? You?"

"This was not our —" Blackwell said.

"Shut up, sorcerer," Sienna interrupted.

I ignored their squabble — hoping it kept them unfocused for a moment longer — and shifted my gaze to the teenagers huddled as far away from the insane adults as they could get in the pentagram. I remembered the last time I'd been faced with a pentagram, and the backlash after Desmond had broken through it. A backlash the teenagers might not be able to survive.

I straightened from McGrowly's prone form, pulled my knife, and flicked my eyes to Kett. "We can't break it or bulldoze through it. But can we counteract it? Like how you held the one in the basement at bay?" My voice was calm and steady. I flipped my knife in my hand. It was a flashy trick for Blackwell's benefit, because Blackwell liked bright shiny objects.

Kett slowly nodded. Then he rolled up the sleeve of his shirt while he walked the perimeter of the pentagram. Blackwell was whispering something to Sienna. She looked to be disagreeing — a lot — but the sorcerer's eyes didn't leave my knife. Good.

"It's cracked here," I said, pointing at the dent that McGrowly had made with his head.

"Dowser," Blackwell said. His voice was as smooth as whipped cream cheese. "A discussion is in order."

"No discussion, sorcerer," I replied. "Sienna should have mentioned I'm not all over this kidnap-my-friends thing. It didn't work out so well for her last time."

"It worked out just fine for me, Jade." Sienna stalked toward Mory and Jeremy. "I wound up here. In case you hadn't figured that out yet. I know everything is just so jumbled in that pretty little head of yours, like all of the time."

"Valencia," Blackwell said. "Perhaps we could —"

"I'm done asking nicely, Blackwell." Sienna grabbed Mory by her hair and hauled the fledgling necromancer backward. Mory hung on to Sienna's wrist as she fought to break away. Tears streamed down her face, but her protests were muffled by the gag.

"First the crack," Kett said as he slid out of the shadows and held his pale arm in front of me. "Which, conveniently for us and perhaps for the shifter, is placed above a point. Then, the four other points. Those are the weak spots."

"I agree," I answered. I could see the magic dancing all around the pentagram. It was thinned at each point — from McGrowly's assault, I guessed.

"Dowser," Blackwell said. "We only wish you to open the portal as you did before."

"The sorcerer is obsessed with the portal, Jadey," Sienna said. Mory twisted and kicked but couldn't get free from my sister's grip. "But he doesn't fully commit to the game. Do you, Blackwell?" Sienna hauled Mory back over the stone altar. The fledgling necromancer's feet scrambled for purchase as my sister bent her backward. "Ah, Jade. Rusty's much more powerful sister. You always bring me the best gifts."

"That's enough," Blackwell said. "We were to negotiate —"

"You're short sighted, sorcerer," Sienna laughed. "You see, Jade? I have a knife too." She pulled out a wicked-looking, jewel-encrusted weapon from her belt. Its blade was two inches wide at the pommel and curved upward into a point. "Blackwell set the spells and provided the knife — one of his collectables. But I'm going to reap the rewards."

Sienna slashed her blade toward Mory's neck as I slid my knife across Kett's forearm. The wound I carved through the vampire's skin closed almost as quickly as I cut.

Sienna's knife hit the protection spell generated by Mory's necklace and glanced off with a spark of magic.

In the same motion as my slash, I flicked the knife toward the crack that McGrowly had created. Droplets of Kett's blood hit and then clung to the pentagram ward.

Sienna screamed in frustration, trying to slash Mory's throat a second time.

Kett and I stepped sideways to the next pentagram point and I repeated the cut-and-blood-fling. This was damn close to blood magic, but as I watched Sienna's knife arc toward Mory a third time, I kept moving and splattering. I wasn't sure how many strikes the necklace could hold against.

Magic rolled in a wave around the sides of the pentagram. Dark chocolate mixed with the cool peppermint of the vampire's blood splatter, as McGrowly transformed into his human form and the alpha staggered to his feet.

Sienna flung Mory to the ground and turned toward Jeremy. Blackwell blocked her passage.

I flung Kett's blood at the fourth point. Right at eye level. The vampire's magic was splattered almost all the way around the pentagram ward now.

"Sienna — " Blackwell said.

"Valencia!" Sienna snarled. Then she hit the sorcerer with her fireblood spell. He staggered, obviously wearing a personal ward of some kind, but it wasn't strong enough to negate the spell altogether.

Sienna shoved Blackwell to the ground and stepped around to grab Jeremy.

I flung Kett's blood on the fifth point and closed the circle by returning to the crack in the ward McGrowly had made.

The fledgling werewolf, still gagged and bound, fought hard. Mory threw herself against Sienna's legs, but with all her stolen power, the black witch was just too strong.

As I thrust my knife through the crack in the pentagram ward, crumpling the protection spell all along Kett's splattered blood, my sister slit the werewolf's throat ear to ear on the stone altar.

Desmond howled as he crashed through the remainder of the protective ward, only to be hit by a blood-fueled pain spell from Sienna. Beside me, Kett also crumpled underneath Sienna's magic. But not me. I didn't fall.

Jeremy's blood gushed across the rune-carved altar while I faced off against my best friend and sister. I gritted my teeth against the power behind the fireblood spell while Desmond, Kett, and Blackwell writhed at my feet.

"Déjà vu, sister," I said, attempting to not simply lose it over the young werewolf bleeding out two feet from me as I pushed inch by inch against Sienna's spell.

"Not quite, Jade." Sienna smiled. I really, really hated it when people smiled when they meant to kill you, drain your blood, and bind your power to their own.

Yeah, I'd figured that part out. She wouldn't need to drag me around to open portals if she could open them herself.

I twirled my knife as if I was loosening my wrist, but I was probably just delaying the inevitable. Then I stepped forward against Sienna's blood-powered spell to strike my sister down.

Except that Jeremy's blood wasn't just fueling the pain spell. Because in the pentagram beside me, dark putrid magic vomited up from the bowels of hell — if there was an actual hell — and spewed forth a freaking demon.

Yes, a demon. Black horns, beady eyes, dark-scaled flesh and all. Demon.

"It is I, Valencia, who commands you, hound of hell. Heed me and you shall be rewarded in the most powerful of blood." Sienna screamed and thrust her knife in my direction. "Bring the blond to me!"

Oh, fuck.

A shitload of shit happened all at once. I gather that's usually the case when dealing with abnormally strong and fast Adepts, it makes for a confused and disjointed understanding of events.

Except I knew every step I took, because they were all toward my sister — until Mory screamed. Because killing Sienna, if I was capable, was the only way to vanquish the demon. Yeah, I'd been studying, so what?

Back up a second.

Sienna had effectively freed the demon from the pentagram designed by Blackwell to call it up and contain it. Containment being the important part of the sorcerer's plan. I guessed that the demon was supposed to be a final bargaining chip. Sienna, by commanding it to bring me to her, released it from the pentagram.

Yeah, bad idea.

She was probably banking on her ability to control the creature because she wielded the knife that made the sacrifice. Either that or she was too crazy to care. It was a stupid move, because technically Blackwell laid the spells and owned the knife. Of course, the demon didn't squabble about who could or couldn't command it. It was unleashed. It simply lowered its blood-red eyes and inspected its prey.

Sienna's pain spell faltered as she commanded the demon. It was too much magic for her to control all at once. Desmond sprang to his feet and leaped the gap between himself and the altar. He batted Sienna out of the way — my sister went flying — and hauled Jeremy off. But no matter the power of an alpha, the teenaged werewolf was dead. There wouldn't be a demon standing fifteen feet away if he were alive.

The demon lifted one clawed foot the size of a smart car and brought it down outside the pentagram. Yeah, there were spatial abnormalities going on, but I only had the time to figure out that I didn't have the time to pee my pants.

Blackwell and Kett rolled to their feet at the same time. Blackwell took one look at the demon's foot outside the confines of its pentagram and then turned back toward me. I shook my head, warning him off the idea of abandoning us in the middle of his shit. He ignored me, clutched the amulet he was now clearly wearing around his neck, and disappeared in a wash of magic.

Freaking asshole.

Kett danced around the demon. It tracked him for a short while, then let out a puff of smoke from its nostrils. Or was that its mouth? Its flat face made it difficult to tell. Either way, it ignored the vampire.

I lunged for Sienna, who was attempting to gain her feet where Desmond had thrown her. She was having trouble putting weight on one leg, but unfortunately was still holding the knife. I was within striking distance, my own knife ready even if my heart was still unsure, when Mory screamed.

I pivoted. The demon's mouth, all toothy and gruesome, was unmistakable now as it loomed over Mory lying on the ground. The fledgling had managed to pull the gag out of her mouth and was frantically working on the bonds at her ankles. She twisted away from the demon, but it pinned her with one claw by the back of her shirt. The cloth was tearing, but not quickly enough.

Two steps and I'd be there. With no idea how to deal with the demon. But I could place myself between it and Mory.

I took one step.

Kett was suddenly on the demon's shoulders, or neck, I couldn't really distinguish the two. With his feet rooted, he yanked on one of the large horns protruding from the demon's forehead. It had four. The vampire, who'd so casually broken my mother's arm earlier, was risking his immortal life for the fledgling. He barely managed to twist the demon's head, but it was enough.

I reached Mory and tried to yank her away as the demon raised its clawed foot to squash us both. Except its downward stamp landed on Desmond.

The shifter, who had leaped in to stand over Mory and me on the ground, took the blow with a grunt and a deep bend at the knees, but he didn't collapse. His shredded clothing was covered in Jeremy's blood. He locked eyes with me, had the audacity to grin, and then transformed into McGrowly.

Mory screamed again. Yeah, seeing a monster boiling out of human skin was pretty scary, but McGrowly was way prettier than the freaking demon.

McGrowly grabbed the demon's foot, lifted, and twisted. I rolled away with Mory clutched to me.

The demon simply closed its claws around McGrowly, picking him up off the ground. It obviously didn't need four feet to stand. It tried to bite the shifter in half while Kett continued to grapple with its horn. This impeded it from getting teeth on McGrowly just momentarily enough to save Desmond's life.

I hauled Mory to her feet — but then had to let go of the teenager to block the knife Sienna had thrust toward the necromancer.

I punched Sienna in the gut while holding her blade at bay with my other hand. She dropped the weapon and grappled with me. She was way stronger than she should have been. More stolen power. I couldn't reach my own knife, which I must have sheathed in my mad scramble for Mory, though I didn't remember doing so.

"Grab the knife, Mory!" I yelled as Sienna got her foot behind my knee. She unbalanced me enough that all I could do was hang on to her.

The demon roared — the first sound I'd actually heard from it. McGrowly had punched it in the eye. Its voice made my own eyes water, but then a glance back at Sienna informed me that my tears were probably filled with blood, because that was what was streaming down my sister's face. The demon's voice was affecting Sienna as much as it did me. Without the knife, she didn't have any more protection than the rest of us.

I rolled away from Sienna and gained my feet. Out of the corner of my eye, I saw the demon finally claw Kett off its shoulder and fling the vampire fifty feet against the far cave wall.

Sienna flung her pain spell at Mory, who'd been running away with the sacrificial knife. The spell hit the fledgling necromancer hard enough that she fell, but she didn't drop the blade.

A bright flash of blue light hit the demon and it roared in pain. I looked up, struggling to see through what felt like the bleeding of my brain, to see my mother and Kandy on the ledge.

Scarlett sagged under the stress of the strength of whatever spell she'd thrown. She fell to her knees with her hands still outstretched. Kandy started climbing down the wall, easily finding the handholds I'd been blind to.

"Take the knife to my mother, Mory!" I screamed. Mory scrambled to her feet and ran. Sienna lunged after her. I got a finger-hold on her — when I should have just stabbed her in the back — and her stupid cloak tore.

Then she staggered back, shrieking, her hands coming up to her face. Small cuts appeared around her eyes and across her cheekbones.

"Hello, Rusty," I said. Sienna shrieked and screamed, in frustration more than pain.

I raised my knife, knowing that Sienna wouldn't stop any other way. My sister, reeling from the attack of her ghost ex-boyfriend, spun toward me. The blackness of her soul had spread through her veins, all across her face and arms. It was obvious to anyone who laid eyes on her.

Even me.

I aimed for her heart. It might be black, but it still had to pump blood.

My sister locked eyes with me. Her mouth formed a small O.

She had no defense against me. She'd killed Jeremy and Hudson and Rusty and others I didn't know. She'd tortured Desmond, Kett, Kandy, Mory, and me.

I was going to have to kill her to stop her.

Then the demon took me out at the knees.

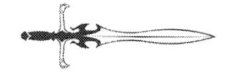

When I came to, Desmond was half dead. Kett, whose eyes were as blood red as the demon's, didn't look much better.

I was lying over the demon's spiked tail. My lungs and organs were definitely punctured in multiple places. They had to be. Not that I could see spikes sticking through me or anything, but it was damn difficult to move. Or breathe.

The demon had twisted around to track Mory and the sacrificial knife, managing to skewer me on its tail. Nice. It was currently clawing at the protective circle Scarlett had managed to erect around herself and Mory on the edge of the ledge. I couldn't see Kandy, but I gathered she'd piggybacked the fledgling necromancer up the cliff wall to get her to safety, and to get the knife to my mother.

Which was great, except that even from my very low vantage point, I could see my mother slumped in the circle she'd raised. Her magic was ebbing with every clawed hit the demon unleashed. The knife, still slick with Jeremy's blood, was clutched in Mory's hands. Mory ... who was a necromancer, not a witch, and therefore had no idea how to command or banish a demon with the magical object she held.

We were totally losing. Badly. If the demon got the knife, no mortal could ever command it, ever. Never again. The humans of the west coast of Oregon, and then the state, and then the entire country were about to be in for a major shock. Most of them would think the devil had risen to walk the earth, and they wouldn't be half wrong.

I lifted myself off the bony spikes of the demon's tail. I tried to not think about the bits of lung and liver and kidney I left behind. Also, I didn't bother wondering why I was still alive, because it was fairly obvious that it wasn't going to last.

I stumbled a couple of steps and fell, noting that Desmond and Kett were both prone by the wall that contained the portal.

The demon clawed at my mother's protective circle again. Scarlett's magic dimmed further.

"Hey, asshole," I gurgled around the blood that poured out of my mouth. "I've got a pretty knife all covered in blood too." I dragged myself to my feet. The demon didn't even spare me a glance. It raised a clawed hand and hit Scarlett's ward again. The magic cracked. Another blow and it would be gone, and my mother dead along with it. Then Mory.

"Wait a second," I said, looking down at my knife. "I was wrong about the blood part. Let me fix that."

Then I cut off the demon's tail.

Well, I got a quarter of it at least.

The demon roared — God, I hated that sound — and turned to backhand me across the cavern. It hurt like my heart might have exploded in my chest, but it conveniently placed me right next to Desmond and Kett. Also, I still had my knife.

Unfortunately, as the demon whirled to face us, none of us were on our feet. I could clearly see Sienna climbing the wall behind the demon. She was about twenty feet below Scarlett and Mory.

Shit.

The demon raised itself on its haunches. In this position, its head scraped the cavern ceiling.

Yeah, scary. Except it got confused, and then distracted, by the magical light spells hanging all around its head.

I laughed. Yeah, insane. But why not? I was certain I was dying, because the pain of my punctured back, lungs, and organs was easing as a warmth spread through me.

Who knew death would be so warm?

The wounds on my back healed. The warmth was spreading through me from the cavern wall.

"The portal," I said. As if it had been waiting for me to acknowledge it, the portal opened behind me in a flood of golden light.

The demon shrieked. The walls of the cavern shook with its pain, but the sound was nothing to me now.

Buoyed by the golden magic, I stood. Desmond and Kett, both still severely wounded, struggled to stand beside me. Even though it meant sheathing my knife, I assisted them.

I had the beginning of a thought ... one I knew better than to think all the way through.

I laced my fingers through Kett's and Desmond's.

"Hey asshole. How's the tail?" I yelled as I took a step back. "Bet it hurts. Like this hurts. Why don't you try to stop me?"

The demon hated the golden magic of the portal, but right now, I was betting it hated me and the missing chunk of its tail more.

I had no idea how the portal worked, but I was guessing it didn't just lead back to the bakery basement in Vancouver — unless I wanted it to — because it was active. Active enough that it had drawn Blackwell's attention. The sorcerer could feel its magic but not open it. I was also guessing, given the presence of the stone altar, that Blackwell had tried many spells here to no avail. At least not until Sienna had come through.

Had Blackwell actually been in the cavern that night when Sienna had come through the portal, guided by my own hand? Or had Sienna simply happened upon the sorcerer in Portland, and seeing him as a powerful ally, told him her story?

The demon snagged me with its claws around my rib cage before I could take a second step back. I couldn't fight it and still hold on to Desmond and Kett. I somehow managed another step. I was crazy strong in the golden light. Impossibly strong. I took a third step.

I had to hope that Kandy was okay enough to get Mory to safety. I had to hope that Scarlett could protect them both from Sienna if I could take the demon out of the game.

"In my pocket," I cried to Desmond on my left as I continued to pull them all back into the portal. The demon hissed and shrieked as the golden magic reached out through me, wrapping itself around the creature's head and shoulders.

Desmond dug into the pocket of my jeans, after checking the hoody pocket and coming up with zilch. He came out with a handful of the jade stones imbued with the skinwalker magic. Their binding magic, to be specific.

I pulled the demon back another step. I could feel blood streaming where its claws were puncturing my ribs and back, but no pain.

Somewhere safe ... take us somewhere safe ... somewhere that can contain the demon ... I chanted it in my head, hoping the portal could hear my thoughts.

I took another step back. Beside me, Kett fell to his knees. He wasn't having a good time in the golden light. I worried I might actually be killing him rather than saving his life.

A flurry of movement behind the demon on the cliff edge drew my attention. Sienna was somehow holding Scarlett and Kandy at bay with her fireblood spell while wrestling Mory for the knife. Damn it.

The demon loosened its claws. I could feel them retracting.

"Now!" I cried. "Throw, now!"

Desmond used the last of his strength to throw the jade stones into the demon's shrieking mouth. Then he also fell beside me.

"Eat that, asshole!" I screamed.

The demon stopped shrieking and fell forward onto me. I had hoped that the lining of its throat wasn't as invulnerable to magic as its hide.

Sienna screamed in frustration. Then, grabbing Mory and the knife, she turned and yanked the fledgling necromancer with her through the cavern wall. Kandy leaped after them, but hit solid rock. Another hidden passageway, probably keyed to Sienna and Blackwell.

With my legs being crushed by the demon and the rest of me floating in magic, I couldn't do anything but wrap my arms around Desmond and Kett and try to visualize the power of the portal pulling us through. I had to get the demon away from Sienna now that she had the knife.

"Take me somewhere safe," I said.

Then I was lost in the sea of golden magic.

Chapter Nineteen

I woke with my cheek pressed against a pure white marble floor and a demon's chin resting across my legs.

Blinking, I tried to lift my head, but I couldn't see anything, except gold, gold, gold. Then, a few blinks later, this resolved itself into golden pillars, golden-carved reliefs, and gold-crusted inlays in carved sandstone walls. Everything was very Asian ... yet not.

I groaned and tried to move my legs. They worked, but the knocked-out demon was crazy heavy. It huffed a spurt of smoke at me when I kicked it in the snout. So not out — just bound from within. Its bloody eyes tracked my movement as I stumbled to my feet.

I was in the middle of an empty round room, its finishings bordering on gaudy with a dose of Greek temple.

Nine doors, each decorated with a different theme I didn't have time to decrypt, led from the circular room, as well as two open archways. Eleven exits. That was good.

The demon lay halfway through one of the doors. The magic of the portal swallowed its body from the shoulders down.

Desmond was trapped under one of the demon's forearms. I freed him, dragging him as far away as possible, but I was too uncertain of where I was and what was going on to just toss him through one of the doors or archways. I wasn't completely sure he was alive, either. But I ignored that part.

I couldn't see Kett. Not until the demon pushed back with one of his smart car-sized clawed feet and shook its head to scream at me with utter rage. Kett had been crushed underneath its chest. I was glad to note that my brain no longer bled from the demon's roar.

It was obviously still fighting off the skinwalker binding magic, because it had a difficult time following me as I tried to dart underneath its legs and chest to grab Kett. I missed the vampire but also managed to avoid being chomped in half as I spun away and pulled my knife out.

At the edge of my peripheral vision, I saw Kett roll away until he lay crumpled by one of the gold pillars. The demon didn't appear to care. But it was pretty pissed when I hacked off one of its toes ... well, claws. It shrieked again and raised its foot to obliterate me.

Someone bellowed, his booming voice cracking mid-note, behind me. I pivoted away from the demon foot crashing down over me, glancing back.

A boy, maybe twelve years old or so, was charging through one of the archways. He was armed with a broadsword that had to be almost as long as he was tall and wider than his arm. Not a child's sword. It looked like actual gold, which had to be heavy as hell.

Wait a second — child's sword? Who gave children swords?

"No!" I screamed, trying to block the dark-haired, insane prepubescent from getting himself killed. But the boy neatly slipped around me, jumped on the demon's foot as it connected to the ground at my back, then sprung off the foot onto the demon's opposite knee.

With another bellow, the boy then launched off the demon's knee and attempted to lop its head off. He managed to hack away a horn, which seriously pissed the demon off. But since his sword was only half as long as the diameter of the demon's neck, I suspected that the boy had been aiming high.

The dark-haired boy hadn't really planned out his landing when he leaped. And unfortunately, the demon was shaking off the binding magic a lot quicker than I had hoped. The boy tumbled to the ground at the demon's feet and was caught in a head-crunching, spine-breaking side swat.

The boy flew across the room, hitting a golden pillar on the far side with a sickening thud. The pillar trembled, which was the first hint of damage I'd actually seen the room take.

The boy dropped straight to the marble floor and didn't move.

I saw red. I flung myself at the demon, whose attention was still on the boy. I executed the same series of moves he had, avoiding the demon's massive maw as it followed my diagonal course. But instead of trying to lop anything off, I thrust my knife through the demon's left eye. Right up to my elbow.

The demon shuddered underneath me — I was perched on its scaled shoulder. Black blood boiled up from the wounded eye, literally burning the skin off my arm. Still, wrapping my free hand around its nearest horn as a counterpoint, I shoved my knife in deeper and deeper. I twirled my wrist in an attempt to scramble its brain, but I was almost blacking out from the intense pain.

The demon finally fell forward. And I fell with it.

One of the doors opened behind me, hitting me with a flood of magic. I wrenched my arm and knife from the demon's eye, half-fell/half-rolled to my side, pivoted, and managed to make it to my knees.

A big blond man stepped through the door. His power — the magic akin to that of the portal — hit me like a sledgehammer to the heart. Which was a good thing because it felt like it had stopped beating.

Oddly, if I'd had a moment to think about it, I would have noticed that his magic tasted of spicy chocolate. But not jalapeño spicy. Spicy like ... like ... Chinese food.

I swung my knife forward to defend myself. I could see the bones of my right arm. My mind screamed with alarm at this reveal, even as my body followed through to protect myself from this newest threat.

Time sped up so quickly — he was that fast — that my mind seemed to slow it for comprehension purposes.

The golden tanned god-of-a-man pulled a broad-bladed gold sword out of thin air — reminiscent of the boy's weapon, but impossibly larger, its pommel encrusted with jewels and pearls. Yes, just out of the air. Not magically sheathed, just out of the air. The absolute power of the sword, an intensely contained replication of the man's magic, made my eyes water. At least I hoped it was water, because in a completely different way than when the demon shrieked, it felt like my brain was bleeding ... or maybe dissolving was the better descriptor.

The blond god was looming over me before I even managed to gain my feet, so I reached up to parry his overhand blow while still on one knee.

Our weapons connected.

My knife shattered.

Somehow, the boy from before — who I thought was dead — was now hanging off the golden god's shoulder and screaming in a language I didn't understand.

Shattered pieces of jade showered down and scattered before me.

My momentum carried me off my one leg and knee. I fell forward to all fours. "Bastard," I said. "You broke my knife."

I looked up through my bloody, dirty curls at the god with his golden-tanned skin that crinkled around his light brown eyes. The boy was standing, quiet now, beside the man. His eyes were on the demon behind me.

"I'm surprised I didn't shatter your arm, witch," the golden god said. His accent was too heavy to be South African, or even New Zealand. "Impressive knife, but certainly you know better than to raise it against a dragon."

Dragon. My mind skipped a couple of million neurons ... though that might have been from the pain in my arm. Dragon.

"Myth," I said.

The blond god — no, dragon — tilted back his head and laughed like someone who loved to laugh, often and fully.

Then the other doors started opening — eight more to be exact — and more magic flooded the room.

Brain-scrambling magic. Blood-vessel-bursting magic that rolled over and under and around me. I clutched at my necklace and prayed for its protection. It flared underneath my fingers as if desperately trying to combat the tide of earth-shattering power.

Voices swirled all around me. Many different languages, most of which I couldn't even identify, let alone understand. I couldn't see Kett or Desmond. I didn't know if they were alive or not. I had no idea if we were all in the process of dying, being killed, or ... maybe ... being reborn.

"What is happening to the witch?" I heard the boy cry.

"Drake!" a woman said. Her French accent was melodic and commanding. "Avec moi!"

"Steady, fire breather," the golden-haired dragon said. "The boy says the witch took down the demon."

"Impossible," the French woman answered, changing to English.

"She's dying." A young man hunched down in front of me. His skin was a light caramel color, his English accented with Spanish or Latin tones. "Too sensitive."

"Not dead yet …" I said.

The man — perhaps he was Brazilian — laughed quietly, his voice soft and musical. Then there was more music as he reached out to touch my cheek, but I wasn't sure if he was singing or if it was a manifestation of his power. I was too overwhelmed to understand the difference.

The room stopped swirling and twirling around me. My hand fell forward as I slumped to catch my fall, unaware that I'd been partially held upright by the power of all the magic before. A long shard of my jade knife cut into my palm, the skin of which was attempting to heal from the demon's blood. I could still see the bone and inner tissues of my arm.

I rotated my hand to look at the piece of jade in my palm.

The conversation continued around me, but I caught only the bits in English.

"Who opened the portal?" an older man with a British lilt asked.

"None of us would invite a demon through," another woman answered. Her English was unaccented, at least to me.

"Actually, this looks exactly like your sort of prank, Haoxin. And you put Drake in danger," the French woman accused.

"Really, Suanmi, you think I would — "

"The witch saved me," the boy — Drake — interrupted.

"Shush!" Suanmi said. "A witch could do no such thing."

"Perhaps you should look closer," another man said, his accent declaring his Asian heritage.

The argument ceased instantly.

I stared at the shard of jade in my palm, mourning the loss of my knife. It was coated in my blood. Under the circumstances — the fact I was obviously dying here — it was a silly thing to mourn. But I'd found the large stone in the river. I'd dragged it home and hand carved the knife from it. All in all, with the spells and the learning to wield it, it represented two years of my life. Out of twenty-three. That was almost 10 percent.

Without really thinking about it, I pushed my senses beyond the barrier the necklace was trying to maintain, and beyond the dragon magic currently frying my mind. I sought out the magic of the knife and I called it to me.

Every shard of jade responded by sliding back across the marble floor and connecting with the piece before it. The knife resolved itself in my hand, as whole as if it was newly hewn.

Someone whistled.

"Impressive," the guy with the British lilt said.

"For a witch," Suanmi said.

I looked up. The Brazilian was before me again, or maybe he'd never left. The music was still playing. He reached for me, brushing his fingers on my cheek and pulling them away bloody. I had been leaking blood, maybe even from my pores.

"Alchemist," the British-lilt guy was saying. He sounded excited.

The Brazilian tasted my blood. I frowned and shook my head at him.

He grinned at me. He was breathtakingly beautiful. Too pretty for a man actually but some women like that. Pinning my knife hand to the ground, he wove his fingers around the back of my head and pulled me into a kiss.

Protest rose behind him, all the other languages in play again.

Healing magic rushed across my jaw, down my spine, and through my limbs.

The Brazilian released the back of my head and pulled away.

"That's some kiss," I said.

The Brazilian laughed, stood, and crossed out of my sight. I felt suddenly like I might be able to stand, but thought that it was probably better to stay where I was.

"You never kiss me like that," the man — no, the dragon — with the British lilt complained.

The golden-haired dragon bellowed with laughter.

"Qiuniu, there was no point in healing the witch —" the French woman began.

"Alchemist, Suanmi —"

"Seeing as all the interlopers must be dealt with —"

"We don't go around killing innocents," another woman interrupted. She couldn't have looked more like Cleopatra if she'd tried. It had to be deliberate.

"No one enters the dragon nexus and survives," Suanmi answered.

I stood and got my first solid look at the nine beings arrayed before me.

"It is an unprecedented event," the dragon with the British lilt said. Oddly, big as a bear, he was swathed in a mink fur coat.

"It is your job to oversee the portals, Pulou," Suanmi answered. "I hold you responsible for a witch gaining access. This never would have happened with your predecessor."

"Alchemist," Pulou corrected. "And, you're barely old enough to remember my mentor. So don't —"

"Not solely," Qiuniu, the Brazilian, said.

"What?" Suanmi snapped.

"She is not solely a witch," Qiuniu answered, completely unruffled by Suanmi's obvious loathing of me.

Nine powerful beings were a lot to take in. Some were dressed in African or Asian attire, seeming to indicate a country or climate of origin. Still others were dressed in modern, nontraditional clothing. The golden-tanned dragon sported shorts and a surfing T-shirt that were completely incongruent with the sword in his hand. The American, who was almost as petite and curvy as my mother, wore a silk peasant dress and sandals.

The dragons — all of which were currently staring at me — were arrayed on either side of an ancient-looking Asian dragon. He smiled at me when I met his eyes. Suanmi stood to his left and the golden-haired dragon to his right. Though a few of the dragons hadn't spoken a word — at least in English that I could understand — they all teemed with the same intense power. I seemed inoculated somehow — perhaps by the healing — from their overwhelming magic.

"Whether she is a witch or an alchemist makes no difference," Suanmi said. "She brought that with her, and they all must be taken care of."

"Not this one," the Cleopatra look-alike said. Desmond was prone at her feet. "He is one of mine." She leaned down and brushed her fingers through the fur of Desmond chest.

He reacted instantly, his body transforming into the huge mountain lion. He rose up on his massive paws and screamed.

"There, there," Cleopatra said. "It's all right, kitty. I'll see you home." The mountain lion blinked up at the Egyptian woman and then sunk down at her feet. She patted his head.

"Fine, Bixi," Suanmi said. "He obviously answers to you."

Drake peered around Suanmi and grinned at me. I had no idea why I was just standing there while the dragons discussed our fates, but I really couldn't think of anything to say.

"And the vampire?" Suanmi asked. I wouldn't have thought that anyone who looked as regal, refined, and expensive as she did would be capable of sneering so venomously. "Who will stand up for the vampire?"

No one spoke.

"So it shall be."

The golden-haired dragon shrugged his shoulders and turned toward Kett. Red-eyed and fanged, he was huddled against the pillar where he'd rolled. He was shaking, but he didn't appear to be wounded. His body healed but depleted his magic as it did, hence his obvious need for blood.

"No," I cried. "I do. I stand up for the vampire, for Kett."

"Nonsense," Suanmi said. "Even if your magic had any power here, you have no right to claim the vampire as your own. You're a witch."

"Not solely," Qiuniu said for the third time. Suanmi turned to glare at him.

The golden-tanned dragon twirled his sword, waiting to lop off Kett's head.

"I do ..." I said, stumbling over my words. "I saw ... he could have run. He could have easily gotten away from the demon, but he saved a girl's life."

Suanmi curled her lip. The golden-haired dragon stepped toward Kett and raised his sword.

"Wait, wait," I cried. "I've saved his life twice now —"

"His life?" A pale blond man with a Norwegian accent snorted.

Suanmi's lip quirked, but she restrained herself — with obvious effort — from undignified snickering.

"He owes me a life debt," I declared. My voice rang through the round room. Desmond screamed his mountain lion call, but I didn't look at him. I locked my gaze with Kett, who closed his eyes as if pained and then nodded his head once. I felt the magic shift between us — tying Kett to me, just lightly.

"And so it shall be," the ancient Asian dragon said. He looked nothing like Buddha, but I gathered from his smile that they shared a philosophy.

"Imbecile," Suanmi said. "Vampires are not pets."

"He is my friend, my mentor," I said.

Suanmi laughed. "Even worse." She nodded her head toward me but her gaze was on the sword-wielding dragon. He spun toward me and my heart skipped a beat.

They were going to kill me anyway —

I felt a blast of hot breath on my back and spun away as the demon raised its head behind me.

Double shit.

The dragon brought his sword down. No fancy moves or jumps needed. He cut off the demon's head.

Severed from its body, the head twisted through the air as it disintegrated into ash and dust. Then the body collapsed similarly.

The ash was sucked back through the portal, which then snapped closed as if it had never been opened or disturbed. On this side, the portal looked like a North American native-carved wooden door.

I just stared in shock at the pristine marble floor.

"Not of our world," the golden-haired dragon said. Then he sauntered back to rejoin the other dragons.

Not of our world ... that explained the demon crumbling to ash, but not why Kett's magic did the exact same thing when removed from his body. Vampires turned to ash as well. I'd seen it three months ago. I turned to stare at Kett. He still had his eyes shut. His face was a map of pain and suffering.

"Sorry to see one of your brethren go?" the Norwegian taunted.

Kett opened his eyes and looked at me.

"Vampires are descended from demons?" I asked. My voice was barely a whisper.

"Created from them. Thousands of years ago. By God, if you believe in such things," Kett answered.

"Now, who will stand up for the witch who can open portals?" Suanmi asked.

I was going to have to deal with the Kett/demon/created-by-God thing later.

"Witches cannot open portals," Pulou said. How he wasn't sweating buckets in that mink coat, I didn't know.

"Well, obviously, your wards have been compromised, treasure-keeper. Perhaps you should question the witch."

"She is not solely a witch." Qiuniu, now grinning like a madman with an explosive secret, said it again.

"Alchemist, then!" Suanmi snapped. "But only dragons should be able to open and travel through portals —"

"Exactly," Qiuniu said.

Silence fell among the dragon group. One by one, they all turned to stare at me. I'd never been so scrutinized in my life. I shifted on my feet. My shoes were ruined. My hair had to be an utter blood-crusted mess. I couldn't remember the last time I'd freshened my lip gloss.

"Impossible," Suanmi said.

"Look again," the ancient Asian dragon coaxed.

Then one by one, they all turned and looked at the golden-haired, golden-tanned dragon with the sword. He continued to stare at me. His face was deadly serious, an expression that didn't suit him at all.

"An abomination," Suanmi said.

The golden-tanned dragon threw back his head and laughed. And laughed.

"Intolerable!" the Norwegian shouted.

"Warrior!" Suanmi snapped.

The golden-haired dragon stopped laughing, though he was now wiping tears from his face. "What is your name, fledgling?" he asked me.

"Jade. Jade Godfrey," I said, feeling a little faint around the edges.

"I'm Yazi," he said. "The warrior of the Guardians."

"The guardians of what?" I asked, not quite believing that was my first question.

"Of the world and all the magic within it, little one," the ancient Asian dragon answered. "I've been waiting to meet you. Impossibilities are supremely interesting."

"A little warning would have been nice, Chi Wen," Yazi said.

The Asian dragon shrugged, though his grin stayed firmly in place. "I see far, warrior. How was I to know that today was that day?"

"Well, the Kalkadoon's have a wicked sense of humor," Yazi murmured, his eyes on me.

"A fertility ceremony!" Suanmi cried. "You're a dragon. You didn't need to answer their summons!"

Yazi laughed. "You didn't see her mother dressed in nothing but the firelight, the moon, and the magic."

Pulou snorted.

"Wait," Drake said. "Half-witch, half-dragon?"

I was really glad I wasn't the only slow one in the room.

"So it seems," Suanmi answered. She tugged the preteen through one of the archways and out of the room.

The other dragons broke rank at the same time but didn't leave.

I gazed at the golden god of a man across from me. My mind was reeling and my thoughts unfocused. He looked maybe thirty-five if I attributed the crinkles around his eyes to age, rather than to sun and laughter.

He let me look at him. His sword had returned to wherever he pulled it from. His arms were at his sides, palms open to face me … in surrender or acceptance?

"I have my mother's eyes," I said, releasing the breath that had been blocking my ability to speak.

"Yes," Yazi, the warrior of the dragons answered. "But every other inch of you is me."

He was right. I was his spitting image.

Half-witch, half-dragon. Well, that was one mystery solved.

I smiled, hitting him with one of my best efforts ever.

"Hi, Dad," I said.

"I have to go back," I said for what I thought was the fourth or fifth time. It was easy for words and thoughts to get lost among the guardian dragons.

"Not today, fledgling," Chi Wen said. All the guardians, except the ancient Asian and my father, had left through the doors from which they'd arrived.

"Dad?"

Yazi, who hadn't yet taken his eyes off me — as if I was some great wonder — turned to question the still-smiling Asian dragon. "You have gazed into the distance, far seer?"

Gold rolled across the old dragon's eyes, seemingly clouding his vision. "Not so far, warrior. Your daughter will choose to remain."

"But —"

"You would bring great pain when you mean to help, warrior's daughter."

"But my mother and —"

"We heed the seer, child," Yazi said. "It is rare that Chi Wen choses to share his visions." Despite his words, my father was frowning at the Native American-carved door over my shoulder.

"I cannot change what is meant to be," the Asian dragon said. "Only redirect what does not need to happen."

"Visions," I scoffed. Yeah, rude, but I really needed to get back to Scarlett and Kandy. And Mory, I was fairly sure I'd seen Sienna get away with Mory.

Chi Wen's smile broadened. He raised himself up on to his tiptoes to lay his hand on my head. The heavily-spiced bitter cocoa of his magic seared through my curls into my brain, and in the briefest of flashes — as if that was all of the vision he thought I could bear — I saw what he foresaw.

I saw myself standing in the cavern before the altar. The stone table was surrounded by the mangled bodies of everyone I loved. Scarlett, Kandy, Mory ... Desmond and Kett crumpled off to one side unmoving. I squeezed my eyes shut as if that would stop me from seeing the streams of blood collecting in a pool at my feet. And Sienna. My sister was sprawled, dead and decaying, across the altar. Her dark blood magic was still writhing in her veins, spilling out of her mouth, and mixing into the lifeblood of those I loved. I could see the blood-coated knife in my hand. I had killed my sister, but not the darkness she'd created, that she'd allowed to inhabit her.

"This is my destiny?" I cried.

"You will stay, Jade Godfrey," Chi Wen said, his voice pulling me from the clutches of the vision. "Train. Learn your magic. You will walk among the humans once again. But not today."

I nodded, tears running down my face unchecked. What else could I do?

Acknowledgements

With thanks to:

My story & line editor
Scott Fitzgerald Gray

My Proof Readers
Leiah Cooper and Heather Doidge-Sidhu

My Beta Readers
Ita Margalit and Joanne Schwartz

For their continual encouragement, feedback, & general advice
Patrick Creery, Kelly Sarmiento, and Jan Schowengerdt

For her Art
Irene Langholm
Elizabeth Mackey

Meghan Ciana Doidge is an award-winning writer based out of Vancouver, British Columbia, Canada. She has a penchant for bloody love stories, superheroes, and the supernatural. She also has a thing for chocolate, potatoes, and sock yarn.

Novels

After The Virus
Spirit Binder
Time Walker
Cupcakes, Trinkets, and Other Deadly Magic (Dowser 1)
Trinkets, Treasures, and Other Bloody Magic (Dowser 2)
Treasures, Demons, and Other Black Magic (Dowser 3)
I See Me (Oracle 1)

Novellas/Shorts

Love Lies Bleeding
The Graveyard Kiss

For giveaways, news, and glimpses of upcoming stories, please connect with Meghan on her:

Personal blog, www.madebymeghan.ca
Twitter, @mcdoidge
And/or Facebook, Meghan Ciana Doidge

Please also consider leaving an honest review at your point of sale outlet

Time to stock up on chocolate.

You're going to need it.

🧁🧁🧁

AVAILABLE NOW
-Amazon-iBooks-Kobo-B&N-
-Smashwords-

Dowser Series · Book 1
CUPCAKES, TRINKETS, *and other* **DEADLY MAGIC**
MEGHAN CIANA DOIDGE

Dowser Series · Book 2
TRINKETS, TREASURES, *and other* **BLOODY MAGIC**
MEGHAN CIANA DOIDGE

Dowser Series · Book 3
TREASURES, DEMONS, *and other* **BLACK MAGIC**
MEGHAN CIANA DOIDGE

Catch a glimpse of the dowser universe through Rochelle's eyes...

The day I turned nineteen, I expected to gain what little freedom I could within the restrictions of my bank account and the hallucinations that had haunted me for the last six years. I expected to drive away from a life that had been dictated by the tragedy of others and shaped by the care of strangers. I expected to be alone.

Actually, I relished the idea of being alone.

Instead, I found fear I thought I'd overcome. Uncertainty I thought I'd painstakingly planned away. And terror that was more real than anything I'd ever hallucinated before.

I'd seen terrible, fantastical, and utterly impossible things ... but not love. Not until I saw him.

Printed in Great Britain
by Amazon.co.uk, Ltd.,
Marston Gate.